"Energy is not lost or destroyed, it is merely transferred from one party to the next." -Isaac Newton

Prologue: A Path Decided.

"This is it," The soft exclamation announced to the darkness, "After all these years under Sheol's rule, we finally have a means to bring it to an end." A lone figure sat in partial shadow, the light from a solitary candle playing across the features of the face like ochre silk caught in a midnight breeze. Without another word the figure rose slowly and with purpose, picking up the candle in its brass holder. The light now caressed further into the black space of the figure's home. It picked out scrolls and books filled with uncountable knowledge, running its soft fingers down their spines and across the ancient bindings, before the figure placed its source back down upon a nearby desk, banishing its exploration with a cloak cloaked torso. Laid out neatly beside the candle were three items; a piece of ordinary white chalk like one might find haunting the classrooms of old, a thick brown tome its leather face a permanent grimace cracked with age, and a round stone the size and shape of a clenched fist that held the engraving of a noble chimera its eyes glinting in the flickering candlelight. The figure opened the book, whose paper folds rustled in protest, and stared intently at a single verse with fierce silence. A moment or two tiptoed by before the swathed figure suddenly broke the stagnant air with a crashing wave of movement. It took the chalk in the right hand and the talisman in the left, and stooped down to the floor in a single, graceful movement that kicked up fine plumes of particles from the gnarled floor and left them hanging with anticipation. With a single, fluid action the figure drew a large circle with a central northern arrow, the chalk's whispers echoing high into the inky blackness of the library. Then, the image complete, the figure stepped forward and turned to face the lonely candle before uttering a single phrase with a voice as thick and heavy as crushed stone. "Simul ire, ad Terram!" It cried, and in an instant the room grew cold and the sound of torrential rain could be heard coming from the within the chalk outline. Thunder growled with barely suppressed rage as the figure vanished with a forked flash of lightning extinguishing the curious candle forever and leaving the scene to be swallowed by darkness' greedy tendrils.

Chapter 1: Our Tale Begins...

Jonathan Rhodes was what you might call average, so average in fact that you'd be lucky to even notice him in a crowd. He was tall and wiry, though whilst he might not have been particularly impressive looking, he was nevertheless contented with his own appearance. Jonathan's pitch-black hair was contrasted by his pale skin, and he wore it short so as to avoid obscuring his vision. His features were sharp yet easily forgettable at a glance, indeed the only thing of mark were his mint green eyes that spoke of hidden intelligence. At twenty-five, with only a small apartment, and no romance of any note, Jonathan's life had been normal and easy going at least until tonight. His lifeboat had been rocked, by Jonathan's standards, and he'd been made redundant as the hotel chain he was employed by had been bought out by another overseas firm. So, for the first time in years Jonathan had spent his evening at the local pub, a slightly run-down looking building with a good history behind it but a sad future. Jonathan didn't want to get drunk, he wasn't the type to 'drown his sorrows' but at times like this he did like to people watch, it helped him to relax and to think about his life, which right now was all he felt like doing. Sitting alone in a corner his eyes wandered over the gathered crowds, and soon he'd worked out a fun little back-story each character present, smiling inwardly he revelled in his contented lonesomeness.

It was nearly midnight when Jonathan thought it was time he should head back to his apartment and get some rest. He grabbed his coat, said his goodbyes to the owner and left. As he did so he was struck by how cold it suddenly felt outside, which was not totally unknown of in the middle of May but it was still rare enough to warrant a second thought from Jonathan, who swiftly buttoned up his coat and pulled the hood up so as to shield his ears from the biting wind that was starting to pick up speed and power. Jonathan lived near the edge of the city in one of the new apartments that had been built atop of an old factory that had once been the keystone of production for the city. It was actually rather amazing to see the transformation from old and disused, to young, modern and vibrant. However, this was also tempered with some sadness as the industries had been a large part of the history of the area and their loss was in away like excising an important part of the city. Jonathan's thoughts on the matter were mixed but ultimately, he understood that the old must in time make way for the new when it is no longer needed, which as depressing as it was seemed to be the direction the world was rapidly headed towards. Still thinking heavily about this doctrine, he continued walking until he reached the well-used matt black stairwell that lead to his flat. Jonathan lived on the top floor of this set of buildings, something he was both fond of and afraid of; fondness for the degree of security it lent him, but also afraid of the isolated nature of his position.

Gripping the corroded iron railing firmly, so as not to slip, Jonathan carefully climbed the stairs to his apartment. When he finally reached the top his front door stood, stoic and oddly imposing, in front of him. Fumbling for his keys, Jonathan suddenly felt a sense of unease creep its knotted fingers way into the back of his skull. Something was approaching; something in the darkness. Panic began to build in Jonathan's mind as his hands, numb with fear and the cold, refused to work as they were ordered to. He dropped his keys twice before finally, after what seemed like an age, they inserted the stubborn key into the lock and opened the door with a deep, metallic 'clunk'. Jonathan practically threw himself inside and slammed the door behind him, before leaning against it in stunned silence, his breaths coming in laboured, stress filled gulps. After half a minute or so he straightened up, closed his eyes and shook his head to steady his nerves. Jonathan, glad that no one had noticed his irrational stupidity, silently chastised himself then set out to prepare for that most pleasant of tasks; sleep.

Jonathan threw his coat over the hat stand that resided next to his front door, removed his shoes, and took a moment to survey his living space. The flat stood just as he'd left it almost seven hours ago. Although a little sparse by most people's standards the space was clearly well lived in, and the available room had been used in the most efficient way, so not an inch was wasted. The living room and kitchen were adjoined into a single area, marked out by a change in flooring. A small television sat in one dark blue corner and flanked by a haggard reading chair covered in light brown fabric that was slightly discoloured with tea stains, which itself stood next to a battered wooden bookcase that of a kind bought in flat pack and self-assembled. Opposite the TV, and serving as a kind of makeshift partition, was a wide green sofa with carved clawed feet and detailing that had seen better years and added to the overall dour feel of the room. Jonathan passed behind the stalwart guard and into the kitchen area, whose faux-rock lino stuck slightly to his socks. Upon being greeted by the sight of the yellowed fridge and cheap plasterboard countertops, Jonathan filled himself a glass of water and swiftly retreated to his bedroom, leaving the appliances to murmur to each other in the inky blackness.

Jonathan's bedroom reflected the rest of his apartment. It was small yet cosy, a little hideaway from the dark dreary world outside, and place of solitude, sanctity, and security. There wasn't a lot of furniture; a low double bed dominated the middle of the room, the sheets ruffled and unkempt, yet welcoming with their promises of a warm embrace and a restful night. The only other features were a small set of white painted oak drawers, to hold clothes, and a squat bedside table that currently served as a balance for a bedside lamp, two empty tea cups, and a set of unfinished novels with folded corners that marked where time and the desire to read had both become scarce. Jonathan took a small sip from his glass and placed it firmly onto the carpet. Reminding himself to move the tea cups in the morning, he quickly stripped off and put his clothes into a neat pile at the foot of the bed. After a quick shower to shake off the day Jonathan set his alarm for 9am and, having now changed into his sleepwear, climbed wearily into bed. It didn't take long for him to succumb to the darkness, all of life's worries and fears melted away before him into the black void of his dreamless sleep.

It was with a loud crash of thunderous symbols that Jonathan found himself suddenly being pulled back into reality. Blinking hard in the darkness his eyes strained to capture what little light there was and give form to the shapeless mass of black that filled his vision. Ears, that had just been assaulted by the thunderous alarm, began to readjust and pick up the sounds of heavy rain pelting the bedroom window. Hands, still groggy from sleep, groped blindly for the bedside lamp but instead of switching it on they only managed to knock the lamp from its stand and onto the floor, taking the pile of books with it as it fell. Annoyed and still half asleep, Jonathan sat up and swung his body round to the edge of the bed. Raising himself unsteadily like some grotesque hunchback, he began to feel for the dislodged light source with outstretched palms. He took a clumsy step forward and felt his fingers brush against the glass he'd planted there last night which, apparently needing little in the way of encouragement, proceeded to gleefully dump its contents onto the previously dry bedroom floor. Cursing his luck with an exasperated sigh, Jonathan ceased his search for the lamp and painfully straightened up before stumbled uncertainly towards the door to the kitchen, somehow managing to avoid the spreading puddle of water that was being hungrily absorbed by the carpet.

Following his mind's eye Jonathan cautiously navigated his way out of his bedroom and around his reading chair towards the kitchen, on the way he almost bumped into his hat stand which was now not by the door but instead between him and the sofa. He was just about to move it out of the way when this realisation struck him with an icy spike of fear.

"Good evening." Said the hat stand, its voice as dry as sandpaper.

Chapter 2: Voice in the Darkness.

Jonathan froze, his mind suddenly sharp and focused. Had he imagined the voice? Thoughts, anxieties, and doubts whirled around his head; a cloud of angry bees growing in number with each second. Jonathan slowly and deliberately moved away from the tall dark shadow of his hat stand, and even as his back touched the cool wood of the bookcase his eyes never ceasing to stare, watching for any signs of life from an object that by all counts should have none. He had almost convinced himself that it was simply a trick of his previously disoriented state when that voice sounded again into the void.

"Are you the owner of this abode?" It asked, politely. Instincts took over and Jonathan, not wanting to seem rude, stammered out a response.

"Th-This is my home, yes. Who are you, wha-what are you doing here?!" The shadow made no sound for a moment, so Jonathan, regaining a little composure, reinforced his questioning. "Tell me who you are, b-before I call the police!" This seemed to intrigue the darkness and it widened as it turned its full shape towards him.

"Very well." The shade rasped, "Allow me to shed some light on your queries." Part of the figure's head began to glow very slightly with a hue of dried blood, just enough so that Jonathan could make out the edges of a deep hood that was pulled over keen, gaunt features. Suddenly there a quiet click as the room's light switch, also glowing with the same hue, turned itself on. Jonathan's vision went from pitch black to blinding white in an instant as artificial sunlight invaded his eye sockets and assaulted his oversensitive pupils. Crying out a little from this invasion, Jonathan instinctively covered his eyes. After a few seconds, when his vision had begun to correct itself, he withdrew his arm and squinted at what was very clearly not his hat stand at all but an ominous, cloak wrapped figure unlike anything he'd seen before.

It stood a few inches taller than Jonathan did, its facial features mostly obscured by the previously outlined hood that he could now see was attached at the neckline to a long shawl made of a cloth that hung off the shoulders and flowed around the figure's form, rather than cling to the body. The mantle stopped a good six centimetres or so from the floor, and Jonathan noticed a pair of well-made leather shoes the colour of coal poking out from the bottom, their dark polished surfaces catching the light. There was little else to mark the being out as the cloak obscured everything and was too deep to make out anything else of note. Fear, although still present in great quantities, was slowly usurped by curiosity as to the identity of this strange man or woman. It made no movement as Jonathan straightened up and withdrew a step or two from the bookcase whose slats had been digging into with his spine.

"Who are you?" He asked, voice now steady and deliberate.

"My name," Replied the dry gravel voice, "Is Greed." The voice paused slightly before adding, "And I am in need of your assistance."

Jonathan rolled the words around in his head, wondering if he'd heard the figure correctly. He was just about to ask if this was an elaborate prank when the figure raised its hands, which were clad with smooth, brown leather gloves, and lowered the cowl. What lay underneath silenced any doubts as to his visitor's authenticity. The man's head was completely bare, not just of hair but also of skin, flesh, ears, nose, everything. Only the skull remained, its cracked bone yellowed slightly from age and the elements. Curiously the lack of flesh only seemed to stem as far as the jaw-line, and Jonathan could clearly see a very human looking neck that disappeared into the cloak's folds. There was also a long piece of brown silk that looped vertically around the head and then behind the neck, before tying under the jaw, though what this was for was unclear. Jonathan's body stood stock still, as his mind processed this new information and tried to make sense of it. Greed stared at Jonathan with deep, empty sockets, seemingly waiting for a response to his statement of 'needing assistance'.

"Who? What...?" Jonathan stammered, unable to form proper questions to the wave of queries that crashed against his mind. Greed, perhaps sensing this problem, spoke again.

"Would it help if I start from the beginning?" He asked. Jonathan nodded, eyes wide with curiosity. "Very well," Continued Greed, a slight impatience in his voice,

"But I cannot linger over this forever, time is short." He motioned for Jonathan to be seated before perching, straight backed and rigid, on the edge of the sofa. He then began his story. "In case you have not guessed by now, I do not originate from this world. I have come from a distant realm that is in great peril and needs the assistance of someone like yourself, that is to say, *not* from my realm." Greed paused for a second, seemingly studying Jonathan for any reaction, who was trying to take all this in. "For as long as we can remember," He continued, "Our realm has lived in harmony with another, emotionally opposite realm. The exchange of energy between both these worlds was constant and in balance." Greed shifted his gaze up a little, seemingly staring above and beyond Jonathan. "That was until recently. We do not know how but a sudden surge of negative energy entered our realm, too much to be converted all at once. It has stagnated and grown, increasing in power and size until it grew large enough to gain consciousness." Jonathan glanced away from Greed for a moment, "This consciousness corrupts all those who call the realm home, no one from our world has the fortitude to resist, and so we are powerless to stop it."

"But, why me?" Jonathan asked quietly, voice barely audible above the rain that continued to throw itself against the apartment roof.

"Your world exists outside of the emotional energy exchange that spawned this great crisis," Greed responded, "You would be unaffected by the power this being has over my realm." Abruptly standing, Greed looked down upon Jonathan. "And so, we must move. Time is of the essence, so to speak." Jonathan just blinked a few times, waiting to see if that was truly it.

"Wait just a minute!" He cried, surprising himself and breaking the air of awkward secrecy that had fallen over the room. "It's all very well you invading my apartment and saying this and that about help and strange realms and such...and I do have sympathy for you...but..."Jonathan's resolve faltered a little, "Well, I don't know *you*, I don't know what you are, where you're from." He turned away from the robed figure, "I'm sorry Greed, but I can't just go."

"I told you all you need to know." Greed stated, matter-of-factly as if that was all the explanation he should need.

"That's not what I mean!" Jonathan snapped, turning abruptly back towards his unwanted guest. "How would you feel if some stranger just appeared out of nowhere in the middle of the night and demanded that they help you save their world?!" Jonathan stared accusingly into the deep-seated sockets, looking for any sign of understanding. Greed took a small step back, relaxing his stance onto his heels, then turned his head very slightly and he raised a gloved hand to his lower jaw as if pondering Jonathan's question. Apparently reaching an answer Greed straightened up and, without so much as another word to Jonathan, turned his back and made for the front door with long, sweeping strides. Jonathan frowned disarmed by this unexpected reaction and followed Greed into the hallway. Upon reaching the front door Greed's head, and the handle, began to glow again with that red hue. The solid construct, locked though it was, nevertheless slowly began to open and invited a biting gust of air to enter the apartment and give a frigid reminder as to the conditions outside.

"So that's it then?" Jonathan stated. He was, admittedly, a little disappointed that this mystery man was leaving so soon.

"What is it you want me to say?" Replied Greed, rotating his head so as to gaze at Jonathan from over his right shoulder. "I need someone who is willing to help me save my world. This is no trick, it is no ruse, my world is dying, and I need someone who I can trust and who trusts me." He turned his skull back to face the open door and pouring rain. "If you thought that me appearing meant you were special then I apologise for misleading you. It was coincidence that the spell brought me to your house, nothing more, and if I can't find a willing assistance here then I shall search elsewhere." As Greed began to walk over the door's threshold Jonathan felt a strange anger bubbling up within him, he'd never been particularly bothered about what other people thought and had never considered himself to be anything above ordinary, however Greed's words had, probably intentionally, hit a rare nerve. The electric feeling frothed and boiled its way through his system, out of his lungs and up his neck until finally, just as Greed was about to descend the iron stairs outside, it erupted from Jonathan's mouth.

"Stop!" He shouted, teeth grinding slightly. "Come back in and close that door. I'll help you with your damn quest." If Greed's face could offer a sly smile Jonathan was sure it would be doing it now, but obediently he returned to the apartment and shut the heavy door behind him.

"You have my thanks." Greed stated, unfazed by Jonathan's outburst.

"Save it," Jonathan retorted, annoyance still on his lips, "Help yourself to refreshments," He sighed, gesturing towards the kitchen, "I've just got to go change. I don't think my pyjamas are suitable for adventuring."

Chapter 3: Where Angels Fear to Tread.

Jonathan emerged from his bedroom around five minutes later, now properly dressed in what he considered to be suitable questing clothes. His chosen attire consisted of an old pair of black mud flecked boots, a relic from his university years, a dull grey shirt, and some worn yet tough, jeans made of thick faded denim and secured around his waist with a simple, notched belt. Having no idea what the weather would be like Jonathan took a cue from Greed and dressed warmly, laying himself within a moth-eaten forest green woollen jumper his mother had passed down to him, and a thick, yet comfortable waxed coat, its colour somewhere between ochre and olive brown. He found Greed perched awkwardly on the edge of the reading chair apparently reading the titles of the many books that adorned the cheap case next to it. He had a mug in his left hand whose contents were in the process of being sucked up through a long, curly straw. Jonathan stopped a few feet away from him and cleared his throat. The noise caught Greed's attention, who put the drink down on the nearest shelf and hastily stood, turning himself towards Jonathan as he did so.

"Are we ready?" He asked, eagerly.

"Almost," Jonathan replied, "I'd like to leave a note or something, on the off chance that someone might drop by. I don't want people thinking that I've run off, which is exactly what I'm doing come to think of it..."

"There is little need," interrupted Greed, "You see time flows differently between realms. Through my studies I understand that you could be gone for weeks in my realm and only be missing a few days here." He crossed his arms, impatiently. "Why do you think I wanted to be gone as soon as possible?"

Jonathan sighed, in truth he hadn’t many friends and his objections were more just stalling tactics than actual concerns. "Alright, alright.” He conceded, “How will this work anyway?"

"It's really quite simple." Answered Greed, who then proceeded to delve his right hand into his thick robes and retrieve a billiard ball sized stone that Jonathan could see was skilfully carved with the noble visage of a strange chaotic beast. "This talisman is currently holding me within this world, all I have to do with break it and I'll be transported back to my point of origin." He looked at Jonathan with his vacant, midnight sockets and extended his left hand, palm upwards, "You'll have to take my hand, unless you *want* to be left behind." Reluctantly, Jonathan brought his own hand up and tentatively grasped Greed's gloved palm. Not hesitating for an instance Greed raised the talisman and threw it against the floor. Whatever it was made from it most certainly was not the heavy, dense stone that it looked to be as it shattered like sugar glass against the soft carpet, tiny shards scattering to every nook and cranny of the tiny living space. The fragments then began to evaporate into a thin velvet smoke that resembled burnt wine in both colour and smell, then the gathered mist rose and enveloped the two figures, before plunging them both into crushing blackness.

Emptiness closed in on Jonathan's stifled senses; there was no sound, yet he felt deafened, there was no light, yet he felt blinded. He was simultaneously too hot and too cold, whilst pin pricks of contact danced their way across his skin in waves of pressure that left him feeling nauseous in their wake. Finally, though all sense of time had been diluted out of him, he sensed something rushing up towards him. He tried to slow himself down but found he could not move his arms or legs. Despair began to overwhelm Jonathan, and he felt himself tumble helplessly over and over into the chasm-like grasp of the void.

"Wake up!" The darkness suddenly screamed, in a voice not too dissimilar from his own.

Jonathan opened his eyes and was surprised to find himself sat bolt upright. His head swam but he managed to get uneasily to his feet. He suddenly remembered what had happened and as he started to look round for Greed, Jonathan noticed that the landscape he was in was nothing at all like the home he'd left behind.

The ground beneath his feet was dry and barren, its loose dirt gathered around his shoes and left deep prints wherever he stepped. There looked to be little if any flora, though a few bare trees were dotted around here and there, their skeletal forms twisted in vain attempts to reach up towards the heavens. Mountains, sharp and stalwart, dominated the distant horizon with peaks that clawed at a sky that was coated in a purple mass of brooding clouds that swirled and moved of their own volition, the rare breaks in the dark layer giving glimpses of sickly sunlight that reached out weakly strike at the parched ground. Somewhere out in the distance Jonathan spotted a writhing sheet of cobalt flame rise from a fissure in the earth, the gout shot into the sky briefly before settling back into its chasm and seething with hidden rage. Finally, as if reinforcing the hostile nature of this world, nearby a huge skeleton lay half buried beneath a small grove of the dead looking trees, its surfaces browned and cracked from exposure, and the long, gnarled finger like bones grinning at him from within their bark lined tomb.

Suddenly, Greed emerged over the crest of the hill Jonathan was standing on, dust swirling around his cloak tails.

"Good, you've awakened." He stated, bluntly, "The experience can be somewhat unpleasant for those new to inter-realm travel. Though I'm afraid it can be an imprecise science." Greed turned away from Jonathan, looking back the way he'd just appeared from. "We're a few hundred meters from where we should be. But not to worry, I have scouted the route and it is secure for now." With no warning Greed set off back down the hill and Jonathan, having no time to question his companion, began to follow him as he led the way to whatever counted as civilisation in this clearly damned world.

It didn't take long till Jonathan could make out a large wooden gate built into a solid looking wall of roughly hewn rock. Reasoning that this must be their destination he took a few jogging steps, so he was side by side with Greed, and matched his pace as they approached the great barrier. Under closer inspection the gate seemed to be made from thick planks of a murky, reinforced wood, at least twice as tall as Jonathan, with no external means of opening it. There were no guards outside the walls, but there was a medieval looking watchtower within the safety of the grey, stone fortifications, just to the right of the massive entranceway. It was from this that Jonathan got the distinct impression that they were not approaching the doors to this settlement unobserved. This feeling was proven correct when he spotted shadows moving within the tower's thin arrow-slit windows, just as he and Greed got to within a few feet of the oaken gateway. With not so much as a word from Greed the great door began to creak and groan on its bearings, and its massive form split neatly in two. Each half then grumbled loudly and retracted into the adjacent walls with great effort, allowing entry into the town beyond. Greed took the lead again and, with Jonathan in tow, entered the settlement.

As they strode into the town Jonathan marvelled at the architecture around him. It was like stepping back into the Tutor era; all the buildings were clearly very old or had been designed with a degree of age about them, their dark wooden beams and cross bars were bold and unpainted, contrasting sharply with the off-white walls that fell between them. Although sagging and drooping slightly every house was still elegantly tall and each was topped with a rustic looking thatched roof that overhung the edges of the building ever so slightly, giving the streets an enclosed and almost malevolent atmosphere. There were cobbled pavements lining the edge of each building, and Jonathan had to be careful not to trip as he picked his way across their uneven surfaces. The inhabitants of this town were even stranger than the town itself. There seemed to be no unifying features amongst them; some were tall, some were short, some big, some small, in fact most of them had no earthly compatriots at all. Jonathan noted a few of the most bizarre specimens as they passed by; something akin to a humanoid griffon, its upper body a sickly grey and its eyes a shining red trotting beside a strange insect like biped with a shiny black-green carapace and double-jointed legs. Beyond them scuttled something that could only be described as a fuzzy brown spider crossed with a small horse that was greeted by a tall, genderless biped whose limbs were unsettlingly long and whose face was hidden by a rubbery, white gasmask that was sewn directly into its skin. Overhead buzzed a group of tiny bat like beings with oval heads studded with countless colourless eyes, but no visible mouth or nose, who gracefully swooped in to land at and browse wares from the stall of a human who looked half melted, and whose face split vertically when he talked to reveal a lining of teeth as long and sharp as the bones of a salmon. Jonathan swallowed nervously, though despite feeling like he was the strange one thus far nobody seemed to pay him and his skull-headed guide much attention until they finally reached what must have been the town's centre. They stood in a large plaza that was dominated by a sizeable open well in the middle of a circle of cobblestone. Greed turned his attention to Jonathan, who was still watching the many strange beings he was seeing for the first time.

"So," he announced, making Jonathan jump a little, "Allow me to welcome you to Anchoridge, one of the last safe havens, and my home." Seemingly pleased with his declaration, Greed continued. "I'm sure you'll be pleased to know that we are nearly ready to begin our mission in earnest, but first I must introduce you to my friends."

Jonathan faltered, he was hesitant to follow Greed any further without a more detailed explanation as to their situation. He stood his ground.

"Who are these friends Greed, and where are we exactly?" He stated sternly, "I agreed to help you, but I didn't expect to be going in blind." Jonathan took a split second to consider his wording, before correcting himself hastily, "Sorry that was careless, no offense meant." Greed's shoulders lowered a little, his seriousness lessening by the barest amounts.

"I promise you, all your questions will be answered in due time." He replied, "I know this isn't easy right now, but once the preparations are complete everything shall be revealed. All I ask is that you wait a little while longer." Straightening back up again, Greed adjusted his cloak. "And for the record, though I have no eyes, I can see just fine." He retorted, a slight softness to his otherwise gritty vocalisations.

Chapter 4: A Will of Iron.

At the opposite end of the town centre stood an impressive structure. Impressive not just for its scale, for it dwarfed the houses that huddled around it, but also in the detailed and delicate carvings that had been worked from its solid stone face. Outwardly the immense building reminded Jonathan of an old Victorian courthouse, complete with tree trunk sized columns supporting a brooding roof that resembled the great maw of a dragon, ready to devour any wrongdoing with its ancient 'jaws of justice'. Jonathan was pleasantly surprised when Greed confirmed his interpretation of the building's function.

"This is Anchoridge courthouse, and it is where we'll find the first of our companions." Greed gazed up at the large clock face that lived above the wide, yawning archway entrance to the building. "In fact, if my timing is correct, she should have just finished her latest case." As if on cue the doors of the courthouse yawned open, and a gaggle of stern-faced figures appeared to melt from the shadowy interior. Most of them passed by without so much as a second glance, but one stopped at the head of the entry-steps and stared at them. It wasn't until his vision was clear of bustling beings that Jonathan could finally see that this individual was not only female, but also oddly human looking.

She was dressed in what could be described as classic 'lawyer attire'. Dark brown shoes poked out from the bottom of a pair of soft grey suit trousers. A woman's blazer, of matching grey, covered the torso, and was neatly buttoned up with two black buttons. Beneath that Jonathan could see a stark, white shirt with an exaggerated collar. There was no neck tie, and the shirt's top two buttons were open revealing the most striking part of the outfit. It was a beautiful golden necklace set with a red, opal-like gemstone that caught and scattered the slight bit of light that struck its surface. The gemstone's deep ruby colouration was reflected seamlessly with a particular feature of its wearer's face; her eyes. The deep crimson irises were perfectly framed by the pale white visage and jet dark hair that followed the contours of the face before curling upwards, and inwards at their tips. Whomever she was, she exuded a sharpened grace, like the beauty of a Black Widow. She walked purposefully towards Greed, stopping a few feet in front of him with a look of sly bemusement upon her face.

“Greed,” She said, her attitude clipped and no-nonsense, “You’re punctual as ever I see.” Her voice was lady-like and calm, smooth as silk yet with an undercurrent that hinted of a deadly intelligence. This was not a woman you'd want to cross.

"Indeed," Replied Greed, unfazed by her bewitching charms, "I trust you have had an agreeable day. Tell me, do you recall our discussion yesterday evening?" He asked. The mysterious woman barely considered his question before chuckling softly.

"Of course,” She replied, answering both question at once. “I have also noticed the person behind you, that you have neglected to introduce to me. Really Greed, must I do everything?" The woman took a step towards Jonathan, her heels crunching the dirt in the now eerily quiet plaza. As she did so she briskly extended her hand, "My name is Pride, a pleasure to meet you, Mr?" She asked politely.

"Rhodes," Jonathan responded, finding the courteous tone to be surprisingly intimidating.

"And do you have a first name, Mr Rhodes?" Pride continued, shaking his hand once with a firm grip.

"Erm yes, Jonathan, or John, whichever you prefer." He smiled, slightly embarrassed at his own awkwardness.

Pride took a slight step back and crossed her arms. "Jonathan Rhodes, not exactly an heroic name." Pride looked Jonathan up and down, her studious visage never changing, "But then again, tis often from the most ordinary of people that true heroes are forged." She returned her gaze to his eyes, "And in that respect, you certainly seem to be qualified." Pride turned her head towards Greed, who was silently observing them both. "I can only hope Greed has filled you in on the situation and such? It’s not going to be a walk in the park."

Jonathan scratched the back of his neck, sheepishly. "Well kind of," He muttered, "He mentioned something about realms, and emotion, and a big evil presence? I admit I didn't understand a lot of it, but it's not often that I get to help beings from other dimensions."

Pride considered what Jonathan said for a moment, before shaking her head dubiously, "You mean Greed has not told you about what shadowy beasts and creatures we're likely to face out there in the wastelands?" She asked, mock surprise cloaking her voice. But before Jonathan could get her to elaborate, Greed interrupted.

"I was going to inform him about that before we set out in earnest." He stated, an edge of unease to his otherwise uniform drawl. "I would have thought you would appreciate the efficiency of not repeating myself seven times Pride." He retorted. Pride just let out a small giggle, enjoying the discomfort.

"If you say so." She responded with sceptical slyness. Not wishing to rise to the bait any further, Greed gestured to Jonathan.

"Come let us make haste to our next appointment. Before anything else, slips out." He turned to leave.

"Yes, the truth has a way of doing that," Pride announced quietly to herself as Greed and Jonathan made their way from the courthouse towards a nearby alleyway. "I'll meet you later for the briefing, I'm *sure* Greed will explain everything then." She called after them, with more than a hint of sarcasm ringing about her words. As Pride faded into the background, Jonathan considered her words and made a mental note to keep his eyes open for anything else that might be being kept from him.

Greed led Jonathan through a series of dark, twisted passageways. The confusing labyrinth curved this way and that, in fact Jonathan was sure that several times the turns should have doubled back on themselves. Eventually however, just as his head was beginning to spin, the alleyways widened out into something resembling an outdoor marketplace. Jonathan could see many bizarre stalls and the curious entities gathered around them, perusing the various goods and trinkets each vendor had for sale. Greed took him to the far-right corner of the market where there stood a small, squat shop. The outside of this crouched building was unremarkable save for a several dozen metal tools that hung in wooden racks under a jutting section of thatched roof. The top of the building also possessed something the other buildings didn't; a tall conical chimney of dark leaden stone that belched a long, wizened beard of smoke up and out to join the swirling vortex overhead. Greed approached the building's sunken door and turned his head in Jonathan's direction.

"Our next companion is just inside, do watch your step." He announced, before he disappeared into the entryway. Jonathan hesitantly followed Greed, stooping slightly as he crossed the threshold, though what greeted him was an almost overpowering wall of heat. Compared to the dry stillness of the market, the inside of the shop felt like a roaring oven, and Jonathan was quick to notice why. A huge furnace, the circular bottom to the chimney embedded in the roof, boldly sat against the back wall, its gaping maw a cacophony of burnt orange and raging crimson surrounded by a lining of clenched jet-black teeth. Such was the fierce heat that Jonathan had to shield his eyes with his hand to make out anything else about the boiling interior. There were few other fittings besides a water trough, a large anvil, a collection of metalworking tools, and a large table just next to the door where Jonathan was standing. Resting on this table was a wondrous white-gold bracelet, with a multi-coloured gem embedding in its surface that danced a rainbow waltz in the light from the furnace.

"This is beautiful," Jonathan stated softly, and he bent down to assess the jewellery more closely.

"Well thanks!" A gruff voice called out, "Nice to 'ear some appreciation." Jonathan jumped a little and spun around on his heels just in time to see someone emerge from behind the furnace. The voice's owner stood a half foot or so shorter than Jonathan, but he as definitely wider, with well-muscled arms and a thick trunk of a torso that strained beneath the white, spark stained vest he wore. The exposed skin was an ashen grey, with the occasional odd looking rusty brown patch. His legs were hidden inside a pair of worn brown trousers with several deep pockets, that were tucked neatly into a pair of black workman's boots. Over the vest, and down his front, he had a robust leather apron whose front pocket held a sizeable hammer for the shaping of metal. The man's face was clean shaven but his hair was done up in an extravagant blood red Mohawk that swept back and down to the base of his neck, like the fin of a great shark. Below the hair, the man's ochre coloured eyes glowed at Jonathan with a fiery, yet stare. Before he could react, the imposing figure stepped forward and thrust forward his hand with unexpectedly welcoming motion.

As he spoke again, Jonathan noticed an Australian twang under the rough cut of his voice, "Sorry for the 'eat, it's been an 'ard days slog." He declared warmly. Jonathan took the offering firmly and was alarmed at the way it felt less like flesh and blood and more akin to steel pipes shaped like a hand; warm as the ambient temperature, yet solid and unyielding. Though he didn't voice it, Jonathan's surprise and intrigue must have been plain on his face. "I can see something's troubling you," The blacksmith huffed, crossing his arms, "Yeah, iron by trade, iron by nature." He stated, rapping his steel knuckles against his forearm. "It's 'andy for my work, but rain's a little inconvenient. Speaking of which," He paused to close the shutter on the great furnace, humbling its fiery temper. "Can't be 'aving the fire going all night. Especially if there's a downpour on the way." He eyed Greed, who was skulking around the shop's circumference, "You're rather quiet Greed, something up?"

Greed raised his head a little. "Nothing my friend, I was just thinking what our next stop should be after we gain possession of the amulet. There is a lot to get through tonight after all."

The man chuckled slightly and shook his head. "Alright, I 'ear you. But I can't 'and it over till it's ready, you know that." He sighed a worn-out sigh and approached the bracelet on the table behind Jonathan. He tenderly picked it up and placed it in the apron's cavernous pocket. "Tell you what, I've only got to finish up the polishing. If I get that done in the next 'our or so, I'll bring it to your little briefing. 'Ow's that?" He placed his hands on his hips, awaiting Greed's answer.

After a few seconds Greed replied. "That is acceptable." He said, coldly, before he strode back through the door with a whirl of his cloak.

Laughing heartily, Greed's companion shouted after him, "No rest for the wicked then, 'ey!" He then turned his gaze to Jonathan once more, "You'd best be off after him mate," He advised him with a smile, "Oh by the way, what's your name?"

Jonathan smiled back, "I'm Jonathan, but you can call me John."

The man nodded acceptingly and picked up a nearby cloth, "Nice to meet you John, you can call me Wrath."

Jonathan followed Greed back outside to find him already halfway across the market plaza.

"Hey Greed, wait a minute!" Jonathan yelled, jogging to catch up with him. Greed stopped for a moment but didn't turn around. "Don't you think that was a little rude?" Jonathan asked, as he came up behind Greed. "I'm no expert on friends, but shouldn't we spend a little more time introducing ourselves before we run off?" Greed shifted his weight onto his right leg and half rotated to face Jonathan, deep sockets burning with hidden purpose. Jonathan faltered a fraction, "I'm sorry," He began, "I don't mean to question how you do things, I just..." He was cut short as Greed spoke.

"This world is dying, and we cannot pass up a single second." He said sternly, "If you wish to waste precious moments on social etiquette there will be chances for that when we set out from this town." Greed crossed his arms and grounded his jaw a little, thinking. Then he spoke again, "However, your point has given me an idea," He announced, uncrossing his arms and pointing to the opposite end of the marketplace, "Follow that path, and stick to the left-hand wall. After a few minutes, you should exit into a large open garden." Greed lowered his arm, "In the middle is a cottage, the home of our next companion. I shall meet you there after I have obtained a few supplies." He turned away again and began to work slowly away, "Perhaps we might save a little time." He muttered as he vanished into a gloomy passageway, leaving Jonathan behind.

Chapter 5: The Heart with One String.

Jonathan looked around nervously, for the first time since this all began, he was alone; alone in a strange world, with strange surroundings, and even stranger inhabitants. He took a deep breath, zipped his coat up, put his hands firmly into his pockets, and walked with as much brisk confidence as he could summon in the direction Greed had pointed. Jonathan quickly located the alley he was to follow and, as Greed had told him, he hugged the left-hand wall. For what seemed like more than a few minutes he doggedly kept his eye on the wall while the thumps of his footsteps reverberated from the dark, dry flagstones, and drew leered looks from the dusty eyes of the surrounding houses. Jonathan quickened his pace, he was starting to get a little claustrophobic, and even though he was certain it was nothing, he couldn't help but heed the shouts from his sub-conscious that he was being watched, and that he needed to get out of this alley and back into the open air. Still gazing at the wall to his left he increased his speed again, moving from a powerwalk into a jog as the windows, doors, and oaken beams of the buildings passed him by in an ever-quickening rush of alternating light and dark. Corners came thick and fast, becoming ever more erratic and random, as Jonathan abandoned his jog and started to flat out sprint his way through the clotted tangle of streets and alleys. It was just as Jonathan thought he couldn't run anymore, that fatigue was going to overpower him and leave him forever lost in this maze of stone and wood, that it suddenly ended without warning as he burst out from the alleyway and straight into the gardens Greed had mentioned.

Jonathan took a minute to catch his breath and steady his nerves bore taking a long hard look at the surprising greenery now cloying for his attention. He was shocked, pleasantly so, as despite the lack of flora and the general decrepit aesthetic he had seen so far, it seemed that these were beautifully maintained, public gardens. The unease of his trip through the alleyways was slowly forgotten as he wandered into a dark, moss green field of swaying, ankle length grass, complete with small stones lining the terracotta pathways. It almost felt out of place to be surrounded by greenery, and to hear his footsteps make the soft 'phut' sound of fresh soil, as opposed to the usual hollow crunch of dry, barren earth. Jonathan began to feel at ease as he wound his way towards to middle of the meadow. It was as he reached the summit of a small emerald coated hill that he saw, stretching out from the slope below, a vast field full of flowering plants, each one bright and blooming. Jonathan would have been the first to admit that only had a layman's knowledge about many things, however he did hold a secret love of botany, and he was pleased that he could identify the names of most of the flora as he worked his way down the hillside and followed the trail deeper into the meadow. Beds of Aloe, Aster, and Honeysuckle led the way, flanked here and there by patches of white Rainflower and magenta Gomphrena blossoms. Delicate Carnations also nestled in the grass, a soft pastel pink in colour, whilst standing like miniature skyscrapers was the occasional amethyst Gladiolus. Lost though he was in his world of flora, Jonathan soon came across a small bungalow that was nestled amongst a thick patch of Coriander flowers. Jonathan began to pick his way through them and quickly noticed something else rising above the sounds of the wind, something emanating from the cottage window. It sounded like someone playing a piano. He quietly made his way through the up to a nearby window, careful to avoid a prickly Broom Shrub that tried to snag his trousers, to confirm his suspicions. He stood on an external beam, and stretched onto his tiptoes to peek through, careful to not disturb the empty plant pot that occupied its ledge. Inside there was not a lot of light but Jonathan could just about make out a lone, female figure sat in front of an ancient, black, grand piano. The tune they were playing was carefully paced, slow yet not arduous. Measured and soft but filled with dismay and clearly of emotional value to the player, who performed it with a practised precision and heart-breaking passion in their deft finger movements. This piece clearly meant a lot to them, and it was at this moment, just as Jonathan thought the melody was winding down, that the figure began to sing a most sorrowful song.

Breath calm, breathe deep
Everything is still there
Don't worry, just sleep
No need to despair
Even though, he said
"Our love is eternal"
You're there, in my head
The change is just external

When this world is no more
Memory is all there'll be
Upon those wings we'll forever soar
I'll think of you, just remember me
And if it all fades, into the night
As long as you're with me, everything's alright

Why can't, I just
Tell you what we're feeling?
I'll do, what I must
You're in need of healing
No words, from prior
My eyes turn to salt
My heart, on fire
Though I know it's not your fault

When this world is no more
Memory is all there'll be
Upon those wings we'll forever soar
I'll think of you, just remember me
And if it all fades, into the night
As long as you're with me, everything's alright

As long as you're with me, everything's...

The music stopped playing. The final notes drifted off into the darkness, which was broken only by the sounds of gentle sobbing as a thin line of tears followed the curvature of the figure's face and fell silently from her trembling chin.

Jonathan didn't know what to feel, the beauty and calm of the outside was completely at odds with the sombre scene he'd just witnessed. Feeling a little guilty that he'd observed something so personal he began to lower himself from the window. He stepped back, but as he did so his foot slipped on the edge of the beam he'd been balanced on and instinctually he shot out his right arm to catch himself on the window ledge. Although he managed to save himself from falling, the same could not be said of the empty plant pot that had, until just now, inhabited the windowsill. The world seemed to slow to a crawl as Jonathan watched the clay cylinder tumble to the ground and smash cleanly in two. The noise might have been fairly quiet, but to Jonathan it had an ear shattering quality that echoed around his head and through the open window, alerting the occupant to his presence. Quickly as he could, without dislodging anything else, he ducked down beneath the window to avoid being spotted.

"Hello?" A demure voice called out, "Is someone there?" Jonathan didn't answer, as his mind frantically tried to think of a way out of this without drawing attention to himself. There was a quiet sniff before the voice spoke again, "It's alright, don't be afraid. I won't hurt you." Jonathan blinked a few times, taken aback. He took a steady breath, accepting what fate befell him, and slowly raised himself, keeping his eyes looking downward towards his shoes. There were a few shuffled footsteps before the voice once uttered, "Oh, hello there" It sounded a little surprised at the appearance of someone, but there was not a single hint of any hostility. The voice sniffed and continued, "What are you doing out there?" It asked in an innocent tone.

"I'm sorry, I didn't mean to disturb you." Jonathan replied, sheepishly, "I was just..." He faltered, his embarrassment beginning to rise again.

The voice's warm, almost mothering tone instilled a sense of calm, “It's alright.” There was a pause, and another sniff, “I was just about to make some tea, would you like come inside and have some too?” Not wishing to compound the rudeness of his spying, Jonathan nodded and walked around the side of the cottage, once again avoiding the various bushes and flowers, to reach the front door. He opened it carefully and quietly entered, gently shutting the door behind him out of respect. The inside of the cottage felt welcoming and homely, with earthly colours and an enclosed, cosy atmosphere. The front door opened into a small hallway that travelled perpendicular to the entrance. To the left Jonathan could see the bottom of a set of stairs, whilst to his right there was a simple wooden door that was ajar, light from the adjoining room was filtering through the gap and around the edges. He took a moment to remove his shoes, placing them beside the front door, before gingerly making his way across the floorboards to the glowing entryway and into the room beyond. It was a quaint example of a living space, and like the hallway it had a bare wooden floor upon which slept a large oval pink and white braided rug. Across and to the left, there was a modest armchair with cream fabric; behind which sat a small fireplace that jutted from the wall, the source of the weak light that illuminated the living area. There were decorations here and there, and a few cheerful paintings hung upon the walls helped to brighten up the room. Directly to his left was the grand piano the Jonathan had watched the figure play earlier, however now that he was stood next to it, he noticed that there were two previously unseen objects adorning the instrument. The first was a single sapphire blue rose, laid out as if in mourning, next to the second object that appeared to be a miniature silver photo frame. Jonathan lent forward to get a closer look. The picture inside was a close up of two people stood together, a man and a woman, both of whom looked very happy and appeared to have been quite close. The man's face was rugged, with short dark brown hair, a sharp nose and shapely chin, though his most obvious and handsome feature was his lilac eyes that hinted of cunning intellect. The female in the picture had a wide mirthful grin, her face was much softer and more delicate looking than the man's, her slender nose and cheeks followed the gentle curves of her face in a very pleasing way. Her hair was tied back into a ponytail and was a bright shade of pink, her oval eyes a pastel blue. Though the photo was mainly of their faces the man looked to be wearing a business suit and tie, which was in contrast with the woman's more casual attire; a sea foam dress with little yellow birds dancing across its folds. There were no clues as the identities of the people in the picture, so Jonathan straightened up. He turned to face the other, half-open door in the room, from which the sounds of tea preparation were emanating. Thinking it might be wise to alert his mystery host to his presence, he called out.

"I'm a...I'm sorry interrupted your singing." There was a short clattering sound before the voice replied.

"Singing? I wasn't singing." Jonathan scrunched his face in confusion, not expecting that response.

“But I saw...I heard you.” He announced, furrowing his brow, “So, why were you crying then?” The question was a little more forceful than Jonathan would have liked, but he was deeply confused as to why someone would so blatantly lie.

“Oh,” The voice started, surprised by the query, “I’m not crying, I’ve just got bad hay fever that’s all. Comes with living in such a beautiful meadow I’m afraid.” Jonathan opened his mouth to object, but then closed it again. He’d obviously seen something he wasn’t supposed to, and whilst it might not make any sense to him why someone would hide it away it really wasn’t his place to demand information out of a stranger, especially from one that had offered him tea.

“Ok, if you say so.” He stated, sighing faintly. The shrill sound of a kettle boiling suddenly echoed from the doorway, after a few seconds there was a click, and the wailing died down.

“Take a seat by the window. I’m just pouring the tea now.” The voice chirped, cheerfully. Jonathan looked round to the open bay and saw a cute, low table and two rustic wooden dining chairs hiding behind the frame. He did as he was bid and sat in the right-hand seat, taking his coat off before hand and hanging it over the back. He didn’t have to wait very long, as barely thirty seconds had gone by before the door to the kitchen swung open and the voice’s owner came into full view, carrying a large tray. She was around Jonathan’s height, if not a little shorter. She was wearing a sleeveless blouse, with a blue and white floral pattern, that went down just past her hips. Below that there was a pair of three-quarter length, navy jeans, which were turned up at the knee, leaving her lower legs uncovered. A pair of ivory sandals with wine red straps completed an outfit that highlighted its wearer’s humble charm. Her face had a pleasantness about it, its curves subtle yet attractive. Her nose was petite, her lips pleasingly thin, and her eyes a soft shade of azure. She wore her shoulder length hair down; a few wayward strands falling across her face and over her ears, and although the style was rather plain, the colour of the hair definitely wasn’t. It shone in a very striking tone of pink, the hue of a blooming rose in all its summer splendour.

“Here we are.” She announced happily, taking the seat opposite Jonathan and placing the tray on the table between them. She reached over, grasped the teapot firmly, and poured out two cups of dark, amber liquid, before carefully setting the china pot back down onto the tray. Jonathan gingerly picked up his cup and brought it to his lips. The smell of hot tea filled his nostrils, the scented air flowing up to fill his head with its wholesome aroma. He took a small sip and was greeted with a wonderfully malty taste that warmed his mouth. He took another larger sip then put the cup back onto its saucer, swallowed the tea, and sighed contentedly. The girl giggled, "Good tea?" She asked rhetorically. "Help yourself to more if you finish it, there's plenty in the pot." She added as she thoughtfully stirred her own cup and gazed out of the window and into the meadow. After a quiet moment she placed the spoon back onto the tray and looked at Jonathan. "I've never seen anyone like you before here in Anchoridge. Are you new here?" She asked, as she took a sip.

"Well, yes, kind of. My name's Jonathan and I'm here with Greed." Jonathan began, uncertain of how exactly to explain the situation. His answer did seem to catch the girl's attention however.

"Greed's coming!?" She blurted out excitedly.

"Yeah, he's the one that sent me; I'm supposed to wait for him here." Jonathan continued. The girl blinked a few times, suddenly aware of her outburst.

"Did he say why or how long he'd be?" She asked, red faced as she straightened her blouse, and tried to hide her enthusiasm. It was then that a realisation must have struck her, as her eyes widened and she sat forward to stare intently at Jonathan who was, in all fairness, beginning to feel more than a little uncomfortable. "Wait a second, you're not?! You are, aren't you?" She whispered fiercely.

"What? I'm a what?" He clamoured, completely baffled. The girl leaned in closer.

"From another realm," She whispered secretively.

"Well, yes I guess I am. But it's not as glamorous as it sounds." Jonathan stammered, raising his hands defensively, "I'm not ever entirely sure as to *why* I'm here to be honest." He rubbed the back of his neck, feeling more than a little underwhelming for someone who was supposed to be so important.

"Has Greed not explained *anything* to you?" The girl exclaimed, genuinely surprised. She leant forward a touch more, her vibrant hair hovering mere millimetres above the steaming tea, and was about to speak again, when a light rapping of knuckles echoed from the front door. Both of them looked towards the hallway, his host's brow furrowed, and she stood. The rhythmic noise sounded again, and the girl moved to answer it this time, muttering to herself as she opened the living room door and made her way briskly into the hallway. Grasping the handle to the front door delicately, she slowly pulled and gazed out of the gap. Almost immediately she seemed to undergo a wide range of emotions, and although she quickly settled on a pleasantly surprised look her face nevertheless betrayed her inner joy towards whomever was at the door. Jonathan heard the edges of a brief conversation, and a voice like parched sandpaper, then after a few seconds, the girl drew back, and Greed entered the hallway still wrapped in his dark grey cloak that seemed to whirl around his form like wood smoke.

"I see you managed to find this place." Greed called out, "I do pardon the interruption but I have what I needed and so I have come to collect you and Lust." The girl behind Greed gave a petite wave which indicated that he was referring to her. "Come now, we must make way to Envy's house, then there are only two more companions to gather." Jonathan quickly gathered himself, though he was greatly dismayed to be leaving the half-finished tea behind, and gave a brief jog to the front door. He pulled on his coat and was just about to slip his shoes back on when Lust appeared at the bottom of the stairs to his right, her hands frantically tugging on a thin pullover knitted from pastel pink wool.

"I'll come too, I was going to head out to Envy's soon anyway." She said matter-of-factly.

"Very well," Greed replied, "Why don't you lead the way?" He suggested, as he stepped through the front door with a single stride. Greed then turned on his left heel and gestured for Lust to take point. Lust looked almost overcome by the suggestion.

"Oh, I'd be honoured, this way everyone!" She exclaimed, beaming ear to ear, as she practically skipped out the door and into the meadows beyond. Jonathan, who paused only to close the thick wooden door of the abode behind him, followed swiftly with Greed at his heels.

Chapter 6: Synergy of Thought.

If Lust's house was the centre of a compass, then she led them westward towards a more deserted looking area of the gardens. The flora slowly grew more and more sparse, and before long there was only the dark and dusty brown earth beneath their feet once more. They were just crossing the boundary back into town when an almighty rumble shook the air; the sound of a terrific explosion. It was so loud that it made the window frames of the nearby houses rattle like maracas and caused a swarm of scrawny birds take flight from the rooftops with startled cries. Jonathan looked round, his eyes wide with fear to the possibilities of what the sound meant. Lust gazed at him, and then at Greed, her finger on her lips as she considered how to proceed. Greed strode to Jonathan's right, his eye sockets fixed intently towards an unassuming alleyway and the houses beyond.

"Come with me," He announced suddenly, "There's been a change to our schedule." Greed began to swiftly proceed in the direction of the almighty eruption, his cloak flowing around his heels like he was gliding along the floor.

"I guess Envy can wait for now." Lust said timidly, her steps echoing in the now deathly quiet town. Jonathan trailed after her, nervous but keenly curious as to what scene they were venturing towards. They entered the alleyway, which was little more of a small ginnel, that only covered a few meters before hastily opening back up into another of the many courtyards that honeycombed the town. At the far end of this plaza, which Jonathan guessed was around thirty meters long, there was a rather unique looking house that they were rapidly approaching. Outwardly it had the general appearance of the other residences that lined the clearing however when scrutinised more closely it looked less like a single house and more like several abodes all stuck together and built into each other, in fact they were so randomly scrunched up that it was difficult to see where one construction ended and the next one started. There also appeared to be a considerable number of piles of assorted junk lining the outer walls and base of the building. As the trio came to within a meter or two from the 'front' of the abomination of engineering, Jonathan suddenly noticed the there was a great jagged, blackened hole in the side of one of the upper floor walls. He was just about to remark that he hoped it was not a load bearing wall, and that perhaps they should knock to warn the owners when a high-pitched, and most curiously Scottish sounding, voice erupted from said hole.

"SLOTHY!" It squealed with the kind of confused whine a frustrated child might use towards its parent. Without hesitating Greed roughly pulled open the lopsided front door and entered the dwelling. Jonathan and Lust promptly followed him and emerged into a wide room that was akin to a workshop. The room itself was broad, with a low bowed ceiling and splayed supporting beams of thick trunk oak that gave the impression that the entire house was sat back on this point, drunkenly resting on its haunches. From every window streams of dust speckled light invaded the cluttered workshop and highlighted great gatherings of sawdust, metal scraps, and discarded tools of all kinds. In every corner, there were half-finished contraptions and broken-down inventions, some uncovered with their inner working exposed and others hidden away and abandoned beneath oil stained blankets. A hefty, solid looking table stood proudly in the centre of the mess, its face buried beneath countless sheets of blue tinged paper; a smorgasbord of schematics and diagrams. As Greed and Lust carefully picked their way around the jumble of miscellaneous items and towards an opening along the workshop's left wall, Jonathan approached the table. He'd just reached it and was about to sort through the curious mess of scribbles upon it when a second very different voice responded to the call of the first. It was similar to Greed's own voice but without the taste of dryness that made it sound like he was gargling gravel. The voice, or more so it's owner, came across as someone speaking from the very edges of sleep, as if they barely had the energy for such things, and that any more exertion might render them unconscious.

"What...is...it?" It responded, with acute pauses between each strained word.

"You said that it was safe this time, that you'd done the calculations for me!" The first voice whined again, its singsong notes leaping around the house at random.

"And I had...but you didn't...follow the recipe...I created...for...you." Laboured the second voice again.

"Well the recipe was long and booooring! I was just trying to create a shortcut. But whatever, guess I'll have to take it from the top. Again." There was a series of quick, light footsteps above Jonathan, they creaked over where he was stood and beyond the doorway at the left side of the workshop. Jonathan followed them and ducked through the opening. This second room was more familiar to Jonathan, and resembled a combined kitchen and dining room, albeit a more rustic looking one. Surprisingly there was little out of the ordinary with this room, it had all the trappings you would expect from its open plan design; the only thing of note was a large system of pulleys and gears that were connected to a reinforced leather swing and a single rope, both of which hung next to the stairs on Jonathan's right-hand side, but what they were used for he couldn't even begin to imagine. The footsteps once again made an appearance and, as Jonathan watched, creaked down the stairway.

The first thing Jonathan saw were a pair of butterscotch walking boots with thick pink laces that were alarmingly undone, in fact the laces were just tucked unto the ankles rather than properly tied, above this Jonathan spotted a rather cute pair of short, walking socks with white frill on their top. From the top of the ankle to just above the knee the legs were bare, with only the subject's milky mocha skin on show, though this was marred by a rather large gash over the left knee that made Jonathan wince a little when he saw it. By this point the person was about halfway down the stairs, and Jonathan could that their torso see was covered by a pair of blue dungarees under which was worn a faded t-shirt the colour of saltwater taffy. Around the waist there was tied a fuchsia work belt with bulging pockets from which hung a pair of dirty yellow gloves, that were frayed at the fingers and had obviously seen frequent use. The figure reached the last few steps and the light revealed a round face, with friendly feminine features. A wide mouth rested at the bottom third of the face, with a natural smile. Above the mouth sat a sweet snub nose that was flanked by two bright, well defined eyes to the left and right, their irises the shade of ripe watermelon, and topped with a softly curved pair of thin eyebrows. A messy nest of curly, coffee coloured hair enveloped the crown of the head, and was haphazardly tied back into a bushy ponytail. She let out an adorable gasp as she for the first time noticed her visitors, then her face lit up into a giddy grin as she moved to greet them.

"Hi Greed! Hi Lust! Hi guy-I-don't-know!" She stated enthusiastically, making Jonathan smile slightly at the jovial nature of it all. "Did the explosion bring you? I'm sorry, I didn't mean to worry anyone. Just one of my usual errors I'm afraid." She scratched her neck in mock embarrassment.

"It's alright Gluttony, I'm glad you're all in one piece." Lust replied, "That was quite the noise just now." She continued as she moved to embrace Gluttony and shed her earlier worries. Once the hugging had ended, Jonathan chimed up.

"Your name's Gluttony?" He asked, folding his arms. "You're not quite what I'd imagine someone with that name to be if I'm honest." Jonathan was not one to normally be so forward, but his curiosity had reached its limit. Gluttony turned to look at him, cocking her head slightly as she did so. She reached into her work belt and pulled out a large handful of black and white striped sweets; Humbugs. She stuffed them into her mouth and began to thoughtfully chew.

"Hmm? I'm not sure what you mean, what did you expect me to look like exactly?" She mumbled, cheeks bulging with sugary goodness.

For the first time in ages, Jonathan laughed out loud. His bubbling calls infected Gluttony, who swallowed her sweets and almost chocked as she erupted into a giggling fit. Lust too was forced to crack a wide smile and join in with the light-hearted situation. Greed remained as unmoved as ever. Eventually after a minute or so things calmed down, and Jonathan could dismiss Gluttony's query.

"On second thought, forget it I was just thinking out loud." He began, wiping away tears. "It's a pleasure to meet you, my name's Jonathan."

"It's nice to meet you too Jonathan." Gluttony replied. She rested back a little on her heels and put her hands into the rear pockets of her dungarees. It was then that Jonathan remembered the scratch he'd seen on Gluttony's leg, he glanced down and sure enough it was still there as fresh and raw as ever.

"Gluttony are you sure you're ok? You've got a nasty looking mark under your knee." Jonathan stated, gingerly gesturing towards it. Gluttony stuck out her leg and looked down in genuine surprise, as if she'd only just been made aware of the frightful gouge.

"Oh!" She exclaimed, "Must have happened during the explosion, piece of debris I imagine. Thanks for pointing it out." She smiled at Jonathan again.

"Well, should we take you to a hospital or something?" Jonathan asked, concerned about the casual manner of her response.

"A hospital? No silly I'll just sort it here and now." She said light-heartedly. Jonathan was about to query further, and maybe even cue Greed for some support, when something truly miraculous happened. As Gluttony closed her eyes, her forehead began to glow with a delicate cyan light, and a feathery tendril of energy emerged from her brow. It carefully trickled its way forward timidly, before arcing downward and latching itself onto the wounded area, smothering the opening with its turquoise glow. As Jonathan watched, his eyes wide with amazement, the split in Gluttony's leg knitted itself back together leaving not so much as a scar to mark that it had ever been there in the first place. "Ta-dah! All better!" She exclaimed.

"Wow, amazing, how did you do that? Is that some sort of magic?" Jonathan stammered, as his brain replied the past few seconds over and over.

"That's one word for it, yes." Greed's gravelly voice spoke up suddenly, "Though the longer the wound is left, the more effort is required to fix it." As if on cue Gluttony's stomach growled loudly.

"Yeah, I'm pretty hungry now, and it IS lunchtime after all." She replied through grinning teeth.

Jonathan suddenly heard the floor creak behind Gluttony, he looked over her shoulder and saw a hunched shape pull itself through the doorway at the bottom of the stairs. Gluttony, seeing Jonathan's curious gaze fall past her, turned her head to see what he was looking at and let out a high-pitched cry.

"SLOTHY!" She squealed, "I'm so glad you're up." She swung her arm wide towards the trio of onlookers. "We have guests." She announced. The figure she was addressing was obviously another of Greed's odd friends. His slouched form stood just over five feet tall, Jonathan guessed, though if he straightened up it was probable he'd be more around six instead. He worn a pair of threadbare grey trousers, possibly denim jeans but it was difficult to notice as they had very clearly seen better days, and an off-white shirt that was partially buttoned up. He had no footwear on and that, coupled with his emaciated and unkempt appearance, only highlighted how badly fitted and baggy his clothes looked as they hung off his shoulders. His sallow skin was an odd grey-beige as if all previous colour had been sucked out of it. Sloth's face reminded Jonathan of an exhausted donkey, with his yellow eyes half shaded by drooping lids and a single cream coloured tooth poking out from under his dry cracked top lip. His head was even topped by an untidy mane of cropped hair the shade of freshly packed earth. Without so much as a twitch Sloth slid open his jaw to speak.

"I can...see...that." The slow drawl of Sloth's words slinked their way over to Jonathan's ears, making him feel oppressed by their owner's mere presence. He barely lifted his head, directing his voice in Gluttony's vague direction, "I'm heading...upstairs...for a rest. Don't...do anything...dangerous...while I'm...asleep." His slithery words were lifted briefly by a hint of tenderness before sinking back into the dusty floor, vocal molasses once more. Gluttony simply beamed at him, apparently unaffected by the treacle-like atmosphere.

"Oki doki, shall I bring you something to eat soon?" She asked. Sloth just dozily nodded before taking a few lethargic steps towards the strange leather strap Jonathan had noticed dangling beside the stairs earlier. Sloth pulled the two sides of the strap open into something resembling more of a hammock, and climbed on board, eliciting more than a few worrying creaks and groans from the suspended apparatus. He gave the adjacent rope a solid tug and began to elevate slowly into a large square hole in the ceiling, a rattling chorus of clicks and clacks applauding his ascension.

"I see you managed to get it working again." Lust chimed, cheerily.

"Yeah, I'm glad too," Gluttony replied, sticking out her bottom lip. "It's still the only thing I've made that actually works properly." She looked a little disheartened, so Jonathan spoke up.

"Well I think everything here's amazing!" He announced, grinning as he did so, making Gluttony's expression lighten somewhat.

“Well, thanks,” She replied warmly, “I’m just happy to have made something to help out Slothy. He’s great at the thinky side of things, but he’s not the best with moving around, especially on stairs.” Gluttony visibly shuddered for effect, as if drawing on some hideous memory. “Aaaaaanyway,” She cried, “I’m going to prep up some lunch now. Can I get you guys anything?”

“That won’t be necessary,” Greed stated, flatly. There was a slight pause during which Lust gave Greed a withering stare. Greed cleared his throat, “Ah, but, thank you very much for the offer.” He concluded, much to Lust’s approval.

“No worries, I’ll be sure to pack up lots of yummy treats for the journey anyway. So, you’ll get to taste my cooking one way or the other!” Gluttony responded with undimmed enthusiasm, skipping towards the fridge.

“Let us leave, it is not wise to be around Gluttony when she’s liable to get carried away.” Greed whispered to Jonathan as he made his way back the way they’d come. Jonathan and Lust followed suite, Jonathan called a solitary ‘goodbye’ on his way out which was countered by a loud crash as something fragile fell to the floor.

Now out of the curious abode Jonathan once again noticed the large, charred hole in the side of the house, along with the large amounts of debris splayed out and strewn across the building’s courtyard. He turned to Greed, a look of concern in his eyes.

“Greed, we can’t just leave all this mess behind. Especially if we’re all to go on some big adventure. What if someone, or something, breaks in through this convenient opening?” His thoughtfulness seemed to catch Greed a little on the metaphorical nose, and he stopped walking to seriously consider Jonathan’s point. Raising a gloved hand to his bony chin he turned to peruse the predicament.

“I believe,” He began carefully, “That you are correct Jonathan.” Jonathan sighed, pleasantly surprised. Greed continued talking, “Our next stop is not too far from here, and Lust knows the way better than anyone. Go there and retrieve our last companion, I shall stay here to assist in repairing this breach then I shall meet you at my own abode.” Greed turned his head towards Jonathan and Lust, “I hope this is acceptable?" He asked, addressing them together. After a quick glad toward each other then back at Greed, both Lust and Jonathan nodded firmly.

Chapter 7: Water of the Soul.

Lust lead Jonathan back through the ginnel that they'd originally squeezed through to investigate the explosion earlier, and out beyond the rows of dreary, huddled constructs towards a more deserted and depressing corner of the ever-expanding township. Their pace was somewhat slower than Greed's and Jonathan was thankful for it, in truth his feet hurt a little from the constant walking and their run in with Gluttony had awakened his hunger. He decided to make small talk to distract himself from its gnawing bite.

"Hey, erm, Lust. Do you mind if I ask you something?" He inquired.

"Sure, what can I help you with?" Lust responded pleasantly.

"What's up with Gluttony and Sloth? They seem very...close." He continued, awkwardly. Jonathan wasn't the type to gossip but with so many things buzzing around his head he needed something vacuous to focus on.

"If you are asking if they're, together, then yes I guess they are." Lust answered somewhat hesitantly. Jonathan was about to push for clarification as to her cryptic answer when Lust spoke again. "But not in the way you think." She slowed her steps slightly, looking deep in thought. "I'm just trying to remember how Greed described it. I believe he called them 'something akin to lichen'" Jonathan pondered on the words for a moment before speaking again.

"Is there some sort of symbiosis going on?" He queried.

"Yes, that was the word he used." Lust announced, pleased with Jonathan's quick thinking. "Gluttony and Sloth are symbiotic. Gluttony is too much of a scatterbrain to think things through, so Sloth does most of the planning for her and keeps her out of trouble. Whereas Gluttony provides for Sloth and keeps him from wasting away, as well as makes him feel useful." She smiled warmly, "It's very sweet actually." She concluded, picking up her pace again. Jonathan smiled too, it wasn't the answer he'd been expecting but he was happy with it, as happy as one could be in his situation anyway.

As they continued walking, and discussing this and that, Jonathan began to hear running water, its soft trickling comforting despite the lack of greenery around him. The duo approached a steep looking hill, reminiscent of a giant earthen bowler hat, its sides wrinkled with shallow troughs of water. Undaunted, his companion started to ascend the hill, so Jonathan took a few deep breaths and followed her towards the weeping peak.

It took a good ten minutes for Jonathan to reach the top of the great mound of earth, a climb that became steadily harder the higher he went as the ground became more and more sodden and the air increasingly choked with moisture. The dust beneath his feet turned to dirt and then to mud that sucked at his shoes and caused him to come perilously close to being devoured by the ravenous ground. For the most part Lust seemed to climb the hill without any signs of difficulty, but then he figured this sort of thing was probably second nature to her. Finally, the steepness began to ease off and they reached the plateau at the top. At first there was little to see, as Jonathan's vision was disrupted by beads of moisture that had formed on his eyelashes, but as the two of them wandered further into the thin mists a small hunched building came into view.

It sat dejected and defeated in the middle of shallow pond whose surface was in constant rippling motion. In fact it looked less like a house and more like a makeshift shack, something purpose built to survive the waterlogged conditions, but which had nevertheless been patched and repaired a fair number of times. The walls were a criss-cross of rough concrete with more than a few cracks marking them, the largest of which had been hastily covered by a large sheet of iron screwed into the wall. The shack's roof was made of the same metal which draped itself over the top like an old weather-beaten blanket. Rainwater danced over the undulating surface and trickled out of the troughs and into the expansive guttering that seemed to hold the whole building together like a makeshift metallic belt. From the base of the guttering there sprouted a thick copper rod that twisted and reached up towards the sky, protecting the shack and its inhabitant from any wayward lightning strikes that might emerge suddenly from the stormy sheets above. Next to that stood a dark iron weather vane in the shape of an animal Jonathan didn't recognise. It looked to be half chicken half snake, though the poor construction was so dented and battered that the shape could just as easily be because of the weather as much as the creator's design. Lust and Jonathan approached the raised front door, which consisted of a sad looking slab of dark tarred wood. Lust stood just to the left of the doorway and spoke softly as Jonathan came up beside her.

"Hello, Envy? It's me." She spoke in a low mothering tone, and there was something about it that seemed to wrap around Jonathan's mind like a cotton wool. Her words warmed and encouraged him, even as the rain fell more rapidly and soaked him to his skin. There was a feeble reply that escaped Jonathan's ears before Lust spoke again. "I've brought someone with me, a new friend." There was another shift in the weather, a frigid chill climbed up Jonathan's spine as the hard rain began to turn into hail and sleet. The door opened a crack as a thin rime of ice started to snake its way across the wood, crystallising the rainwater. There was another faint response from the darkness to which Lust replied, "You don't have to be afraid, he's very nice and I know he'd love to meet you." In answer the door opened a little more and Jonathan could just see a tiny, frail looking figure sat silhouetted against shack's interior. It spoke, this time just loud enough to hear over the half-frozen raindrops still hammering the tin roof and pond to the sound of miniature applause.

"Who is he? Why is he here?" The voice inquired, as thin and fragile as glass. Jonathan straightened up a little and cleared his throat.

"I am..." He started to say, but Lust cut him off with a glare and slight shake of the head.

"Why don't you come on out and introduce yourself first?" She implored diplomatically, though there was no reaction from the faceless shade beyond the door. They all waited in increasingly awkward silence before Lust spoke again with a little less patience in her voice, "Envy, I don't want to rush you, but this is something very important. I'd hate for you to be left behind again." The temperature suddenly dropped, and the air itself felt like it was freezing solid. The sharp cracks of fracturing ice began to echo from the pond as tendrils of frost sprouted from the edges and rapidly worked their way over the surface. Jonathan's breath appeared as thick puffs of steam, and he pulled his coat tighter around himself. Lust was visibly uncomfortable, biting her lower lip. Jonathan felt a twinge of empathy for the diminutive inhabitant of the shack, in many ways he had felt the same set of emotions himself only a few hours earlier. He stepped forward, in front of Lust, and lowered himself on one knee as flakes of snow replaced the hail.

"Hey there, I believe your name is Envy?" He directed his voice towards the shadow in the doorway, which appeared to nod its head. "I'm Jonathan, it's a pleasure to meet you." He briefly glanced back at Lust before continuing, "This weather's fantastic, did you do this?" Again, the figure nodded. "Well, colour me impressed, and a little jealous. I wish I could make it snow like this, I'd never want to go inside again if I could, it's so pretty out here." Jonathan lent forward a little, "You don't have to if you don't want to, but it would be great if I could meet the person responsible for this amazing power." He noticed that the air was starting to feel less frigid now; even his breath was no longer condensing as thickly as it had been. "I'd love to thank them for making something so beautiful." Jonathan smiled warmly, before Envy's voice gently echoed from the shack.

"You...you're..." The silence hung for a moment before Envy settled on a single word. "Funny." Almost at once the cold oppression lifted and the clouds rose, dissipating into the atmosphere. Envy's silhouette shuffled as she stood and left the darkness of their home.

She must have barely reached four feet five inches tall, perhaps four feet eight if she stretched on her tiptoes. Though not quite as short as when he'd first seen her shadow, Envy was still much shorter than Jonathan, who peaked at around six foot himself. Her pixie cut, forest green hair was pretty in its own way, and her long fringe was brushed forward over the left side of face. Her eyes, of which Jonathan could only see the right one, were tired looking with slight purple shadows under each pale orb; however, her irises shone with the hue of purest jade. Her round, pale face was completed with a tiny bulb nose and diminutive mouth, whose thin lips were bent slightly downwards in a half frown. She wore a thick, long-sleeved jumper which looked to be three sizes too big for her and covered not only her upper body but her arms and hands as well. Its cotton alternated between two sad shades of pine green and mint in thick horizontal stripes. A pair of dark green shorts poked out from under the bottom rim of the turtle-neck, and beneath those she wore two ochre coloured wellington boots with black laces. She stood slightly hunched, her feet pointing inwards with her right arm across her stomach and holding the elbow of her left, in a nervous, protective stance. She refused to look anyone in the eye, her gaze forever pointing downwards towards the sodden floor. Jonathan, trying not to be overcome by pity, raised his right arm slowly and offered his hand to Envy who placed the very tips of her fingers, which were hidden inside her jumper, on his palm. Jonathan smiled as a single ray of weak sunlight poked its face through the purple vortex above and, slowly, he led Envy away from her hut step by meek step, as Lust watched on in a tense mix of anticipation and amazement. When Jonathan and Envy were by her side, she gently took Envy's other hand and together as one they made their way back down the waterlogged hill and the town beyond.

Chapter 8: Wood for the Trees.

Lust, Envy and Jonathan carefully worked their route back through Anchoridge, never once breaking contact. At times, they had to walk in a single long line and at other times they could spread out a little and enjoy the stroll together. Jonathan didn't know where they were heading exactly, but he picked up on subtle cue and hints from Lust. He did initially worry that people would think it odd the way they were travelling, but that feeling of unease slowly drifted away the longer it went on, until eventually he was left with only his enjoyment of the very human moment he was a part of.

Eventually, after many alleyways and turns, the trio came to yet another large open square, and there in the middle stood a great and terrible oak tree. Although it was not overly tall it was impressively wide, and its many leafless branches reached out in stark defiance of the violet maelstrom, their gnarled shapes standing dark and imposing as a netted web of skeletal fingers.

'It truly represents this world; a negative, twisted version of my own.' Jonathan mused to himself as they drew closer, 'Or, is my world a twisted version of this one...' He pondered.

Such thoughts were quickly silenced however as they came around the mighty oak and it became apparent that this was no mere tree; it was a dwelling!

Built into the roots there stood a wide wooden door, painted in a deep blood-red colour, which was reinforced by an ornate iron frame that bent back and forth, imitating the growth patterns around it. From the top of this frame, parallel to the ground, there sprouted a metal pole that was capped with a hanging lantern that had been shaped into a grinning skull. Surrounding the thick knotted trunk, the curled, warped branches held a multitude of framed fractal windows of many irregular sizes, from which an eerie orange light was filtering, that gave the whole organic construct the impression of an enormous jack-o-lantern. Looking upward into the tangled mess of sticks and twigs Jonathan spied a small balcony nestled within, upon which was balanced a miniature telescope and some sort of jet-black globe. Puzzled but unable to form any meaningful conclusions, Jonathan joined Lust and Envy as they approached the front door of the oppressive tree. He reached forward to knock, but before his knuckles could make contact, it opened before him and bathed all three of them with the soft amber glow of candlelight.

"Please, come in." A deep gravelly voice called to them. Jonathan and Co entered, and the door shut behind them with an audible clunk of metal on wood. The three of them stood in what amounted to a giant circular library that had carved its way up inside the centre of the oak; its shelves spiralled upward towards the roof and were filled to the brim with all kinds of books, manuscripts, and artefacts. A few scattered ladders hung onto the wooden frames, poised to lend their sliding assistance in the pursuit of knowledge. In the middle of this treasure trove of words stood a tall-backed reading chair, and in front of that there waited a familiar 'face'.

"Glad you could make it." Greed announced in his usual gritty tone. As he spoke to Jonathan he raised his left arm sideways and gestured palm out to a set of stairs that descended beneath the great tree into the root system. Lust and Envy made their downwards and as Jonathan approached Greed, he spoke again. "The others are already waiting downstairs, let us join them." Jonathan took a moment to gaze into Greed's cold empty sockets before proceeding the way indicated.

As he made his way step by step down the flat wooden steps, Jonathan could make out the sounds of conversation that floated up from the room below. It was not long before the spiral passageway, with its thick root wall twisted and knotted against the earth beyond, opened into a sizeable spherical room, and joined with its circumference. Though the space was underground it was still adequately lit by an old, yet beautiful golden chandelier that hung proudly and spread its warm bronzed light to every nook and cranny. The solid earthen wall that lined the room was reinforced every several feet by hefty oaken beams pressed into its surface, and carved into a few of these Jonathan could make out miniature alcoves that held objects and artefacts that must have been important enough to warrant their own personal storage space. The middle of the room was dominated by an enormous, circular table that appeared to have been created from a single colossal piece of wood. It was covered with a bewildering array of foodstuffs, snacks, and pitchers of drink, some of which Jonathan thought he recognised, but most of which were completely alien to him. The cacophony of smells from the buffet reminded Jonathan as to just how hungry he was, something that had until now been suppressed. Around this feast, and recently joined by Envy and Lust, were sat all of Greed's mysterious friends. Pride was shaking her head and picking up the crumbs that were being strewn about the table by Wrath, who was heartily wolfing down handfuls of tiny pastries. Lust and Envy had taken seats next to each other by the bottom of the staircase and were being greeted by Gluttony who was excitedly showering them with homemade purple Bonbons. Sloth, for his part, was asleep just to the right of her though the food around him untouched. Jonathan spied an unoccupied place at the far side of the table and made his way round as swiftly as he could. He sat down in the elegant wooden chair and had only just removed his coat when Gluttony bounced over to him, spilling sweets and savouries from the several bowls in her arms.

"Hiya Jonny, glad you could make it!" She exclaimed excitedly, a look of genuine glee on her face. Jonathan hadn't the heart to tell her that he'd always hated that nickname, and instead just nodded and mumbled a greeting. Gluttony practically threw the bowls, which thankfully were sturdier then they looked, on to the table top and then pulled up a chair beside him. Greed finally strode into the gallery where he stood tall and imposing at the head of the table, which considering the table was completely round was an impressive feat. All conversation drew into low, hushed tones as slowly and deliberately Greed raised his elbows, brought his hands to his chest, and with one fluid motion removed the robe that Jonathan had assumed was his signature attire. Jonathan stared in fascination at the clothing that had until this time been hidden from view. Beneath the robe Greed wore a stylish double-breasted pinstripe suit, complete with a folded violet handkerchief in the breast pocket, a cobalt-blue tie with speckles like starlight and an immaculately pressed white shirt. Jonathan could not help but admit that, even with the skull head and wrap, he looked exceedingly dapper. Greed placed his gloved hands on the back of his chair.

"My friends, please make use of this modest banquet, we must prepare for our long quest. Afterwards, I shall proceed to explain to our honoured guest the full extent of his purpose here." As if on cue everyone began to fill their plates with whatever food items took their fancy. Wrath, the remnants of his pastry feast still scattered upon his top, helped himself to a hearty ladleful of stew from a large pot, and took several rolls of speckled bread each the size of his fist. His enthusiastic slurping only seemed to irk Pride who was sat beside him. She had opted for a more restrained platter and had instead picked out a few choice morsels including a few slices of dark red meat accompanied by several types of green and white root vegetables. Unlike Wrath's aggressive munching, Pride ate her meal with all the grace and poise Jonathan would have expected. As he glanced around the table his eyes fell upon Envy and Lust. Envy it seemed wasn't much of a big eater and was timidly picking at an assortment of h'orderves from tiny crackers with cheese, to wraps resembling puff pastry sausage rolls. Occasionally she would raise something to her mouth and take a nibble or a sip, but otherwise she seemed disinterested in ingesting any of the snacks and drink. Lust was busy trying to juggle mothering Envy and eating her own meal, which was more or less a bit of everything, though she did seem to favour a tall, iced glass of what Jonathan assumed was tea from the colour. Sloth was being tended to by Gluttony who was feeding him forkfuls of flaky pasta. Unlike Envy, Sloth was dutifully eating each bite that came his way though it took him at least a minute to finish chewing each heaped mouthful. The large pauses between administering Sloth's meal did however give Gluttony breaks within which to shovel various items of confectionary into her wide mouth.

Jonathan brought is gaze back to his own empty plate and reasoned that he had better follow everyone's lead and eat well. His eyes flitted back and forth trying to find something within arm's reach that he recognised. Jonathan was not afraid of new foodstuff and new experiences, but if the meals here were as odd as the residents then Jonathan didn't know how well that would sit with him. From the assembled bowls and serving platters in front of him Jonathan selected a modest variety consisting of; three broad dark green leaves that he hoped was lettuce, a spoonful of a chunky white mixture that resembled potato salad, several diminutive rolls with various meat fillings, two heaped servings of plump berries the size and colour of red grapes, a thick slice of grain flecked bread, and a half-glass of something that smelt like pink lemonade. Jonathan's stomach growled nervously as, with a quiet sigh, he picked up his utensils and began his culinary journey. The fern green leaves had a texture like lettuce but tasted more like crunchy spinach, he managed a mouthful or two before deciding that they definitely needed eating with something and not on their own. Next, he tried the creamy chunky sauce and was pleasantly surprised to find that it was indeed some otherworldly variety of potato salad, albeit a little sweeter than he was expecting. The puff pastry rolls were light and crispy, and the interiors delicately spiced to fully compliment and boost the rich almost lamb-like flavour of the meat. Unfortunately, the dumpy little berries were unbearably sour and it was all Jonathan could do to not spit out his mouthful, instead he took a swig from his glass to wash them down and noted with relief that the beverage he'd picked closely resembled lemonade although it carried a heady wine-like aftertaste. After refreshing his mouth with a few more of the delectable rolls, Jonathan finished off a 'lettuce' and slaw sandwich of his own creation and sat back with his glass in hand secretly glad the experience was over for now. Nevertheless, his belly gurgled in appreciation, grateful for the sustenance no matter where it came from.

Jonathan suddenly felt a tap on his shoulder, he swivelled himself round and was greeted to a cheery beaming face and a pair of hands that held out a purple silk bag, bursting at the seams.

"Take one!" Gluttony chimed innocently. Jonathan was sceptical and raised a questioning eyebrow. "Why the face? I just thought you might like an after-dinner mint." She clarified, pulling the pouch open. Inside were dozens of marble sized sweets, Jonathan extracted one and examined it more closely. It was perfectly round and had a pretty tricolour swirl of amber, hickory, and pearl.

"What flavour is it? Jonathan asked, "It doesn't look to be *just* peppermint." Gluttony giggled.

"Of course not silly, that would be boring." She clapped her hands together, "It's plantain, hazelbutter, and mint. It's a new recipe I've been trying out in my space time." Gluttony stared at him with equal parts mischief and eagerness. Jonathan, who was admittedly curious to sample the strange combination, braced himself and put the sweet into his mouth. At first there was very little to it, but as it began to dissolve and coat his taste buds a wondrous flavour erupted across his tongue. The joy from the ongoing experience tentatively blossomed forth onto Jonathan's face, eliciting an adorable squeal of triumph from Gluttony.

"Wow!" Jonathan exclaimed between sucks, "You've got talent, this tastes amazing." Gluttony, overwhelmed by the positive feedback, threw her arms wide with absolute glee.

“Aww I’m so glad you like them. I dunno about talent, I just do it as a hobby.” She turned to the rest of the table, “I’m going to see what the others think too.” She said, bounding off towards Lust and Envy with an air of determination about her. Jonathan chuckled and turned his attention back towards Greed, who had just finished consuming a deep bowl of rich savoury broth and was contentedly lent back, a metallic straw still clasped between his front teeth. Greed breathed deeply, expulsing a satisfied sigh seemingly unaware of the room around him. After a few moments he straightened back up, and reapplied his cold, emotionless mask once more. Everyone one else finished their respective meals and sat waiting on Greed expectantly.

“Now then, Mr Rhodes.” He spoke slowly, his words full of purpose. “I believe it is time everything became clear.” Greed rose from his chair with one deft motion and, using his ruby telekinesis, retrieved a large scroll from a shelf to his left. “As I have already explained, our world exists in parallel with another world. Equal, yet opposite.”

“Opposite energies, positive and negative, yes I remember.” Jonathan said, contemplatively. “Something’s gone wrong though, right?”

“Many years ago, unknown to us, a great vortex of energy appeared in our realm, too much to be converted.” Greed explained. “It gained its own consciousness, becoming akin to what you would call, a god.” He lent forward on the table and opened the scroll completely for Jonathan to see. It was a vast map complete with lakes, forests, trackways, and a vast horizontal Y-shaped mountain range that split the map in two. Greed pointed to a spot nestled at the point where the two upper prongs of the Y connected.

“This is where we currently reside. Anchoridge; a little sanctuary from the world. At least, for now.” He shifted his finger to a point near the top-right corner of the map, north-east of Anchoridge, an array of ancient ruins surrounded by forest. “This is where we believe this being to be spreading from.” Pride cleared her throat.

“It’s called Sheol.” She blurted abruptly. “There’s no harm in using its name.” She glared at Greed dispassionately.

"Yes, quite." Greed stated as he seized control of the conversation again. "Regardless, that point there is where we must go if we are to stop this...thing...from corrupting everything." Jonathan peered up from the map.

"What happens then?" He asked, apprehensive of the answer. Greed gritted his teeth, pondering the best way to address the question. "Ok, ok, it would be really bad. Forget I asked." Jonathan waved his hands, regretting his query. "What about this then, why do you need me?" He asked nervously, changing the subject. "Before you said that I wouldn't be affected by Sheol's power." Greed nodded, slowly.

"Everyone in this realm and its twin unconsciously feed from the energy exchange, we are shaped by it, and grown from it. This being casts a great shadow, a shadow that can tap into and eat away at the willpower of anything connected to the exchange." A heartbeat passed. Greed and all his friends gazed at Jonathan, was that hope in their eyes? "Anything, except someone from a world that sits apart from the flow. Someone like you." Jonathan suddenly felt the full weight of their stares, and although he'd never been the type to self-loathe, he definitely didn't believe he was anything above ordinary.

"But why me? You said yourself that I was nothing special Greed, just a happy coincidence." In response to this everyone shifted their attention back to Greed, with a few accusatory looks and baleful expressions at Greed's callous use of words. Greed raised his hand to stow any outbursts.

"Yes, I did say that, because it is the truth Mr Rhodes. You, when compared against your world's population, are not out of the ordinary by any means. However, that quality, or lack thereof, is exactly what this quest demands. A more self-centred person would have refused the call outright; a more selfless person would have been determined to do this alone. Both of the extremes are useless, I needed something in the middle." Though Greed's reasoning seemed a little odd to him at first, after running it through his head a few times Jonathan had to agree that it did make a kind of sense. This was not the time for emotional heroics, but for a logical solution to an illogical problem. Jonathan smiled, and nodded understandingly.

"Ok, so if this Sheol being can corrupt anything born of this world. What's to stop it controlling all of you when we get closer to it?" Wrath let out a snort and stood up.

"That's where I come in. I've been working on a little something special for this trip." He reached into his apron's vast pocket and pulled out the bracelet that Jonathan had seen earlier in his workshop. Wrath came around the edge of the table and gave Jonathan the finished piece to inspect. It was still the same beautiful white-gold as before, but this time Jonathan could see there had been intricate and arcane looking knotwork carved into the body around the twinkling gem. There was even a delicate copper inlay on the inside of the bracelet loop that made the hairs on back of Jonathan's hand stand on end when he ran his fingers along it.

"Is this for me?" Jonathan asked, aghast. Wrath nodded and gave a wide smirk.

"Aye, try it on." He urged. Jonathan rolled up the right sleeve of his jumper and slide his wrist into the bracelet. He creased his brow, aside from a very faint static feeling from the copper inlay, he didn't feel any different.

"Do not worry if you cannot feel any immediate effects." Greed spoke up, clearly noticing Jonathan's disappointment. "Unaware as you may be, your kind projects an aura of nullness, you exist as a kind of void in the energy flow."

"Which is why I'm unaffected by Sheol's shadow. Right?" Jonathan replied, putting two and two together.

"Exactly," Greed continued, "This charm amplifies that void and enhances it. Allowing you to act as a kind of metaphorical umbrella that will allow us seven to remain safe, as long as we are within a decent radius around you."

"Should keep us pretty safe. What Greed lacks in looks, 'e makes up for in smarts." Wrath announced jovially, crossing his arms. Lust shuffled uncomfortably in her seat as Jonathan eyes caught Pride's doubtful expression. It was then he remembered what Pride had said earlier about the wastelands and their dark denizens. Considering his words for a moment, Jonathan turned in his seat to face Greed straight on.

"There's one last though, this might keep us secure against Sheol. But I remember talk of...shadow beasts?" Jonathan watched as Greed rubbed his jaw, deep in thought, before he settled back down in his chair. He placed his elbows on the table and knotted his fingers together before securing his chin atop the arch. Jonathan glanced at Pride, who had lent back a little and folded her arms across her chest. A look of smug amusement wiped across her face, she was clearly eager to see where this exchange would go. Greed let out a contemplative sigh.

"There have always been dangerous creatures that have prowled the wastes." Greed's voice hung lower, a glint of danger surrounding his words. "However, with the shadow's influence ever present these animals have begun to take on more aggressive behaviour, as well as darker, more terrible forms." He lowered his hand arch to the table, keeping his head where it was. "That is also the matter of the Shadow People." Greed's skull glowed blood-red, again retrieving a tightly coiled scroll from its holdings to his back left. This time the scroll did not contain a map, but instead what looked like a detailed blueprint or autopsy report. Notes were scrawled along the edges and margins of the many frightening diagrams that depicted many kinds of hunched, mutant humanoids and warped skeletons that got more and more disturbing the longer Jonathan looked at them. "We have catalogued a few different variants," Greed continued, tone still as dark as thunder, "The most common type appears to be this one here." He brushed his right hand across the page and pointed to one of the larger drawings in the upper corner. The image, though intricately drawn, was too misshapen to be anything other than grotesque. The main portion of the picture was concerned with detailing the attributes of the thing's skeletal features. The structure looked to consist of two gangly arms that were capped with horrifying razor-edged fingers, four per hand. Each razor was at least the length of Jonathan's forearm and were depicted as being able to be drawn up together like some quad-pronged pair of scissors. A cage of solid ribs made up the thing's chest, though Jonathan could see something resembling a carved opal or ruby depicted inside the ribcage protected by the sternum. A bald skull could be seen mounted atop the neck, though exactly what it resembled Jonathan could not completely tell as instead of a face the being was wearing a ghastly black iron helmet, a kind of half-helm with a single visor like eye opening that was obscured by a jagged metal grill. The abomination's macabre grin poked out from underneath the helmet's flat nose guard, both otherworldly and yet disturbingly familiar. The creatures were shown using their hands for locomotion, as the skeleton had neither feet nor legs, in fact it simply terminated with a lengthy, pointed spine. Clearly these spawns of Sheol dragged themselves forward to eviscerate whatever hapless soul stood in their way. Jonathan shuddered as an imaginary breeze snaked its way up his back. This quest was getting more twisted by the minute.

"What are these things?" Jonathan asked as he looked away, disgusted by the diagrams.

"From what we've been able to deduce these creatures are not born, but made." Greed rolled up the offending scroll and retied the bindings. Wrath strode forward a pace or two, powerful hands resting atop his hips.

"I've only been able to look at bits and pieces, but them skeletons are definitely made of a steel alloy, maybe chromium but it's 'ard to say for sure." Wrath crossed his arms again, "That's the easy part though, the tricky bit's what's 'idden inside that metal body." Jonathan shot Greed a quizzical look.

"Wrath is correct, though they may be varied in structure these Shadow People all have one thing in common; their cores." Jonathan frowned slightly, but kept his eyes firmly fixed on Greed who continued speaking. "The cores of these beings are made of a peculiar stone called Carnelian. This stone is also known as Soul-Stone, and for good reason, for it has the power to capture and contain the souls of the dead." Jonathan swallowed, this throat suddenly dry as he unravelled the meaning behind Greed's words. "Indeed Mr Rhodes, these infernal beasts are driven by the souls of all those who have perished under this mad god's shadow."

"C-can't they be destroyed?" Jonathan stuttered, his mouth parched with horror, "Can't the s-souls be released?" Jonathan's pleas were only met by a solemn shake of the head from Greed.

"Whilst destroying the core will indeed allow the soul of the operator to be set loose, such an act only delays it does not permanently solve anything." He answered monosyllabically, the topic clearly wearing on him.

"What he means is," Lust's sweet tones echoed across the table, "Although we might grant the soul temporary release from its torment..." Her eyes sank low as if in mourning, "...the soul is soon recaptured by Sheol and...reused." Jonathan let out a hefty sigh and scratched the back of his head nervously.

"Greed, I must admit, this sounds fairly hopeless." He admitted. His feelings were not helped by the dank dreary atmosphere of this realm, which seemed to thrive on his doubts and fears. Greed however, stood up and peered at Jonathan through his empty sockets.

"That is where you are wrong, Mr Rhodes." He announced, a little more life in his gritty voice. "For that bracelet will not only keep us safe from corruption but also allow us to move unnoticed by minions or master. Well, as long as we do not do anything too conspicuous." Greed stepped up to Jonathan and, in a rare moment of heart, placed his hand on Jonathan's left shoulder. "We will protect you Mr Rhodes. We will do our job, so that you might do yours." Jonathan could not help but give a nervous yet determined smile. As uneasy as all this made him feel, he could not let these people down. They needed him, and he would deliver.

Chapter 9: Fire and Frying Pan.

It took a further half hour to clean up the remains of the banquet, and then begin to prepare for the journey they were about to undertake. Thankfully Greed had done most of the work for them and had already assembled everything he thought vital to their quest in the form of personalised travel packs for each companion. Jonathan's pack contained back-up food rations, water rations, a compass, a smaller version of the map scroll from earlier, a bed roll, a fold up parka that doubled as a blanket, several bandages, and a twelve-inch foldable knife for 'emergencies'. Jonathan unpacked, checked, and repacked everything until he was satisfied that he could access things even in the dark, as he had no clue what kind of environments they were likely to face. By this time everyone except Wrath and Lust had gathered back at Greed's house and were doing their own final checks and training. The master of the abode had retreated upstairs to gather a few final important belongings. Pride had been busy meditating, necklace in hand, her lips occasionally moving to mouth the odd words or phrase. Sloth, as ever, was asleep his pack beside him untouched from the moment it had been given to him. His stalwart companion Gluttony was hunched on the ground nearby trying to attach a dozen or more colourful bags of confectionary to her pink work belt. Envy, who was awaiting Lust's return, was perched on the table itself, her sombre stare fixed on a landscape painting on Greed's wall, her face reflected in the painting's burnished brass frame.

Jonathan gingerly made his way over to Envy, trying his best not to break the unsteady air that had fallen over the room. He parked himself beside her, her gaze never once leaving the image she was intently watching.

"Hey," Jonathan spoke, softly, "Mind if I join you?" He asked, playfully. "It must be a terribly exciting painting to warrant such scrutiny." The corner of Envy's mouth turned up ever so slightly.

"This is how life began." Envy's soft child-like voice was so quiet that even in the relative calm of the basement Jonathan had a tough time fully hearing her.

"All life?" He asked her gently.

"Yes," She replied, "In the past." Jonathan took a moment to properly look at the painting Envy was referencing. It was indeed a landscape, albeit not one that Jonathan would have recognised. It depicted a great wintery forest of spiky charcoal pines surrounded on two sides by steep rocky cliffs. The upper half of the picture was devoted to the sky, and a fantastic black and violet whirlwind. The centre of the tempest was painted a brilliant contrasting pearl, in the shape of a star with four prominent spikes and four diminutive ones. From this eight-pointed badge were painted seven streaks in a whole spectrum of colours, each streak being projected outward towards the very edges of the frame. It was certainly very masterfully done, but the true cryptic meaning was lost on Jonathan.

"I've never been one for fine art I'm afraid." Jonathan admitted.

"I like it," Envy whispered, "It makes me remember where we came from." She moved her eyes to stare at Jonathan. "Don't you think that's important?" She asked quietly.

"Oh, very," Jonathan replied to the seemingly innocuous question. "It's never a bad thing to know and value your heritage." He turned to look at Envy compassionately, "Those who forget the past are doomed to repeat it." He quoted, secretly proud of himself for sounding hopefully wise. Envy just giggled softly for a second.

"I was right." She decided, "You are funny." And with that she turned her gaze back towards the painting. It was just as Jonathan was about to change the subject when he heard a most dreadful bang from above.

He realised it was Greed's front door being violently forced open from the outside in. There was a chorus of muffled, concerned voices and before Jonathan could react, he heard frantic footsteps descending and Lust's face appear at the apex of the stairway. She was white as a sheet, her eyes wide with fear.

"Everyone come quickly, we need to move!" She called down, her normally demure voice shaking on the edge of panic. She disappeared back upstairs, leaving Pride, Sloth, Gluttony, Jonathan and Envy to hurriedly gather their things and follow her.

Back in the central library, Greed was conversing with Wrath in hushed concerned tones. The larger man had a few weapons at his feet and his chest was heaving as he recovered breath from what must have been a hard run. As Jonathan, how was the last one to get reach the top, emerged Greed turned to address everyone. His voice gravelly was firm yet for the first time had an edge of uncertainty to it.

"My friends, there was been a complication and we must move fast. The enemy has found us and we must evacuate, we must get Mr Rhodes to safety." He picked up a heavy leather satchel from the reading chair to his left and made for the door. "Gather what you can carry and follow me!" He called, leaving the house with his signature long strides. A hectic ten seconds ensued as everyone grabbed their kit bags, as well as anything else that looked useful, and set off through the door.

Once outside Jonathan was bathed in pale moonlight, its beige glow illuminating softly the manic scene in the square before him. A distant bell was tolled mournfully as villagers ran to and fro. Beings of all shapes and sizes were gathered across the square and formed into a loosely organised band armed with everything they could get their various appendages on. Jonathan saw everything and anything being thrust into service to protect the township; pitchforks, swords, hammers, a pole-arm or two, knives tied to broom handles, some of the denizens weren't even visibly armed instead relying on their own brute strength or natural weaponry that sprouted from their multitudinous forms. Jonathan might have felt afraid, terrified even, but as he studied the faces of the villagers he saw nothing but grim conviction. If they were afraid to face death, they did not let such trifle feelings manifest. Not wishing to tarry more than needed, Jonathan left the villagers to their preparations and hurried after his own companions who had rushed off towards one of the larger warren-like ginnels that comprised the guts of Anchoridge. Jonathan saw Pride jogging just up ahead of him, and he picked up pace to match her speed.

"Pride," He called, "Where are we going?" His breathing had become a little heavier, and Jonathan briefly regretted not taking his personal fitness more seriously. Pride looked back over her shoulder.

"There's a secret passage behind the gatehouse, come with me Mr Rhodes." She called back, her own voice steady, clearly Pride was more accustomed to this sort of thing than Jonathan was. She sped off, picking up speed with Jonathan trailing behind her, as he followed her lead through the twisted labyrinth. It took a few minutes until the two of them reached the gatehouse, by which time Jonathan's lungs were burning from the exertion.

"I...just need...a second..." He spluttered through deep gasps. Pride stopped her advance and doubled back, grabbing his arm to heave him forward.

"We don't have time for this Jonathan!" She spat at him clearly frustrated with his lack of stamina. A series of frightful splintering impact sounds made Jonathan look up, and he could clearly see she was right. The noble gatehouse with its impressive entryway was being blocked and barricaded by a mob of armed and armoured townsfolk. The dreadful scraping blows of metal on timber were coming from the other side of the hulking oaken doorway that he and Greed had passed through barely a few hours ago. The unnerving thing was, aside from the beating of sharpened steel against wood, there was no noise at all to be heard from the attacker's side of the gate; no shouts, no battle cries, nothing except the relentless assault on the steadily fracturing lumber obstacle in front of them. Jonathan, still in Pride's grasp, stumbled into the shadow cast by the stone bastion and was half dragged half pushed behind the right gatehouse tower to where Greed and the others were waiting.

"Ah Mr Rhodes, so good of you to join us." Greed stated dryly. Jonathan hadn't the breath to mutter a response, so he elected to remind quiet. Pride let go of his arm and impatiently strode over to Greed, stooping down she began counting the cobbles away from the base of the slate grey wall. Upon reaching the fourth stone she ran her fingers down its length and sank them into the dirt between it and the fifth pebble. Her digits ate into the earth with comparative ease and she slowly began to lift a meter-wide section of the ground. Wrath bent to help her, and together they uncovered an inky black shaft going beneath Anchoridge. Without hesitation Wrath removed a torch from the wall and, his sombre face aglow with the firelight, descended into the murky shadows. He was subsequently followed by the vexed looking Pride, a worried Gluttony who was holding hands with very nonplussed Sloth, and a terrified Lust dragging a reluctant Envy. Greed motioned silently for Jonathan to head down next as the rhythmic metallic drumming against the gate was being frantically hypnotic. Jonathan placed his feet, somewhat unsteady with adrenaline and the physical exertion of earlier, onto the ironwork ladder and lowered himself down into the musky, claustrophobic pit. After several steps Greed followed him down and it was just as the trapdoor above was being heaved shut that Jonathan heard the blood curdling sound of the once-sturdy timber gate crunching and exploding outward as it finally gave way. A chorus of dismayed voices rose in a wail of doom as the villagers met their silent foe, only to be suddenly and forever shut out with the closing of the secret stone hatch. Jonathan's heart sank and he shut his eyes as he tried to blot out the echoed memory of that terrible moan. There was no going back now.

Chapter 10: Unknown Depths Below.

For a few minutes, darkness reigned. There were precious few sounds, save for the plinking of shoes on iron, and nothing at all from the surface as the trapdoor blotted out everything above them. The stench of stale air permeated his lungs, and Jonathan could do nothing except feel his way down, putting one hand below the other, one foot beneath the proceeding foot. He felt cold, alone, helpless to do anything but descend lower and lower into the bowels of the underworld. His mind, frayed by the stress of recent events, began to play tricks and games with him, creating shapes and faces in the stale blackness. Bit by bit, neuron by neuron, Jonathan feared he was going mad.

Eventually the air of chaotic melancholy was shattered by the quiet shuffling of boot soles hitting solid, dusty ground. Jonathan squinted downward and could make out fractured shapes silhouetted against the base of the ladder. As he slowly approached the hallowed light, he felt the oppressive, shade induced insanity begin to leave him, and his own self return. Jonathan finally reached the end of his climb down, and gingerly stepped off the ladder. His breathing and natural rhythms returned as the gentle caressing glow from the burning torch in Wrath's grasp, banished the imaginary daemons back to the mental pits from whence they came.

Jonathan's eyes quickly adjusted to the soft flickering light source and as Greed emerged from the shaft behind him, he peered round to inspect the cavern they had arrived in. While not as large as Jonathan would have liked, it was nevertheless much more spacious than the way in and was easily wide enough for the group to walk two-a-breast. The walls were ancient rock; dark, dusty, mottled grey, and Jonathan noted that the original area must have been somewhat narrower as it was clear from the pick marks and engravings that it had been worked and widened over the centuries. He stepped closer to Wrath so as to utilise his light, and could make out alcoves and deep-seated pits carved into the walls. Though they were too strewn with old debris and cobwebs to identify their holdings, he did recognise the purpose of the repeating pattern of their appearance along the cavern's sides. These were catacombs, and they had not been used for a very long time it seemed. Jonathan straightened back up and felt Greed gently push past him and to the head of the group. Greed turned swiftly on his heels, causing a sprinkling of dust to raise up from the floor, and faced everyone.

"These catacombs and tunnels should eventually bring us to the other side of the mountains. From there we can make our way back to our original route, and then onward to the northern forests." He rotated his head slightly back and forth, scanning their faces with his non-existent eyes. "I trust everyone is ok with this slight change in our plans?" He asked. Though the question seemed rhetorical a single gentle, yet strained voice piped up in answer.

"What happened Greed? I thought we were safe, I thought Anchoridge was safe!" Jonathan turned to see Lust staring at Greed, her moisture-stained eyes glaring accusatory daggers. Greed just met her gaze, eye for eye. She took a few steps forward, as tears began to form a new and run in staggered drips down her cheeks. The catacombs rang silent and Jonathan heard them tip-tap onto the stale, chalky floor. "The villagers Greed, they were all..." She faltered, her breathing ragged. Her voice cracked and she stopped looking toward Greed, her head steadily lowered as the horror of her words ran through her mind. "And we just left them to their fate...we just ran away...all those kind men, and women, and...and..." She started to sob in earnest and Jonathan felt a pit of regret open in his stomach as Lust hiccupped and the dripping of a tap became the drumming of rain. Greed just stood there, no sign of reaction or understanding. Lust raised a horrified hand to her cheeks, in a vague effort to stem the flow of tears. Jonathan glanced at her and back to Greed, powerless to do anything but watch the exchange unfold. Greed let out a diminutive sigh, and ground his front teeth softly, Jonathan wondered what it was he was thinking so deeply about, and clearly something was weighing on his brilliant if cold mind? After a few anxious seconds Greed spoke.

"Their worries are over. But ours are not." He announced, "We must press onward or it will all have been for naught." Jonathan got the impression there was more he perhaps wanted to say, but instead Greed simply turned around and motioned for them to follow his lead further into the dank tunnels. With a shake of his head Wrath preceded after Greed, then Lust who was being consoled by Gluttony and Envy, Sloth trailed behind them dragging his feet, which left Pride and Jonathan at the rear of the column. Jonathan didn't know what to say in a situation like this, so instead he just watched Pride out of the corner of his eye, waiting for the right moment to ask a burning question in his gut. After a good fifteen minutes of walking he had almost given up hope of ever breaking the frigid silence when Pride broke it for him.

"I know what you've been thinking." She spoke in a low whisper.

"What, and how?" Jonathan asked quietly.

"No, Greed was not always this cruel." She replied, ignoring his second query and answering his first. Jonathan opened his mouth to protest, but Pride raised a hand and shook her head to stow his complaint. "It is ok. Cruel is the correct word here. But understand that cruelty is not Greed's game."

"What do you mean?" Jonathan asked, "I can understand his logical approach, but surely there are times when a little compassion is in order?" Pride laughed under her breath, but it was not a joyous sound, it was one born of a bitter, pain-drenched memory.

"Did it never occur to you to ask why he looks the way he does?" She suddenly retorted. Jonathan lowered his eyes and was surprised to find that it did not.

"I guess I just didn't want it to seem like I was judging someone based on their appearance." He answered, honestly. "And I also guess that once we arrived here, it just sort of fit the mould for this world." Jonathan added, sheepishly. Pride smiled sadly.

"A rare answer and only one a true outsider could give." She whispered. Pride turned to Jonathan, "The truth is Greed was not always this way, his looks, his behaviour, they used to be very different." She turned away again, recalling something from the forgotten mists. "But that has long since passed, needless to say do not judge him too harshly Mr Rhodes." She concluded, looking back at him once more with her crimson spheres. Jonathan sensed a vein of pain behind her calm, reminiscent expression but decided not to dig. If she wanted to relive the past with him, he was sure she would do so when the time was right.

Hours ticked by in silence, and the more time Jonathan spent in the tunnels the more he came to realise just how vast the complex was. The group passed numerous side passageways and junctions all carved out the underground, all now long forgotten and left to rot. He began to wonder if perhaps it was not the townspeople who had built them but instead some long-lost civilisation and that Anchoridge had simply been built upon them, ignorant as to what lay beneath their feet. He continued to ruminant on this hypothesis when the group passed under an impressively ornate sandstone archway and entered a cavernous vault like one might find in the centre of a cathedral. As they crossed the boundary of the arch the whole space was softly lit with a smooth ice blue glow as curious wall-mounted orbs blinked unsteadily to life. Though not wonderfully bright, the orbs did provide enough light to see by so Wrath, muttering something about magic, extinguished his torch to conserve it. The group spread about a little, no longer being constrained by the narrow tunnel.

“We will take a short break, now that we have room to breathe.” Greed declared. Jonathan and the rest of the party settled to the floor as Greed made his way to the middle of the vault to inspect where they might be heading next. He was thankful for the brief respite and was pleased to note that the air in this expansive room was a little less stale than the catacombs they’d come from. Wrath unburdened his large, conical, tough leather backpack, which reminded Jonathan of a golf club case, and opened it up to carefully slide out the contents. He removed four very different objects; the weapons from earlier.

“I’m sorry I couldn’t grab ‘em all, I barely had time to finish sharpening this lot before we had to up sticks.” Wrath explained as he spread out the four weapons in front of everyone. Jonathan took a closer look at each one in turn.

The first weapon was a slender and regal looking rapier. Its silver-steel glistened as it caught the glow-orb’s light, and Jonathan admired the careful craftsmanship that went into every detail, from the elegantly contoured hand guard through to the very tip of the graceful yet deadly blade. The ‘pommel’ of the guard cradled a cut crimson ruby, and there was some kind of inscription along the rapier’s length, but it was too thin and the light too poor to make it out. The second weapon was a curious contraption akin to a crossbow but with a few modifications. It held an extra string on its curved compact frame and just above the locking point there was a thin oblong box that held several black iron bolts. The chunky stock held an interesting flywheel that hooked into the trigger. Its sturdy construction gave it a rugged and slightly haphazard appearance. Jonathan concluded that this particular crossbow must have been altered for repeat fire, or at least auto loading. The third item was by all accounts an ordinary broadsword that, while not as decorated or intricately forged as the rapier, was still beautiful in its own ordinary way. The blade was at least three times as wide as the rapier, and its short grip was wrapped in black leather with a wide egg-shaped pommel. This was an honest and trustworthy sword. The final piece was a sizeable, heavy war hammer that looked similar to an everyday work hammer but had an acute point on the reverse side instead of a rounded bulb or nail remover. Its tempered surface was made of ashen grey steel that reflected little light, and the long, rugged handle had been carved from a tough, dull wood that matched the whole weapon's theme of simple yet powerful.

One by one each weapon's owner came forth to claim their property. Pride retrieved her rapier, handling the dangerous article with practised, familiar hands. She brought the blade up the sit parallel with her face before delicately securing it in her belt.

Next was Gluttony who, with wide-eyed wonder, picked up and inspected the crossbow. She removed the bolt cage, aimed upward and released the trigger causing the dual strings to snap forward with an impressive whip crack. The fly wheel then spun into motion and restrung the device. The whole operation took less than a second.

"Wowee!" She exclaimed, "It's even better than I'd imagined." Her awestruck face continued to beam even as she retreated back to her previous spot. Wrath was next, picking up the hefty war hammer. His iron hard muscles heaving and flexing, grumbling with internal power, and he let out a chuckle.

"Heh, it ain't pretty, but neither am I. But still I'd rather carry it and not need it, than need it and not carry it." He announced, with wise gruffness. That left just the broadsword, there were a few heartbeats but none else moved. Wrath tutted, stooped and picked up the blade. Cradling the weapon in his hands he turned, and thrust it pommel first towards Jonathan, who just blinked and glanced back and forth between him and the sword. “This’uns for you Jonathan.” Wrath disclosed, as if it was not obvious already. Jonathan tentatively reached forth and grasped his fingers around the ebony grip, lifting it from Wrath’s hands. It was lighter than he’d expected, and perfectly balanced around the simple yet ample crossguard.

“Erm, thanks.” Jonathan exclaimed, still surprised by the unexpected gift. “I promise to use it with respect.”

“Let us hope you don’t have to use it at all.” Pride declared coolly. “That sword is for self-defence only.” She folded her arms, her stance confident. “Let the rest of us handle the heavy lifting.” Jonathan heard a crunch of footsteps over his shoulder and looked round to see Greed coming over to address them all.

“I have identified the best route to the surface. If everyone is ready, we will commence.” Everyone nodded morosely, got up and made to leave. Jonathan sheathed his sword in his belt, gave a determined huff, and set off with Greed at the head once more.

Chapter 11: Thought Enclosed By Caves.

The group ventured out of the catacomb vault, leaving the glow-orbs to fade away once more, and joined a passageway across from the one they'd entered by. This crack in the wall was more primal and jagged than the other tunnels, and Jonathan heard Sloth muttering steadily to himself about how this was perhaps a natural cave formation that had eroded and collapsed its way into the purpose-built vaults beyond. Jonathan was once again at the rear of the troupe, this time flanked by Gluttony and Sloth, Pride having decided to watch Greed's back as they wandered further from civilisation. Even ignoring the structural differences, it was obvious that this tunnel was of a very different vein to the ones before. Its path twisted and turned sometimes feeling as if it were folding back onto itself, the width was inconsistent at best allowing the group to walk three in a row at times and having to shuffle awkwardly through gaps the next, the height also fluctuated, mostly remaining above head level but occasionally dipping down and forcing the party almost to a crawl to continue onward. After a half hour of spelunking Jonathan noticed that it had gotten chillier in the cave system which made him thankful he'd dressed warmly, as the occasional wisp of frosty air swept past his head and teased his hair playfully.

"We must be getting closer to the outside again." Jonathan announced to himself, his voice joining the now solid echoing of footsteps as the dirt and debris on the floor became sparser and instead the dry, compact rock beneath came to the fore. After a further five hundred meters Jonathan heard the gentle whooshing of a distant waterfall and soon after that the blanket of noise was joined in harmony by the delicate, rhythmic bloops of water droplets falling in rhythm from nearby stalactites, like a damp xylophone playing to the darkness.

The caresses of air collected into a near constant light breeze as the group emerged not into daylight but into a truly enormous underground chasm. The gaping maw before them opening up and dropping away steeply, almost swallowing Gluttony who wasn't looking where she was going and nearly stepped full tilt into the yawning void before Wrath grabbed her and pulled her back to safety. Jonathan stepped up to the edge, enjoying the chilly flow from the darkness, and gazed out across the chasm. Becoming alarmed that he couldn't see anything except shadow he reluctantly tore his eyes away, just in case the gloom started to stare back at him. To his right he could make out their path, which was weakly highlighted by Wrath's relit torch, and the hooded form of the falling river that smothered it.

"How are we going to cross that?" Gluttony asked, shouting to be heard above the deafening blur of the waterfall. Greed rubbed his chin and nodded. Approaching Lust, who by now had at least waylaid her earlier fears, Greed whispered to her and gestured in the direction of Envy who was gently tapping loose stones over the side of the chasm. Lust smiled wistfully and joined Envy at the path edge. Firmly grabbing Envy's hands from within her jumper sleeves she leant down to be at eye level and relayed Greed's instructions, Envy's face becoming more morose the more she was told. Nevertheless, Envy nodded her agreement and wandered to the cusp of the flowing water that blocked their advance. Lust took a deep breath and released Envy's hands. Steadily the atmosphere in the cavern became sharp and frigid, wayward liquid spray blossomed into flurries of snowflakes, and the blanket rumble of the waterfall started to be punctured with the unmistakable crack of ice fracturing and forming under pressure. Jonathan watched on impressed as the underside of the waterfall progressively froze over, freeing the path from its influence and allowing safe, and dry, passage to the other side.

"Quickly, everyone get across!" Lust demanded, waving the group onward. The party hastily ducked under the sheet of frozen water and, with firm steps so as not to slip on the sodden rock, continued onward till they were a safe distance from the waterfall. Jonathan glanced as Envy as he passed and saw she had eyes closed, tears forming rime laced trails down her pale cheeks. Lust was the last one to leave, and lifted Envy onto her shoulders so as not to leave the tiny girl behind. Once they had re-joined the group Jonathan flinched as the fragile ice shattered and sprinkled everything within a meter or two with slender silver stars that quickly evaporated in the rapidly warming air. Lust lowered Envy to the ground, who was still wiping the wetness from her face, and Jonathan, when he noticed her watching him from the corner of her jade eyes, put a calming hand on her shoulder coupled with a reassuring grin and complimentary thumbs up.

Their way clear for the moment the party resumed their travels, this time the path doggedly hugged the steeps sides of the chasm. Not daring to look down

Jonathan followed close behind Lust and Envy as the group snaked up the steadily inclined pathway towards what looked to be an opening in the cavern wall. Whether or not it lead to the outside Jonathan no longer cared, he was getting nervous of the dark void all around them, and though Wrath's light kept it at bay he was beginning to think that they were being watched by devious eyes, staring, plotting even, waiting for a moment to swallow them all up. His doubts nagged, prodded and carved their way bit by bit into the back of his mind until it was all he could do to concentrate making sure to put one steady step in front of the other.

Step. Step. Step.

Would that he could just leave this cursed crack in the ground and feel the sun, no matter how weakly, on his skin again.

Step. Step. Step.

The wind in his hair, not this stale recycled air from the bowels of the earth.

Step. Step. Shuffle-Scrap-Chitter. ...

Jonathan stopped walking briefly and held his breath as his terrified ears strained to discover if the noise he heard was real or just a figment of his stressed mind crying out for a break from the monotonous shadow. He quietly continued forward so as to not be left behind, his brain on high alert, and looked up to see that Greed had reached the opening and was being surrounded with a silky purple glow of daylight. He watched as each member of their entourage vanished into the heavenly sight and started to power walk, as he did not want to be taken by whatever was following him, but also did not want it to catch on to the fact that he was aware of the its plan. He glanced back into the void and then back to the opening that loomed before him as he triumphantly stepped through into the late afternoon air, driven by paranoia and not stopping until he was a good ten feet at least from the cave's exit.

Jonathan sank down into the dry yet welcoming soil and sucked in oxygen as the adrenaline of those last few moments had made him feel nauseous. Everyone else said not a word and waited patiently for him to recuperate. After a minute or two Wrath came up and stood over him before offering a hand up. Jonathan took it appreciatively and was yanked to his feet in a rough but reassuring manner. He smiled at Wrath and gave a nod that he was ready to continue. The mood was much brighter now that they were outside, and the group began to chatter quietly amongst themselves for the first time as they rounded a nearby corner. Just before Jonathan crossed it however, he risked a look back so as to prove to himself that the monster was all of his own creation, and was about to look away convinced when he saw something in his peripheral vision. It was a collection of six half almond eyes, their glowing tone an angry red like a half dozen open wounds. They glared at him for a split second before vanishing back into the nameless void. An instinctual chill marched up Jonathan's spine, and he made double time towards the front of the group, away from the apparition.

Chapter 12: Path of the Mined.

The overall good mood did not last too long however, as although they were now freed from the cramped, confined conditions underground the group of adventurers still made frustratingly slow progress. The hillside they had emerged onto was nestled at the base of one of the mountains to the east of Anchoridge, and its winding trail zigzagged back and forth across the lower faces which meant they spent more time travelling side to side and less going forward. The path was also constantly obstructed by debris and dangerous terrain features that sapped the party's time, energy, and willpower. Greed, perhaps sensing the fractious nature of his troupe, called a temporary halt.

"My friends, I have good news," He announced, "We are nearly to our first stopping place of this trek. I understand that this has not been easy, but soon we shall be able to rest and gather our wits come the 'morrow." A half-hearted cheer went up from a few of the assembled members, though it was hardly what Jonathan would call inspirational. Greed gave everybody five minutes to collect themselves before they were once again up on their feet, trudging onwards. Jonathan took a swig of his water and pulled out the mini map that Greed had left for him in his pack. The wizened parchment unrolled with a scratchy whisper and he quickly located Anchoridge, which was flanked by the two prongs of the mountainous Y just as before. Jonathan traced his finger around the peaks that surrounded Anchoridge, trying to deduce where Greed might be referring to. It took him a few minutes of searching before Jonathan noticed a tiny settlement to the east on the other side of the ridges. He squinted at the puny scrawled name on the paper. 'Nox' it read, quite simply. He rolled the name around his head for a while but had to admit that he really had no bearing on it whatsoever. Jonathan bound the map up again and stuffed it in his coat pocket for easy access later. He upped his speed a little till he was matching pace with the group's forerunners, Wrath and Greed, who had been speaking intensely to each other for most of the leg down the hillside. Jonathan caught the end of their exchange.

"I'm just sayin' Greed that I'm not sure if it's really as safe as we're led to believe." Wrath was saying with a measure of concern. "We've 'eard neither 'ide nor tail from 'em for weeks now, and I..." He stopped mid flow, noticing Jonathan drawing level with the both of them. He flashed a grin of fake confidence and nodded towards him. "I think Jonathan 'ere wants a word." He stated.

"What can I do for you, Mr Rhodes?" Greed acknowledged, not shifting his sights from the road ahead.

"Well, I'm sorry to interrupt, but I think I know where we're heading towards, and I was just wondering if you could tell me more about it." Jonathan queried, hoping Greed wasn't mad at him for possibly overhearing some secret conversation. Greed just responded in the same barren, gritty tone he always used.

"Are you referring to Nox?" He responded, answering a question with a question. Jonathan nodded, prompting Greed to continue. "It is a mining hamlet to the direct east of Anchoridge, though not sizeable it is remote. We can overnight there." Wrath sighed heavily and shook his head. "Wrath however does not agree with my assessment." Greed declared, bluntly.

"It's not that I don't agree with ya," Wrath started, defensively, "It's that I don't think you've considered all angles 'ere." Greed turned his head to stare at his friend, Jonathan was sure if Greed was capable of it he'd have raised an eyebrow too. Wrath just frowned, insulted at not being taken seriously.

"Ok, why do you say that, Wrath?" Jonathan asked, trying to be diplomatic.

"Well," Wrath began looking him dead in the eye, "Nox may be small, but it's got a prominent trade in Blackice Steel and we've always 'ad groups of miners 'eading back and forth trading and selling the stuff. 'Owever about a month ago we lost all contact, and I think it's cos they were attacked just like we were this morning." He shrugged his massive shoulders, "Greed doesn't believe it though." Jonathan motioned towards the skull headed man and asked his opinion of Wrath's idea.

"For once Wrath is being too cautious, I have pondered all approaches to the query of Nox's silence and I can only come to the conclusion that they have not been the victims of an assault as we were, perhaps they have willingly shut themselves off?" Greed declared. "It is the very fact that there has been no communication at all that leads me to this deduction. Nox is much too small to make for an inviting target, and even if they had been overrun suddenly then there would have been reports of such from survivors, refugees, and the like." Greed crossed his arms, his eye line back on the path ahead of him. Jonathan was about to offer his own thoughts when Wrath let out a heated cry and threw up his arms in defeat.

"Fine Greed, fine, but when this all comes crashing down around you." He pointed a hefty finger in Greed's direction, "Don't say I didn't try to prevent it!" Wrath stormed off towards the back of the group, ignoring Pride's attempts to ask him what was wrong. Jonathan was left aghast and Greed just sighed gently and shook his head.

"Do not worry about Wrath, sometimes he is his namesake. He forgets that he is not always right." He affirmed. Jonathan also sighed and continued walking by Greed's side, internally despairing at the simultaneous arrogance and lack of self-awareness.

For the rest of the hour-long journey down the rubble infested hill things were quiet and uneventful. Jonathan kept himself busy admiring the many oddly shaped rock formations and organically carved features protruding from the side of the cliffs around him; he drew particular amusement from his pareidolia and the numerous warped faces it produced out of simple shadow play between the weak sun and the mud brown buttresses of rock. When he grew tired of those games Jonathan shifted his attention to the sky. The slow-motion maelstrom of lavender vapour swirling above no longer seemed so alien, and in fact it was comforting and oddly beautiful in the way the indigo clouds drifted lazily in and out of each other's embrace. When even this wondrous ever-changing vista opened the way to boredom Jonathan decided, after wantonly kicking a few wayward stones in frustration at the tedium of this leg of the journey, to reopen and peruse the map that sat in his pocket. He quickly found himself lost to the delight of exploring a land completely unknown to him. Jonathan scanned the map, from the Great Plateau to the north with its flanking guard of forests, to the swaying path of the Ourobor River at the eastern edge, and around past the Central Grasslands, and back up to the Western Plains and Anchoridge. Sparse though they were, he particularly adored the names of the few cities and towns that dotted the map; names like Nox, Weirwood, Mesaton, and Bitterhaven just seemed to speak so openly of this land

and its inhabitants no nonsense way of dealing with its trials. Even the names of the land features, such as Snake's Head Lake, Northern Prong Pass, and Boreale Jungle, carried the theme of naked, honest simplicity. It was just as Jonathan was seeing if he could predict their path to the northern ruins, that Greed had alluded to much earlier as their eventual destination, when he noticed that they were no longer descending a slope and were instead traversing on flat, almost even ground. He looked up from the frayed paper in his hands and was surprised to see something that could have been a settlement jutting off in the distance, skirting the edges of a sheer crag. Though to him it looked more like a close-knit ring of charred, broken teeth sprouting from the ground at the base of a limestone cliff Greed recognised it for what it truly was.

"At last," He muttered, pleased they had left the hillside behind them. "Nox awaits us."

Chapter 13: Mined over Matter.

As they drew closer to the fabled town Jonathan felt a sense of relief as his eyes picked out more details, and realised that Nox had not been burned to the ground, as first impressions were lead to believe, but that the bleak objects he'd first spied were in fact thick metallic sheets set up as make shift walls to keep out intruders. Even better was that the closer they travelled the sturdier and more impressive those walls seemed which caused Jonathan's heart to lift at the prospect of once more being safe and secure. He looked round at his companions, Lust and Envy were together, as always, and looked just as hopeful as he was, Gluttony and Sloth looked oblivious and were more interested in their immediate surroundings than distant townships. Pride looked somewhat apprehensive, and next to her Wrath simply frowned with a look that spoke of a deep feeling of unease. Greed, who was still beside Jonathan, gave off a glowing smugness, even without a face to plaster it upon. Jonathan sighed, there'd no doubt be a confrontation soon, and he vowed to stay out of it this time and get some rest.

The group pulled up to the walls, expecting a greeting or query as to their purpose, they were left wanting. Curious, but still not unhopeful, they skirted the settlement's circular walls, which Jonathan could now see were indeed composed of a dark, featureless steel that was surprisingly cold to the touch and felt like it was actively pulling the heat from his hand. After several meters a simple gatehouse, comprised of the same black material as the walls, loomed ahead of them. They rounded the corner of the first tower and were surprised that there were no guards to be accounted for, in fact there seemed to be no one around at all, and to make this even more perplexing the gate was wide open. Greed 'hmmmed' to himself and raised a pondering finger to his lower jaw.

"Perhaps they've all gone to dinner?" Gluttony suggested, hopefully.

"At the...same...time?" Sloth retorted.

"Oh, yeah that would be weird." Gluttony realised. Wrath stepped forth.

"It's like I said, they've been attacked and the enemy's moved on." He sighed heavily, "We're too late Greed." If Greed heard his friend's statement he paid it no mind, and instead studied the gatehouse and its gaping, abandoned entranceway. Without warning he suddenly strode through the gate and into the main street beyond. Jonathan let out a tiny yelp of surprise before chasing after him. The rest of the party followed hastily.

"Greed?!" He cried, crossing the threshold, "What are you doing?"

"Something does not make sense." Greed replied suddenly, spreading his arms wide and looking at Jonathan "If they were attacked, then where are the signs of battle?" Jonathan opened his mouth to argue, but swiftly shut it again as he glanced round and noticed that Greed was right. If the assault on Anchoridge was anything to go by then there should be debris littering the ground, and Jonathan didn't even want to consider the bodies that would have been left over from the bitter conflict. Wrath appeared over Jonathan's shoulder, his visage unchanged from before.

"So are ya now sayin' this place isn't safe?" He asked, accusingly. Greed shook his head.

"I never made illusion to that in the first place. I simply stated that I believed they had not been attacked." He declared, with more than a hint of smugness still about his demeanour. Wrath just glowered at him, but did not continue his assertions, as much as he might have hated it Greed was correct on both counts. Jonathan was about to question if maybe they should consider moving on, when he heard a rustle behind him. He turned rapidly, to face an empty stone house, his hand unconsciously hovering over the hilt of his sword. Pride, seeing his readiness to draw, stepping in front of him her own weapon in her hands and raised in a high guard. The second rustle drifted from the shadows inside one of the open windows as Pride took a cautious step forward.

"Show yourself!" She yelled firmly, "You've already announced your presence." She lingered a couple of steps from the window frame and slightly raised her left foot to venture closer when something small and blurred suddenly leapt from the darkness and landed on the cracked earth in front of her. Pride swung low but managed to catch herself before the blow connected when she realised that the something was not armed. In fact, it did not even look dangerous at all but looked suspiciously like a cat, albeit one with double the number of legs and a black fluffy rabbit tail. Jonathan relaxed, his palm drifting from the pommel of his sword and back to his side as Lust let out a gasp at its cuteness.

“Awwwww!” Gluttony cried. Sloth had to put a firm hand on her shoulder as she was overcome by the animal’s charms and tried to pick it up.

Pride however was not so easily convinced and pulled her blade down so that it pointed chest level at the diminutive creature, ready to skewer it should the need arise. The cat however just cocked its head to one side and studied the blade for a second before padding softly forward and cleaning the tip with tiny licks from its adorable salmon pink tongue. Jonathan laughed under his breath at the ridiculousness of the situation, and at the alleviation of adrenaline. Pride finally released a controlled breath, relaxed her shoulders, and pulled her rapier up and away to no longer threaten the rustler, now deemed harmless.

The cat, still completely oblivious to the near death it just encountered, slipped over and started to rub against Pride’s ankles. Pride bent over slightly and reached a hand down to pet the creature’s head, eliciting gentle, appreciative purrs and an expression of glee from its otherwise vacant face. Jonathan squatted low and tutted at the animal to draw it closer to him. While all this was going on Greed and Wrath, under a temporary argument truce, had retreated further into the town and had been scoping out the abandoned buildings that lined the main street and plaza. Nox was not very large at all, and after a brief fifteen minutes the duo returned to the rest of the group, by which time Jonathan had been forced to sit crossed legged in the dirt as the cat had decided that he was its favourite and would now use his lap for a catnap. Wrath chuckled to himself as he and Greed came upon the scene.

“So, did you find anything?” Pride asked, straightening up from the wall she was leaning against. Wrath shook his head.

“The place is just abandoned, there’s no sign of a fight, but there’s also no sign that this was planned.” He answered, perplexed.

“It is as if everyone just vanished into thin air.” Greed stated, “Which is, of course, impossible, but there is little to go on at this time.” He looked round at the group, and then centred his gaze on Jonathan and his furry friend. “It seems your companion has the right idea Mr Rhodes." Greed nodded towards the cat nestled between his legs, "We have identified a suitable abode further along that can serve as a base and place of rest, at least for tonight." He turned ninety degrees to his right and raised an outstretched arm. "Shall we?" He asked rhetorically. Jonathan did his best to get up without distressing his new fluffy ally, who simply pushed out its eight legs, shook itself and sat by his feet awaiting his next move. Greed, Jonathan, troupe, and cat, all walked briskly up the eerie, vacant street towards their chosen accommodation, which resembled a three-story stone house similar to what Jonathan imagined homes in the old west to be like. Its slate walls were solid, squat and speckled with peculiar amaranth lichen. The front of the dwelling had a quaint wooden porch complete with overhanging roof that was constructed out of a pale, ashen wood. Six boxy windows were arranged on the building's face, murky pips on a domino, though Jonathan could make out little of the interior through them save for the dreary shadows that leered at him as he approached. Greed mounted the porch, which creaked in protest under his weight, grasped the doorknob firmly and pulled. Anticlimactically the door opened with only a pathetic squeak from its hinges, something toward which Jonathan could not help but be a little disappointed about, though as the party shuffled in the floor continued its chorus of dismay. Once everyone, cat included, were inside Greed closed the stubbornly quiet door behind them.

Now isolated from the outside world the group steadily split up to claim a sleeping space for the night, Jonathan however decided to explore the vacant house and get a bearing as to its layout and escape routes, should the need arise. He wandered the house's three floors bottom to top, and although the simultaneously familiar yet alien atmosphere was intriguing, he just couldn't shake the feeling that he was being watched. The ground floor consisted of a spacious living room and a narrower dining room, there was no dedicated kitchen, but an ancient cast iron stove dominated the living room's far corner its copper flue pipe burrowing upward into the ceiling like a metallic beanstalk. Though overall furniture and decoration was sparse, the longer he studied the area the more it gave off a warm, inviting, lived in glow. The second floor was made up of two equally sized bedrooms and one miniature bathroom. Here there was more evidence of the home's original owners, a cracked photo of a bright couple on a dresser, simple jewellery laid out on a bedside table, the odd piece of clothing escaping from a drawer, a discarded child's doll, an empty cot. Unlike the lower floor, the more Jonathan searched the more depressing it got until he finally ceased his scouring, too pained to continue, and ascended to the final floor. The last area was a surprisingly well-kept attic space built into the house's roof. Its broad low beams crisscrossed at head height, and though he had to duck to avoid connecting with them, Jonathan felt the securest up here amongst the rafters. Deciding not to indulge his curiosity amongst the piles of old belongings, he relegated himself to let sleeping ghosts lie, and instead knelt to unpack his travel bag for the evening, arranging a cosy resting place nestled amid the neatly stacked cases and crates. He stood his sword, point upward, next to his sleeping space and sat back on the mat, just as the tender sound of padded footsteps caught his ears. The cat from earlier slunk into view, it let out a pitiful mew and settled on the end of his sleeping roll just by his feet. Jonathan smiled and leant forward to run his hand over the feline's head.

"Oh cat," He muttered through a pained sigh, "What happened here?"

The creature paid his words no mind but curled up and began to purr pleasantly, Jonathan felt a little more relaxed and removed his shoes before lowering himself prone, on his back, beside it. Fatigue set in as he crossed his hands over his stomach, his eyelids drawing heavy and, taking advantage of the restful break, fluttering closed.

Chapter 14: False Dawn Breaking.

Jonathan's eyes slowly opened to an unusual and unfamiliar sight. He was no longer in the old house in Nox but was instead laid down on the cold floor of an ancient cathedral. He sat up and drunkenly swung his head round, the grasping strands of sleep falling away piece by piece, to observe these new surroundings. The place was a huge vault, a chasm of a building with enormous ribs of carved basalt arching along the entire length of the chamber to meet in the ceiling. Thin arrowhead windows were cut into the walls between each rib, the glass stained midnight black and undercut with ripples of violet. The indigo haze carried over into the shards of light that leapt from the openings and stabbed downward, sparkling as they caught patches of swirling dust. Behind where Jonathan was sat a monumental brass door was fitted, the surface smooth but reflectionless and devoid of any means of opening it. Jonathan hauled himself to his feet and brushed the stone dust from the back of his legs before turning his attention to the far end of the cavern, where only shadows seemed to live.

As he started to walk he could make out the distant sound of water slapping against stone, and the dry staleness of the air was gradually replaced with the scent of damp rock, a few steps more and a something emerged out of the black. The void peeled away to reveal a great altar and a wall of bare granite the face of which was pitted and marked in a thousand places, as if someone had taken a chisel to it and intricately chipped away layer upon layer, transcribing countless unknown words until the entire piece was one giant mural of scratched out lettering. To either side of the stone slab stood the source of the pattering water drops; two marble statues one in black and the other in white, one a facsimile of a daemon the other the classical likeness of an angel, both had their eyes covered and water flowed steadily from their mouths and down their fronts before trickling away at gem studded bases and into circular grates in the floor. The altar was actually more like a reading podium, though the wide, chiselled design spoke of many varying uses, upon which rested a vast tome of unmarked leather. The tome was open to around mid-way through and the yellow parchment pages looked to be half filled with writing, curiously each side seemed to be being written separate from the other, like each side of the book was telling a different story. Jonathan rounded the altar, which faced outward back the way he'd come, and tried to read the harsh, runic script but to no avail, the words just made his head swim and caused pain to blossom from behind his right eye.

Suddenly the immense brass doors released a shuddering echo as they were slammed shut, and the shuffling scrap of footsteps could be heard coming towards him. Jonathan, not knowing what else to do, strained at the darkness waiting for a figure to dissolve into view. Squinting at the haze, his view became to cloud over and even rubbing his eyes did not help to clear his view. After several seconds the blindness was almost complete, and only the sound of the being's footsteps could be heard.

Shuffle-Scrap...

The noises echoed into his head.

Shuffle-Scrap...

Jonathan shot open his eyelids with a start, and for a brief almost blissful second he saw his old room. The afterimage slowly dissolved before his eyes however as his brain awoke from its restless sleep, to become the decaying attic space once more. Jonathan released a throaty groan as he released he had been dreaming, sat upright, and rasped his parched lips with an equally dry tongue. Pale, sickly moonlight filtered through the attic windows in broad shafts, catching particles of dust and illuminating their silent dance. Jonathan observed them for a second, sparkling midges in the night, before he sluggishly turned his head to the pack by his side, and reached In, bringing out a water packet to slake his thirst.

Shuffle-Scrap-Chitter...

Jonathan froze, senses suddenly razor sharp. His eyes groped at the shadows, trying to grasp at any faint movement that might betray the source of the terrifyingly familiar noises. His hearing strained at the void, whose blanket of silence was deep, and oppressive. Carefully, so as not to make any utterances himself, Jonathan put the empty water packet on the floor, and squirreled closer to a stack of boxes, hoping to obscure himself until he identified whatever was scrabbling around.

Shuffle-Scrape-Chitter...

He flinched on instinct, the sound as loud as gunshots, and travelling over the roof above him. The moonlight caught a solitary sliver of dust as it escaped from the cracks in the ceiling, drawing Jonathan's frantic gaze just in time to catch a glimpse of a sizeable shadow flitting past, interrupting the flow of silken light. His heart skipped a beat, and in a split second his mind was made up.

'Time to leave.' It sang, ringing clear.

Jonathan moved solidly, quickly, fear driving him. Without hesitation he stuffed his bedroll and sleeping mat into his pack, grabbed his sword, and made for the stairs.

His footsteps reverberated against the bare wooden steps, and Jonathan swore he could make out the eerie scrap of metal following him from outside. Fingers of steel drumming along the slate and stones of the outer walls, as their owner moved spider-like across their surface, awaiting the opportunity to secret itself inside and work its havoc. Jonathan shook his head to clear such destructive thoughts, now was not the time to lose hope, he had to get the others, they'd know what to do.

He rumbled his way down to the ground floor and skipped several of the bottom steps as he jumped, running on memory more than sight, as there was little hazy light available for his strained senses to use. The living room door was slightly open, and Jonathan threw himself through it, jarring the hinges and shaking the frame. Pride was awake instantly and pulled herself upright from her bed roll on the sofa. She looked around, her face vaguely illuminated by the scraps of moonlight, and her eyes asking questions her mouth could not yet form. Jonathan stumbled into the back of the lacquered wooden sofa, sucking in gasps of air to feed his aching muscles and terrified mind which was only held at bay by an instinctual layer of logic and a singular vision of finding help.

"We-we have a problem," He stuttered, hyperventilating a little, "Th-there's something, ou-outside."

"Can you be more specific?" A gravelly voice rolled from the fireplace as Greed hoisted himself up out of the deep armchair that resided there. Jonathan took a few more exaggerated gasps before answering.

“I was having a drink, and I heard a noise from outside. On the roof.” He replied frantically.

“What do you mean ‘a noise’?” Pride responded as her mouth finally engaged, annoyance ringing about her words. Jonathan realised that he probably didn’t sound very convincing and was about to try and emulate the frightening sound when the fireplace took the initiative and did it for him.

SHUFFLE-SCRAPE-CHITTER...

Jonathan frowned, for although the noise was the same it was now much, much closer, almost as if...

Everyone’s heads steadily turned to look at the previously empty ashen alcove as an amorphous, charcoal shadow slowly unfurled itself before them.

Though it was still desperately dark, they could make out a half dozen piercing red eyes watching all three of them at once, as four slim legs cracked and revealed themselves, more than doubling the thing’s width. The bone chilling sound of creaking chitin sent a chill up Jonathan’s spine, and the legs were swiftly accompanied by a pair of sleek, murderous talons. Then two whip-like antennae emerged from the creature’s back and swished through the air, sensing the new environment. A dull glow began emanated from the being’s armoured chest and Jonathan swallowed, his mouth dry again, as the horrific insect form straightened up in the dim twilight; a mechanical mantis amongst its prey.

All feeling and colour drained from the room like ink in the rain, leaving sharp, noir dread in its wake. The creature raised a limb, and the glint of razor-edged steel in lunar luminescence caught the corner of Jonathan’s eye. Reflexes kicked in pushing him back and down out of the way of the mantis’ talon as it scythed the air, missed his scalp by an inch and buried itself in the timber frame of the sofa. Pride, who had until the moment been sat upon the now skewered settee, rolled off, simultaneously drew her rapier, and stood up blade across her chest in one fluid, graceful movement. The shadowy assailant yanked its caught limb free and jabbed towards her head, but Pride smoothly sidestepped and knocked the claw away before reposting with her own lunge at the shoulder joint. It was a strong, well-executed attack but unfortunately the only response was the distinct, jarring ringing of metal as Pride's rapier rebounded harmlessly, throwing her arm off awkwardly and opening her guard. The being took advantage of her disorientation and dealt Pride a savage blow with the back of its opposite talon, not enough to badly wound but certainly powerful enough to knock her back into and over the sofa, severely winding its opponent and leaving her temporarily dazed. Jonathan crawled over to her crumpled form and cradled her shoulders and head as he attempted to bring her round, aside from a probable concussion she appeared unharmed for the moment. A fearful shade spread over the two of them forcing Jonathan to turn a pitiful gaze upward as he winced, preparing himself for the inevitable assault but the pain never came. After a few terrified heartbeats he opened his scrunched eyes and was astonished to find the creature partially frozen in a halo of blood red light. Greed edged his way around the sofa to stand over them, his skull glowing, and his hands raised in a powerful, protective stance.

"Mr Rhodes, take Pride and the others and flee this place." He called out, his strained voice betraying the invisible duel he was enduring just to hold the thing in stasis.

"But..." Jonathan started, conflicted, but Greed interrupted him.

"Do not argue with me, I will cover your escape, but I cannot hold this creature at bay for long." As if to illustrate his point, the luminous field around the mantis sputtered, causing the creature to jerkily try and force itself closer to them, like some stop-motion puppet. "There will likely be more of these creatures on the way. So, you must all flee, the darkness will disguise your flight." Greed turned his ruby enveloped skull slightly towards his indecisive friend. "Jonathan. Please." He whispered. Jonathan shut his mouth and nodded sadly. Wishing he was somewhat stronger, he half dragged half carried the stunned Pride along the floor and out of the living room, pulling the door shut with his foot.

As he entered the hallway, he noticed a dozy Gluttony apprehensively coming down the stairs, obviously drawn by the noise, and rubbing her eyes to clear them of sleep. It took her a few moments to focus herself onto what she was seeing.

"Ohmygosh!" She screamed, the reality of the situation hitting her, "Pride, Jonny, are you ok?" She stumbled down the flight of steps, concern overriding caution, and helped Jonathan attend to Pride who was beginning to come to her senses, a pained scowl creasing her face. Jonathan shook his head and tried his best not to convey his overwhelming distress. Right now, he had to follow Greed's instructions and get everyone out, fear be damned.

"Gluttony, look after Pride." He pointed to the front door, "When she can stand, get clear of this place. I have to get the others." Gluttony started to bite her lower lip and Jonathan could see she was becoming deeply uneasy, so he placed a calming hand on her shoulder. "We'll all meet by the gate, ok?" He asked. She just nodded, uncharacteristically quiet, but nevertheless she replaced Jonathan in supporting Pride's upper body and head. He stood to leave; however he felt a tug on his trouser leg as Gluttony tried to get his attention.

"Where's Greed?" She asked meekly.

"It'll be ok, I promise." Jonathan replied. Knowing he didn't have time to explain everything. He gently pulled away from Gluttony and proceeded to climb the stairs three at a time.

Jonathan headed for the master bedroom first, where he was sure he'd seen Lust and Envy setting up shop earlier. As he reached the door he heard and felt something large and heavy impact the walls below him, the sound made him hesitate for a split second as his mind flitted back to the image of Greed holding the creature back. However, there was nothing he could do except try to carry out Greed's last instruction and get his friends to safety. Telling himself, unconvincingly, that Greed would be fine, he tugged open the thin wooden door and stepped inside. Moonlight streamed through the uncovered window before him, once delicate and comforting but now harsh and contrasted. Jonathan peered round the room, and saw Lust and Envy sat together, the latter being cradled in the former's arms, huddled afraid and unsure at the foot of the bed.

"Jonathan is that you? What's going on?" Lust asked briskly. Jonathan took a breath to help swallow his misgivings.

"Something has found us, and we need to leave now." He answered, trying his best to sound sure and confident. "Gluttony is downstairs with Pride, go help her, and we'll meet at the gate." He saw movement in the corner of his eye and was about to jump back when he saw it just Sloth pulling himself up from his sleeping mat. Sloth let out a yawn and levelled gazes with Lust.

"Pride...must be...hurt," He droned, "Go...I'll gather...our bags...you carry...her..." He turned his hung head towards Jonathan. "Beside you...a weapon...take it..." He stooped and proceeded to collect up his bedroll. Jonathan looked down to his right and saw Gluttony's crossbow, he smiled and grabbed it before making to leave with Lust and Envy at his heels.

They crossed the landing in two hasty strides but as they were about to part ways at the top of the stairs, Jonathan felt a tug on his coat sleeve. It was Lust.

"Where's Greed?" She asked delicately.

"Don't worry, he'll be fine." He responded, dodging the question somewhat. She just stared at him, worry diluting her pleasant features. He nodded determinedly and made for the second bedroom and Wrath, leaving Lust and Envy to descend into the darkness.

Jonathan burst into the bed chamber and was relieved to find Wrath was already up and packing his bags. Jonathan approached him, invading the glittery trails of moonlight from the window, and picked up Wrath's weapon. It was weighty, but not so much that he could not carry it over to where Wrath was preparing to leave, and Jonathan presented it to him hammerhead first. Wrath gave an appreciative nod but said not a word to Jonathan as he finished placing the last few items safely away, and reached for his hefty hammer. Just as his fingers touched the tip however the window in front of Jonathan exploded inward and he threw up his arms instinctually as he was overcome by a fearsome crash, an unyielding weight pushing him back, and a flurry of broken silver shards. He released a gritted cry of pain and crumpled backward as hot, sharp wetness creased his raised limbs, marking where a half dozen of the glass needles had pierced the fabric of his coat and scored deep grooves to the soft skin within. Jonathan cracked open an eye to bear witness to his attacker and could just about make out the shape of the same kind of creeping, chitinous horror that had infiltrated the house downstairs. It raised itself up threateningly, silhouetted against the crisp amber curtain of the night, and peered around the room it had invaded. Jonathan could barely move, the fresh throbbing sensations in his arms blotting out most higher functions, and he could only grind his teeth in frustration and pain as the creature scanned for him lying prone in the gloom. It wasn't that Jonathan was a coward, but he'd never been in a real fight and had certainly never experienced pain like this before and on such a large scale. The entity stopped and tilted its arrowhead shaped face downward to glare at him with its six menacing, blood drop eyes. It twitched its head, cocking it slightly for a second as it studied him then brought its right claw up for a final skewering strike, hoping to pin him to the floor in one blow. Jonathan's eyes widened, his brain recognising its rapidly closing fate, and it was just as his heart skipped what could have been its final beat when a flash of movement caught his peripheral vision and Jonathan watched in disbelief as the beast's head crumpled in on itself like an aluminium can. It jerked backward and flailed its razor shape talons in random directions, slicing thick gouges out of the surrounding walls, before a second blow split the abomination's ribcage like a walnut and send chunks of metallic material scattering all over the room. The shadow beast stumbled and collapsed to the floor, its crimson crystal heart beating weakly as the unseen saviour stepped up and swung their weapon downward with all the force they could muster. The blow rang true and shattered the radiant gem at the being's core into a thousand tiny fragments. The insect form made one last spasmodic jerk and then finally lay still, as thin oily black smoke trickling out from between its fractured ribs, and Wrath stepped forth into the ochre light, his trusty hammer grasped firmly in his powerful iron hands.

"Now we leave." He announced his usually laid-back face straight and serious.

Chapter 15: Darkness onto Darkness.

Jonathan followed closely behind Wrath as they left the bedroom and the smoking ruin of their adversary behind them. He hugged his wounded arms to his chest, trying to smother the creeping pain, but could slowly feel his sleeves sticking to him as they absorbed the blood seeping from the slashes. They descended the stairs and Jonathan was vaguely pleased to note that the bottom of the stairway was empty and the front door wide open. His friends had escaped, and he had done as Greed bade him.

"The others are waiting at the gate Wrath," Jonathan said, the aching discomfort straining his voice slightly, Wrath nodded and made to leave. Jonathan took one last look at the living room door, which was ringed with a fine ruby halo, turned his back, and proceeded with Wrath out of the house leaving the remaining inhabitants to their fate.

The night air greeted him with its bracing, bitter coldness, and whisked him and Wrath away into the veiled darkness and tentative safety. Jonathan kept his gaze on the path ahead, not daring to look back, and thankfully they reached the gatehouse without issue, rounding the corner and coming face to face with the other five companions who were huddled at the very cusp of the town's entrance. Pride, who had now awakened and was laying propped up against the base of the Nox's walls, stared at him with her piercing crimson gaze, silently asking the question they all were thinking. Jonathan shook his head regretfully, and she lowered her stare her face dejected and full of scorn. He was about to attempt to offer some kind of reassuring sentence, when there was a crumpled bang from back within Nox, and a faint cloud the colour of rusted burgundy rose wistfully into the pale night sky. All eyes turned to Jonathan, who, the edges of his face marred by the throbbing pain of his hidden wounds, simply made his way past the group and towards the open, dour wasteland. Without a pronounced noise, only the timid scraping of feet on dusty earth, the group followed him as he led them out and away from the midnight disaster.

They wearily walked in tepid silence, not a word being given nor asked for. Jonathan's frayed mind running on automatic until they finally approached a secluded rocky outcrop sat upon the crest of a downtrodden hill like a being deep in troubled thought. Jonathan and company spread out and slumped down into the relative safety of the verge, their low morale finally catching up with them and halting their progress for even the merest glimpse of a respite from travel. Nobody spoke not wanting to be the first to break the air of silence, everyone just sat or leant, drawn out, still very much shaken, and on edge. The pattering of a few estranged raindrops began to sound off from the surrounding rock, the tell-tale voice of a downpour threatening to break, as Jonathan dumped the belongings he'd escaped Nox with, sank to the cool earth away from the group and carefully removed his coat with its shredded sleeves and dark stains. He winced as he at last saw with his own eyes the damage caused by the glass shards as they had wrought a bloody path across his flesh, parting his pale skin like a knife through butter and leaving crisscrossed dried rivers of red to mark their passage. Gluttony approached him timidly and knelt to examine his wounds, strained worry and fear warping her usually round and welcoming features.

"I can help, if you want me to?" She whispered, as her bubble-gum eyes gazed at him wearily. Jonathan sighed appreciatively and brought his arms forward, and Gluttony gingerly handled them as she tried not to cause any undue discomfort. She squeezed her eyes shut and bit her lower lip in concentration as, just as before, a thin crystal blue line of energy snaked its way lazily from her forehead and towards his torn limbs. The soft glowing feeler split in two and wound itself round his scarred arms; relaxing them and making them feel warm and cosy like they'd just been wrapped up in a blanket fresh from the dryer. The sensation was a blessed relief from the last half hour of tortured, and even managed to elicit the fringe beginnings of a smile from the edges of Jonathan's mouth. He watched in blissful amazement as the deep scored lines knit themselves closed, the split flesh zipped up, and even the dirty copper smears of blood retreated back into his skin's muted surface. Finally, after a few extra seconds of care, the azure worm of energy ceased its caresses and retracted back to its origin winding down its nightlight glow till there was only the moonlight once more. Jonathan flexed his now unharmed arms, feeling a rekindled strength return to them. Though his coat was still in tatters the flesh beneath was as clear and pale as it had been but twelve hours ago, the surfaces unharmed, even the muscle fatigue had abated for the time being.

"Thank you, Gluttony, I feel...refreshed. How you can do such an amazing thing is beyond me." Jonathan chuckled quietly. Gluttony put her right hand behind her head and smiled a weary, but genuine grin.

"Oh, it's nothing really." She replied modestly. "It works and it helps people, that's good enough for me. Greed said something about time manipulation or something, but..." Her voice trailed off and her gaze drifted south towards the gravel strewn earth. "Greed, is he...?" She began, fearful of the answer she hoped was not true. Jonathan shook his head.

"I don't know." He muttered sadly, trying to think of something inspirational to say but drawing nothing but blanks. Gluttony drooped lower and started to draw circles in the dirt with her finger to distract herself from the apparent futility of the situation they had been landed in. Jonathan watched her for a few moments before own eyes started to descend as the gravity of this situation dawned on him. There was no Greed, no guide, no plan, and no way back. Wrath sat hunched and aimless, Pride kneeled nearby cradling her bruised body, for once Envy seemed to be comforting Lust who just sat and her eyes boring a deep pit into the ground before her, Sloth was lent against a light brown boulder watching the horizon with a hooded stare as his stalwart companion crouched a few feet in front of him still scribbling pictures into the parched dirt. The gravity of the situation was dire, and even though this was their land they all seemed truly lost.

For a fitful time, Jonathan's mind ran with depressing ideas, turning them about in a whirling maelstrom of thought. It didn't help that not one of his new companions could offer any sort of solution, in fact they seemed listless and defeated without their enigmatic leader, as aimless as a snake without a head. Jonathan began to seethe in an inner strength he didn't know he had, or at the very least had never been used until now. Perhaps Gluttony's magic had awakened it, or perhaps it was there all along but had never been needed until now, but whatever it was it began to curdle and solidify his scattered, sour thoughts into something more streamlined until a sudden logical thought thrust itself into the limelight. There was no way back, but what about forward? A spark of resistance crackled within Jonathan. The plan may have gone off track, but it was by no means derailed. The spark began to grow and spit, reaching out for something in his chest. Jonathan reached into his pocket, pulled out the crumpled map and opened it; he then found Nox and worked eastward towards Weirwood. It didn't seem so far away, and he was sure the six of them could find their way there. Cinders began to fly deep inside Jonathan's heart, igniting tiny, determined embers. Greed might not have been with them, but they were still all alive and mostly unharmed. It would be a waste to his memory to allow the quest to crumble now. They needed to continue onwards, to try, even if they failed it was better than doing nothing. Jonathan's eyes flared as the warmth spread within his breast, fully rekindling that which was thought lost by his mind; the fires of hope. He knew he was no one's superior, and he could not lead them, but by god he would hold them together and stand with them no matter what!

Jonathan shook himself off and straightened up, hoisting himself to his feet with newfound strength he turned towards the defeated group. Though he said nothing the inferno inside him must have glowed strongly as everyone's gaze slowly gravitated towards him, transforming from glowering looks of despair to stares of curiosity. Jonathan took each face in one by one before addressing them with fiery conviction.

"Everyone, I have an idea!"

Chapter 16: Firmly in His Court.

Jonathan gathered everyone around a particularly wide, flat rock, and opened the parchment map out fully. After pressing out most of the creases with his hands, he began to explain his thought process and ideas to the apprehensive group.

"It seems to me, if it was not obvious already, that this being," he began, gesturing to the dreary, purple sky.

"Sheol." Pride interjected.

"Exactly," Jonathan responded, disarming Pride who had been prepared to defend her interruption as before, "This 'Sheol', is aware of our mission and is gathering its forces to stop us however it can." There were a few nervous nods, as Jonathan continued. "We may have lost Greed, but from his brave sacrifice our path shines as brightly as ever." Wrath, looking puzzled, raised a curious eyebrow.

"What do ya mean? Did Greed share his plan with ya?" He asked, pre-emptively surprised.

"Not exactly," Jonathan replied, shaking his head, "However, I do remember him talking about how our impromptu retreat from Anchoridge had caused him to alter his original plan." To highlight his point Jonathan brushed the map with his right hand and pointed to a small settlement nestled between two mountainous prongs. "That's Anchoridge, and this," He slid his finger a few centimetres due east, "Is Nox." He paused for a second to check everyone was listening. "Does anyone have a pencil?" He asked.

"Right here." Pride spoke up again, as she reached into her top pocket to retrieve the writing implement and then present it point first to Jonathan, who took it with a grateful smile.

"Now, if I was a betting man, I'd put money on our original route being something like this." He gently jabbed the pencil nib into Anchoridge and drew a thin graphite line northwest that travelled through the Northern Prong Pass before heading due east, straight for Mesaton and onwards towards the Boreale Forest and its ruins. Jonathan paused for a second to raise his gaze and study the surrounding faces, before continuing with his theory. “However, as we have had to make a major detour through Nox, I think our new course was going to be this.” Again, he started the pencil track at Anchoridge, but this time headed directly east and through the mountain range a short distance till he reached Nox. From there the pencil followed the mountainous line eastward till it reached Weirwood and then veered north, through Weirwood Falls, and terminated its sketchy line again at the Boreale Forest. Again, he paused to allow the group to study the route, before concluding, “If I was Greed, this is what I would do.” Pride lent forward and put her palms on edges of the map, scrutinising the proposed plan closely. She gracefully traced her finger along the graphite route, running the landscape through her own mind’s eye, before sighing with heavy conviction and straightening up once more. She rotated her eyes towards Jonathan, staring for a moment with her intimidating ruby gaze.

“As far as my own knowledge goes, this is as good a plan as any right now.” She announced carefully, much to everyone’s surprise especially Jonathan’s. “We all knew this quest was going to be hard, but the loss of someone...even Greed,” She hesitated ever so briefly, a lump caught in her throat that was quickly hushed away with practised calm, “Should not stop us from bucking up and carrying on until our mission is complete.” She paused, and a dark visage clouded her sharpened beauty, “Or we all end up in the ground.” A storm cloud rumbled ominously overhead as the mysterious world demonstrated its perchance for timely meteorological utterances and reminded everyone that there was more rain on the way soon, and that they should really prepare to meet it. Wrath, who had until now been half-listening, half watching the horizon, stepped forth.

“That’s good plannin’ mate. So ow’s about we follow that after a good night’s rest, eh? There are still many hours till daybreak, an’ besides I don’t fancy trudging towards Weirwood in a downpour.” He suggested, eliciting a few tired nods. Jonathan looked round again, and for the first time noticed that everyone was watching him. Not in fascination or curiosity, but for a glimpse as to his own thoughts on the matter, and for a sign as to what their next move was going to be. He creased his brow, considered Wrath’s proposal, and found himself in agreement with it.

“Yeah, I think you’re right.” He stated, with newfound confidence. “We’ve all had a tough night, and I agree that it would be better to start our journey after we’ve had time to properly rest, and process what’s happened.” The weather, also in agreement, started to lazily spit thin drizzle down from the heavens and dampen everything beneath it, which was to say everything. In response everyone steadily, but without the remorse that blighted their recent past, dispersed to find somewhere covered where they could settle down for the night. Jonathan knew they should appoint guards for the night and so, as he’d been thrust into the role of leader, he decided to do a quick tour of the ‘camp’ to check everyone’s morale and see if anyone would volunteer. Wandering the small, rocky area he noted how pleasingly defendable is was; there were many places to hide, and the area was raised ever so slightly giving a greater vantage point to view the surrounding landscape. He took a moment to survey the route from which they’d come, the jagged teeth of the distant mountains seemed to taunt him with their lies of safety, their peaks standing jaunty and bleak against the violet sky. Aside from those immoveable titans there was little else of interest in the dusty, rock strewn, and steadily moistening wasteland, Jonathan thought he could potentially make out the beginnings of a forest or large patch of trees to the east but the darkness and thin, misty rain made it impossible to be sure. Sighing softly, he continued his tour but stopped when he heard hushed reassurance to his right. Turning towards the soft words, he saw Lust and Envy had found shelter underneath a particularly large and curved rock that crouched over them like a figure deep in prayer. Jonathan approached, shoulders relaxed to not cause any alarm, until he could make out what Lust’s calming voice was saying.

“I know what I said before Envy, but I really don’t think we should worry.” She spoke quietly and with reassuring purpose, but Jonathan could not help but catch an edge of uncertainty and fatigued pain to her words. He watched as she kindly made sure Envy was cosy and comfortable in her sleeping roll, and that their sleeping area was both tidy and organised, she then brushed the front of her roll down before sliding inside up to her waist. “We must not dwell on the negatives but find comfort in the good.” She continued, perhaps more to herself than Envy who had already turned her back to them both. She looked Jonathan dead in the eyes as he came up beside them and crouch down, the edges of her stare red ringed with the remnants of tears that had been hastily rubbed away. “That’s right...isn’t it?” She asked in a wintery whisper barely audible over the background murmurings of the environment. Her outward aura spoke of calm collection, but her internal struggle seemed very real. Jonathan hoped it was just over analysing things with a pessimistic bias.

“This area is nice and sheltered, and we’ve not been followed. Besides I’ll get Wrath to join me on look out.” He announced softly, “Try to get some rest.” He patted her gently on the shoulder before standing up again. Lust released a sorrowful sigh that told him more than any actual words ever could and settled down to sleep. Feelings conflicted and unsure, he moved on.

Chapter 17: Rust of the Soul.

The lethargic drizzle shown no signs of slowing down as Jonathan wandered the circle of the makeshift camp, and he was thankful for his coat's waxed nature that fought to keep the worst of the wetness at bay, even with its tattered sleeves. He passed each member of the group in turn though by this point no one was up for talking, or worse already asleep, and he felt he lacked the conviction to descend on any one of them for guard duty. Wrath, whose actions at the house hinted that he'd not slept at all until this point, was already face down on his sleeping mat underneath a makeshift bivouac, his muffled snoozes drifting out to mix with the static of the raindrops. His bedroll sat beside him, hunched and unopened, neglected and left to sadly watch its master like a forgotten puppy, and Wrath's mighty iron hammer napped to the left, parallel to its owner. Jonathan cursed his luck a little as he would have liked to have spent more time with Wrath, but for now he let the powerful man snooze till he was called upon. Gluttony and Sloth were just across from Wrath and had also built a temporary shelter from whatever materials were on hand, though admittedly it looked worryingly more unstable than Wrath's. Sloth was, shockingly, curled up in his bedroll and asleep whereas Gluttony was, shockingly, wide awake and reading from a messy collection of pages that she held loosely in her hands. Jonathan shook his head and, following his better judgement, decided not to disturb her. That just left Pride, who he found sat facing the horizon back where he had dumped his belongings, knees to her chest with a pained and dejected look on her face. He was grateful to see that she'd pooled his stuff together and erected a small black parasol to shield them and her from the thin, filmy excuse for rain that continued its half-hearted fall from the heavens. She glanced round as he approached, straightened up and rose to her feet steadily to regain her usual composure. Her gaze wandered over him as she spoke.

"I'm afraid that was all I could escape Nox with." She gestured to the noir umbrella, the slightest taste of sheepishness about her. "Not that it matters, as I was planning on suggesting that someone should stay on watch." She continued, her blood red eyes settling on his face. "I can think of no one it should be than me."

Jonathan smiled at her suggestion, even in her current state Pride put the safety of everyone else first. In her own unique way, she cared deeply about everybody.

"As luck would have it, I was thinking the same thing," He replied jovially, his knuckles on his hips, "And if it's ok with you, I was thinking that I'd take first watch." He took a few steps to his shaded pack and retrieved his bedroll that had been hurriedly thrust inside. He quickly tried to make it more presentable before offering it to Pride. "Here, you can borrow my spot for the night; it probably won't be long till daybreak." She took the offered roll with uncertainty, as he stood back up. "Anyway, with your injuries you need all the sleep you can get." He stated with a tone he hoped was laced with enough authority. Pride relaxed an inch and glanced at the floor.

"You are probably right." She muttered, a half smile creeping its way onto her lips. Jonathan moved past her and on a few meters, leaving her to set up for the night, as he approached a hollow fallen log and got ready for his night's watch. He'd only just gotten settled on top of the dead wood when he noted a graceful figure coming up behind him. "As it stands, I don't feel much like sleeping yet. Do you mind if I join you, if only for a short while?" Pride's voice queried. Jonathan as caught off-guard by her genuine and friendly manner, but he overcame his internal caution and nodded firmly.

"Truth be told I could use the company." He answered, honestly grateful to not be alone. Pride pulled up carefully next to him and they sat together in silence for a while staring out at the distance mountains that silently slumbered through the night. After what seemed like a good half hour or more the pathetic pattering of rain gave up and abated, clearing the now refreshed air. For the first time since Jonathan had arrived, patches of the dusty, lavender sky cleared of cloud allowing him to take in the foreign stars that twinkled behind them. Through one particularly large patch of sky a low and oddly beautiful moon peeked timidly round the clouds, its amber light picking out highlights on the ground below it and setting a sombre and contemplative mood. Pride inhaled beside him, enough for him to hear but not to break the atmosphere that had gathered.

"I can't believe he's gone." She said, quietly.

“Who?” Jonathan asked on reflex. Pride either didn’t catch the thoughtlessness of his question or didn’t care.

“Greed.” She responded with a wistful exhale.

“Sorry, I...knew better than to ask that.” Jonathan replied, covering for his carelessness. Pride just delicately shook her head.

“It’s ok. We’ve all had a trying day.” She remarked as she metaphorically waved his mistake away. A few moments passed before she spoke again, even softer than before. “I never did tell you about him, did I?” Pride asked rhetorically. “Maybe I should have done. Maybe I should have made more of an effort.” She added, more to herself than to him.

“You never really got time.” Jonathan stated in an attempt to deflect her guilt lined addition.

“No,” She started, watching him from the corner of her right eye. “I had time, plenty of time for it all.” She let out a ragged breath, tinged with pain. “I just didn’t think it would have made any difference.” She licked her lips tenderly and stared towards the moon. “I kept putting it off.” Pride closed her eyes. “And I was so wrong to do that.” Jonathan’s own emerald gaze wandered the sleeping landscape, not knowing what to say. In truth her words confused him, though he guessed there was more to what she was saying, and that it wasn’t all for his benefit. He settled his view onto his shoes. He wanted to say something to soften whatever it was that was hurting her, but he found he just couldn’t think of anything comforting that didn’t sound foolish with the lack of context. Finally, he settled on a simple phrase.

“You can tell me now, if you wish.” Pride, head still pointed towards the ochre orb of the moon, opened her eyes and nodded smoothly a few times. She opened her eyes and spoke, not breaking sight grip on the celestial guardian before her.

“As I said,” She began, “Greed was not always as you knew him. He was once like you or me, a proper whole person full of soul and life, with goals and dreams besides his own survival. Even...” The words caught in her throat, awakening a bitter memory. She swallowed and composed herself a little. “Regardless, Greed always had a fondness for knowledge bordering on the obsessive.” She chuckled humourlessly, “You saw his house, all those countless books and scrolls.” Jonathan nodded, it had been a veritable ocean of paper and must have taken a lifetime to collect and organise. Pride continued, “Well one day he came across something that troubled him, something dire. He wouldn’t tell me the full extent of what it was, he wouldn’t tell any of us, all he said was that it showed him what was in store if he kept up this relentless pursuit of knowledge.” She paused again, seemingly gathering herself and settling on phrasing for the parts to follow. “Needless to say, it scared him. So he went back into his archives and found a...spell. It, ah...” She stumbled on the words, her eyelids flickering as a thin silver line emerged to frame the white and crimson spheres within. “It...stopped his urge to collect, to gather. It removed his need to hoard information, and with it everything to do with greed.” Pride lowered her tone, bitterness and remorse coating her voice. “The spell left him scarred, not just physically,” She gestured to her face, “But also left him unable to feel anything linked to his name sake. He just, forgot about it, about it all. It wasn’t just that he couldn’t remember the feelings, he couldn’t remember how to feel them.” Pride drifted her head downwards to glare at the floor, her true vision buried in the past. “I tried so much in the beginning. So much, to help him remember her...” The silver line extended down her pale cheeks to her chin, and she stopped, reluctant to torture herself any longer, silence once again blanketed the scene. Pride wiped her cheeks and blinked away the silver speckles that remained. She pulled her knees up to her chest and rested her head upon them, eyes shut. After a few minutes Jonathan raised a respectful whisper.

“Did you...love him?” He asked tenderly. Pride smiled a sad smile.

“Like a brother,” She replied. Jonathan ruminated on the unexpected information, wanting to pry more but unable to find the correct line of questioning. Fifteen minutes wandered slowly by before he came to a simple question.

“Then, who...?” He started to ask in a hoarse whisper. But as he turned his head towards Pride he noticed that exhaustion had overcome her and she had fallen into a deep sleep. Deciding that it could wait he quietly removed his coat and carefully placed it over her to keep her warm, before resting his hands behind him, and leaning back to observe the silent moon.

Chapter 18: Curative Distraction.

The remains of the night passed without incident, slipping by and melting into dawn like water down a canvas of ink. Still haunted by the odd dream, not to mention the terrifying events thereafter, Jonathan stayed awake and vigilant until the meagre sun crested the mountains to the east. Though the daybreak was by no means spectacular but it did hold a special meaning for Jonathan, who had watched it emerge and mature from violet haze to golden lavender glow, as this was the first time he'd witnessed a sunrise in this world and it marked the beginning of a new leg of their journey. Weak though they were, the sun's rays blossomed outward from the east and spread through the filtering clouds like tendrils from a great heavenly beast. They crossed and converged to fill the whole sky with their glow. The cloud cover seemed minimal, though there was still plenty of it and the huge swirling vortex that marked their eventual destination was as bold and menacing as ever, as it leered over the distant peaks. Jonathan stood up and brushed his feet against the gritty ground, which had absorbed all the night's moisture and was now bone dry. He shook himself in an effort to remove the stiffness from his lonely vigil and peered around to see if anyone else was stirring. Pride was still where she had been last night, though Jonathan had made the effort to cushion the log perch with his sleeping matt so she wouldn't be too uncomfortable, and she was now laid on her side upon it. Wanting to give her more time to rest and heal Jonathan did not disturb her but turned to survey the rest of the 'camp'. He could already see a thin, reluctant trail of smoke leaking from between rocks where Lust and Envy had bedded down, and he watched as a stocky, grey skinned man emerged from behind a nearby boulder, his blood red shark fin Mohawk standing stark against the pale sandstone. He was carrying a pair of spoons and two deep wooden bowls, one in each hand, and he smiled warmly he approached Jonathan and the sleeping Pride.

"So 'ow was sentry duty?" Wrath asked jokingly, as he offered one of the spoons and bowls to Jonathan and placed the other duo on the ground beside Pride. Jonathan took the carved crockery and was pleased by how warm it felt. It was full of a hearty stew in a light brown broth with a chunk of hefty granary bread that was making headway in devouring the juices. Jonathan's stomach gurgled appreciatively as the meal's rich, herby aromas bid him good morning and he smiled; someone had obviously worked hard to prepare breakfast.

"Nothing to report," He replied, digging into the food. He chewed a lump of tender meat thoughtfully and swallowed. "Which is something I'm very thankful for to be honest." He added before taking another mouthful. Wrath chuckled and made himself comfortable on the ground to Jonathan's left.

"Ya should 'ave woken me for my shift." He stated.

"Well you looked like you could use the rest, it was a stressful night and I'm pretty sure you hadn't rested at all till we got here." Jonathan responded between mouthfuls of broth-soaked bread. Wrath rubbed the back of his head slightly embarrassed.

"Hah, so you noticed huh." He replied grinning widely, "I just didn't feel at all safe in Nox..." He caught himself, "Ahh, not that I wanted to be right of course." Jonathan just nodded and swallowed.

"No, it's fine." He said, finishing the topic as he finished off the stew and balanced the spoon and now empty bowl on the log next to him. Changing gears to a darker topic Jonathan spoke again. "Wrath, what were those things last night?" Though still good natured, Wrath's face took an overcast tone.

"We call 'em Stalkers." He said his voice a low menacing rumble. "And 'til last night they were just a rumour. We didn't think they were a real thing." Wrath rubbed his chin thoughtfully. "Though, I guess it makes sense."

"What does?" Jonathan asked quizzically. Wrath rested his hands on a raised knee.

"We knew that the big bad could capture souls, and we'd encountered 'is foot soldiers before." Wrath began. Jonathan shuddered as he recalled the images he'd been shown back at Greed's house, but nodded affirmatively. "Well, it stands to reason that there'd be other, more specialised forms." Silence reigned for a few moments, making Jonathan regret bringing the topic to light. "'Owever!" Wrath announced suddenly, breaking the tension. "We now know about 'em, so they've lost their biggest advantage; surprise." He nodded determinedly, "And anyway we shouldn't focus on the bad stuff aye?" He grinned again and lent back in the manner of a man confident of his convictions.

Pride began to stir from her slumber, disturbed by Wrath's booming voice or perhaps the mouth-watering smells from the bowl in front of her, and she let out a reserved, quiet yawn before sitting up slowly causing the Jonathan's coat to slip from her shoulders like a snake's discarded skin.

"Good mornin'!" Wrath announced cheerily. Pride, whose usually pristine hair was now all messy and stuck up along one side, shot him the look of someone who'd not yet fully woken up.

"Is it?" She replied grumpily. Wrath just let out a hearty laugh and ignored her jibe, causing Jonathan to release a small snicker of amusement. Pride was most definitely not a morning person.

She leant down to pick up the aromatic broth and, once her lap had been suitably covered with a pocket handkerchief, began to gracefully tuck in. After a few mouthfuls she wiped her chin delicately and turned to Wrath, who was still smiling at the earlier altercation.

"I don't suppose someone had the forethought to bring any coffee, did they?" She asked him.

"I saw a pot or two boilin' away, yeah. Shall I bring you one madam?" He asked with more than a pinch of condescension cutting through his bemused voice. Pride, to her credit, did not succumb to the bait.

"Yes please." She simply said, bluntly. Wrath held up his hands in mock surrender and stood up sharply before heading back the way he'd come only a short while before. Jonathan wisely decided that it was best not to disturb Pride until she'd fully caffeinated herself, and so took the opportunity to go through the things he'd had the sense to grab back in Nox. He went over to the parasol, leaving Pride to finish her breakfast, and knelt with his pack between his knees. He carefully pulled the top of the pack open and nearly jumped out of his skin as a dark, six-legged fuzz ball erupted from the mouth of the bag, and brushed past his face. Jonathan's startled cry petered out as he recognised the black shape as the cat from last night; so instead he smiled and sighed in relief that it was not something that meant him any harm while the cat just looked at him with its vacant stare. Indeed, the animal seeming no worse for wear for being stuffed inside a backpack all night and just shook its fluffy fur before bouncing off and away from Jonathan, and rounding a large rock to its left. There was a brief pause where only the breeze could be heard drifting lazily by, until it was rudely chased away by a screech of delight as Gluttony caught sight of the furry friend. Allowing the unexpected but pleasant respite to make him temporary forget last night's woes, Jonathan lent back on his palms, let the ridiculousness of the situation overwhelm him, and laughed long and hard.

An hour or so later, after everyone had woken and eaten breakfast, Jonathan gathered the group back around the large central stone to go over the new plan in more detail. As he leaned on the large rock awaiting everyone's attention, his coat caught a slight breeze and billowed out behind him. He'd taken to wearing it more like cloak, not just because the blood caked sleeves were now useless strips of cloth but also because he felt it made him in his own words, 'more leader-y', which was something Pride, despite having a mind to, had refused to comment on. Regardless though, as soon as everyone seemed ready Jonathan dramatically unfurled the map once more and loomed over it, hands on corners, his stance confident and assured.

"So, we all know the new route correct?" He asked to a silent chorus of nods. "Excellent, however I have a thought that I would like to put to you all. It appears to me that so far the mountains have provided us with nothing but peril and second to that, if I were Sheol and I knew we were coming from I'd definitely send my forces along the quickest routes, which includes this." He ran his finger against the pencil scribble from last night, the straight graphite line from Nox to Weirwood that scrapped along the bottom of the mountain range. To his immediate right Pride suppressed an arrogant sneer, like she knew what his next words were going to be, though she stayed quiet and kept her focus on the map before her. "My question, therefore, is this. Would you all be against going through these woods instead?" Jonathan indicated to an expansive forest the covered the entire area south of their position and ran all the way to the Ourobor River and Weirwood.

“Wouldn’t it take longer to reach Weirwood though?” Lust asked nervously. Gluttony nodded in agreement.

“We only have supplies for a few days travel.” She added, placing a lollipop in her mouth and twiddling the stick thoughtfully. Sloth, surprisingly, stepped forward.

“It would be... safer however...” He interjected with his trademark drawl. “Perhaps even...unexpected...”

“I can see the merit, yeah.” Admitted Wrath as he studied the map. “And I ain’t against a little foraging.” He leant forward across the rock, on the opposite side to Jonathan, and looked him square in the eye with his fiery orange stare. “You ‘ave my vote.” Jonathan nodded and studied everyone else, letting them come to their decisions.

“You, ah...have mine.” Envy’s wispy voice drifted across the table. Lust smiled and added her own agreement to that of her friend’s. Gluttony whispered a few words to Sloth, who drowsily nodded before muttering back into her ear.

“You have mine Jonny!” She declared happily, “Oh, and Slothy’s too.” That just left Pride who had still not said a single word and whose crimson eyes were still ejecting daggers into the outstretched map. He found her demeanour to be rather odd, considering the tender glimpse he’d witnessed last night. Perhaps it was the proximity to her friends that brought up her stern, reinforced exterior, or perhaps it was simply the situation had no demand for softness. Jonathan feared he would never know. Finally, Pride stopped studying the routes and straightened up.

“It needs a little refining.” Her clipped tones cut through the still morning air. “However, you have my backing.” Her frank appraisal was not unexpected, but Jonathan welcomed it.

“In that case,” He began, secretly pleased with himself that he’d thought up this eventuality. “I’d be happy for you to assist me, Pride. You can be my second-in-command.” He smiled a genuine smile. Pride’s tough veneer momentarily cracked at the sudden invitation, though she covered it extremely well and patched it in an instant.

“Indeed, I think that is a splendid idea.” She concluded, not missing a beat. She spun on her heels to face the rest of the troupe, who all seemed more than happy with Jonathan’s decision. “Ok everyone, go and make ready while we fine tune the route. I want us all back here in fifteen minutes.” She gracefully turned back to Jonathan, leaving her orders to be carried out, and together they delved into the world of paper topography.

Quarter of an hour later, with the pale sun rising with uncertainty into a hostile sky, everything was packed, and the group was ready to head off. Jonathan, with Pride beside him, took one last look back the way they’d fled, before slinging his pack on his shoulders and beginning the journey south eastward away from the mountains and into the safer, but still decidedly perilous, woodlands of the negative realm.

Chapter 19: Deadwood Calling.

The forests of this world were no less strange than its flatlands, though there was a familiar presence to them that spoke to Jonathan's childhood years spent exploring the woods and trees that surrounded his parent's old detached house. He had fond, if now life jaded, memories of the time he'd spent amongst the branches and leaves before he'd outgrown such pursuits and moved away to begin his own life anew. Perhaps it was this nudge of nostalgia that made the forest paths more unsettling and reinforced the oddities they encountered, throwing them into sharp contrast with what his mind expected, and keeping his nerves on a constant fizzing edge. A twisted plant stalk here, a misshapen shadow there, a bleating strangled cry from an unseen animal high in the canopy, it all ran contrary to what he was used to and, even though he had begun to acclimatise to the nature of the world he had been thrust into, it didn't allow him to truly appreciate what his rekindled childhood memories would have lead him towards. However, the woodlands were in their own way, truly beautiful when compared to what they had left behind. The dry wasteland ground begrudgingly gave way to a softer, spongier soil, and shifted from the colour of grave dust to a less pallid brown tone of strained but well-watered land. Jonathan started to notice a peculiar smell, as the journey thus far had been mostly devoid of strong odours, it entered his nostrils and grew in strength the closer they got to the forest-actual. It took him a few minutes, but he finally recognised it as the inviting smell of damp earth mixed with the increasingly cloying, yet welcome, aroma of leaf rot. Jonathan smiled as a gentle breeze began to blow, ushering them onwards deeper into the woodland's embrace.

There was a fantastical variety of plant life that the group passed by as they delved deeper into the shaded relief of the treeline. It began with scattered groups of thin, chest high plants which resembled miniature Birch trees in the way their bare, sickly white bark was roughly wrapped around the withered trunks. It looked ill-fitting and on some of the examples Jonathan saw it hung loosely or gathered at the base of the plant like a pile of shed clothing alongside discarded oval leaves the shade of custard and spikey clusters of coarse grass that crunched like broken glass when stepped on. The parchment-wrapped Birches began to grow in height steadily, and become more and more numerous, the ground beneath them being smothered with their unwanted skins and leaf litter. It was now almost impossible to see out of the ocean of bone-white trunks that surrounded the troupe, and even the silicon grasses had retreated from view under the onslaught. Fifteen minutes or so went by and as the Birches started to reach somewhere around seven-foot-tall, Jonathan noted their number finally begin to thin, and other tree-life and plant-forms take their place.

Apart from some unremarkable species of squat grasses and shrubs nestling under the boughs of Ash, Beech, and the occasional Oak, along with analogues of Heather, Holly and the odd Gorse, there were also a few unique specimens that piqued Jonathan's interest. Firstly, there were tall, thick trees with swollen bases to their dark, gnarled trunks. Their raindrop shapes shot up perpendicular to the undergrowth for many meters before opening into hundreds of long needle-like branches which supported thousands of tiny butterfly leaves that rustled and sang as the wind brushed past them. Where they fell, and they did so in regular flurries, they twirled and passed by silently leaving only the faint whispers of mint to mark their passage. Occasionally Jonathan could see curious bushes comprised of domes of delicate purple flowers. They swayed gently in the breeze, and from close range emitted a heady fragrance like dried camomile and nettle, he leaned in close and was about to take a deep sniff when he noticed a thimble-sized moth land on the dome in front of him. The insect had made contact for less than a second when the flowers it had purchase upon violently snapped shut and trapped the struggling insect in a vice-like grip. The blooms sank silently below the outer layer and emerged a few moments later, the poor moth nowhere to be seen. Jonathan grimaced and shuffled back to the group, reminding himself to keep his botanical curiosity strictly beyond arm's length. Aside from them, there were also climbing plants that coiled around the bodies and branches of the larger trees, as well as themselves, twisting and growing in a single long, intertwined strand like a piece of organic rope. The plants, with their broad leaves stuck flat to their host's bark, rarely climbed higher than perhaps ten or twelve feet before terminating in a bulbous growth the colour and shape of an unripe pear, that dangled like the head of someone who'd fallen asleep whilst standing up. Jonathan noted several varieties of this plant, with differences ranging from subtle changes to the leaf shape and the maximum height to which the rope ivy grew, to the colour of the 'pear' being rich red, deep fern green, or even crystal blue. Something they did all have in common however was that each growth had a wide hole on the butt of the 'pear'. As he watched he noted with surprise and wonder as a small chipmunk-eske mammal emerged from one of the growths nestled at the midpoint of a large Ash tree, let out a high-pitched chirp and glided a dozen or more meters on pale, membrane wings that had sprouted from its sides like a pair of organic parachutes.

Jonathan shook his head and chuckled to himself, within the space of an hour he'd seen competition and co-existence, with both life taken, and life extended within mere meters of each other. Despite its first impressions this land was very much alive and breathing, and it gave Jonathan a renewed sense of duty and a humbling respect for his companions, they weren't just fighting for themselves they were fighting for everything's right to exist and to play out its story according to the unseen whims of the universe and not some mad god of otherworldly energy who's only recourse was destruction and decay.

Heedless to his internal thoughts, the group marched onward through the pleasant coolness of the forest, the moist soil and leaf litter making wet crunches beneath their collective feet.

Chapter 20: The Past's Tense.

The late morning sun stabbed through the multicoloured boughs of the woodland, stained glass in the ceiling of an organic church. The hard, cool light filtered into chaotic shafts that danced as the wide spread arms of the trees above them shuffled and muttered at the caress of the wind. Birds played overhead, whistling and calling as they dove and swooped around the outstretched limbs of plant-life, and the occasional furry mammal could be spotted scurrying up and down the barks of the various trees, nibbling at seeds and chasing each other. Everything smelt faintly of cut grass and earth.

After another hour or so, as the sun began to reach the apex of its arduous climb through the heavens, the tree layer abruptly thinned out and opened into a large clearing. The group entered tentatively and spread out, caution edging its way back from the peaceful journey thus far. With Gluttony, Sloth and Wrath to his left, and Pride, Lust and Envy to his right, Jonathan advanced carefully. The clearing was a sizeable oval that had cut into the woods rather than evolved naturally. The grass was short, yet rough and uneven in its care, with speckles of yellow and white weeds that suggested that the original caretakers of this meadow had been gone for some time. At the other side of the clearing, offset to the right, Jonathan could see a solid looking, stone house with an open wooden outbuilding attached to its side. He motioned towards it and started to lead the group across the tough grass. He'd made it perhaps a third of the way there when his foot connected with something small and metallic. Jonathan halted in his tracks, though by then his unintentional kick had sent the object spinning away in a low arc, a thin trail of disturbed dirt following in its wake. He looked down to see if there was any trace of what had once been and noticed something partially buried in the green carpet at his feet. Perplexed he crouched down and reached out to pick it up. As his fingers touched the cool surface, he realised it was a piece of dented armour, partially rusted and apparently trampled into the ground. There was some kind of symbol etched into the surface of the piece and he lifted it up to get a better look when something, loosened by his intrusion, came away from within and fell into the grass before him.

It was a skull, cracked and bleached with age, black rot creeping from its empty sockets.

Jonathan fell back onto his behind, startled, and dropped the salvage. Wrath chuckled and helped him up with a quick pull from an offered hand.

“Not what ya were expecting huh.” He joked quietly. Jonathan brushed himself off and stooped down to pick up what was now obviously an old helmet. He held it out to Wrath.

“Do you recognise the symbol here?” He asked. Wrath took it from him and ran his hands across the corroded surface.

“Maybe, but this ‘elmet’s pretty far gone.” He passed the piece to Pride, who had gathered everyone round when Jonathan had stopped walked. She daintily took the bent metal and, without touching the rust and taint on its surface, delicately turned it over in her hands.

“I’m afraid,” She said with a sigh, “That I’m drawing quite the blank.” She reached out to give the metal back to Jonathan. A low voice suddenly emerged, a snail unfolding from its shell.

“I might...be able...to help...” Murmured Sloth, his words flowing like cold treacle from his cracked lips. “Let me...have a closer...look.” He held out a jaundiced hand towards Pride and she turned towards him, doing as he had asked. Sloth grasped the bent metal firmly and placed his right palm upon its surface, spreading his fingers wide and disturbing flecks of rust and corrosion. He closed his eyes, and his expression changed from its usual look of fatigue to one of intense concentration. Sloth’s eyes darted about under his heavy lids for several seconds, their bulges flitting back and forth, searching for something. They suddenly stopped, apparently finding what it was they were looking for, and Sloth opened his mouth very slightly drawing a smooth breath from between his clenched, discoloured teeth. The air suddenly felt dry and stale, and everything from the colours of the trees to the calls of the frolicking birds became downcast and muted.

“This way! Through here!” He suddenly called, in a voice that was most definitely not his own for it was powerful and strong, and lined with a curious sing-song accent. "Beltay, Drahvo, take your scout units and flank south I want to pincer them against our main shield wall. Then our Crayven allies can crush them from the north with their cavalry." Sloth's head rotated left and right as he stated the odd names, as if he was talking to ghosts that only he could see. He smiled and nodded, looking at Jonathan but also past him. After a few moments he spoke again in the same wood-song voice. "Yes?" He asked, responding to an unheard question. "No, we'll hold here, our backs to the woods." Sloth tilted his neck up and to the left. "Men and Women of Venestra, we make our stand here!" He stated, full of purpose and poise, "This is where it ends, where we crush the foul machinations of the dread lord and secure the future of our lands." Sloth swept his head round, like he was addressing an assembled row of people. "History will long remember your names here today, and it will long remember the part you played in crushing the forces of evil. Your heads may be filled with fear, and plagued with thoughts and doubts, and I know well this cloud for it hovers over me too." He paused for a second, "But know this, though my head may cower my heart soars forth with wings of courage and a will that cannot be extinguished. So, I ask you to join with me, join your heart with mine and send these foul beings back to where they came from!" There was another longer pause, where presumably there would have been much cheering, but instead the silence rang out as more awkward and chilling. Sloth's head sank a little, and his eyes began to twitch and jump against the confines of his lids once more. Half a minute slunk by, with everyone on edge and waiting for his next utterance. Finally, his closed eyes settled again, and he parted his chapped lips and drew a steady breath just as before. This time the voice was female, with a husky quality that quite took Jonathan by surprise.

"Arr, this is bad..." The voice muttered through clenched teeth, clearly trying to stave off pain from some unknown wound. Sloth's head twitched, uneasily. "Captain? Captain!" A pause. "Captain, thank goodness, here I think you dropped this. By the gods what happe-?" Her voice stopped suddenly as if she'd been speaking into a microphone that had been forcefully unplugged.

"-ank you Sergeant." The male voice returned abruptly, and Sloth's head snapped from looking to the right to looking to the left. Jonathan surmised that he was now speaking as the Captain again. "I'm not entirely sure. Crayven's forces just turned on us." Sloth shook his head sadly, "I'm sorry Sergeant but I don't know what to say.

For now, we must..." He trailed off before suddenly opening his mouth wide and yelling. "Look out!" What followed as a brief series of grunts, moans, and general sounds of exertion that would have been amusing coming from Sloth's utterly motionless form were they not so worrisome in meaning. After a minute or two the sounds ceased. "Damn it all, Sergeant I'm so sorry." The voice now sounded full of sorrow, and regret. Sloth, his head bowed low, nodded. "Yes, I'll tell them, how you fought with honour and strength." Sloth's head dipped lower, so his chin almost touched his chest, and after a short time he raised it up again. "Enough of this, we may be beaten but we're never broken." He whispered. Jonathan could not see his eyes, but he was sure that if he could, they'd be aflame with rage. Sloth proved him right a moment later when he turned to look out into the clearing and released a cry of pure hatred that with even their muted surroundings could not help but increase everyone's pulse in empathy. Sloth opened his eyes and returned to his usual hunched stance.

"I do not think...you want to hear...the rest." He mumbled solemnly. "It...does not...end well." Sloth produced what amounted to a grimace however, despite the apprehensive looks of his fellow, refused to comment further. He handed the corrupted helm back to Wrath who took it with a creased frown upon his brow, as colour and sound gradually returned to the world.

"Aye, I thought 'ad an idea about this symbol." He stated with a knowing nod, as he once again brushed his fingertips against the rusted iron. "Judgin' from Sloth's recollections there, I'd say this is the crest of Hammerswell." Wrath's frown increased, and he shook his head slightly. "But this 'elmet really old, older than any of us now." He gestured to the gathered Sins.

"Is that a problem?" Jonathan asked puzzled.

"Not a problem per say." Pride said, her tone layered with concern. "But it does open up a few, unpleasant queries." Lust shuffled her feet at Pride's words.

"Like our origins." She said softly, almost afraid of her own voice. Jonathan scrunched his brow in confusion.

"Your origins?" He asked. Lust nodded gently, but timidly.

"Y-yes. I don't know if this makes any sense but, well, none of us know exactly where we came from." She replied. Now Jonathan felt truly lost, he knew this world was odd but now he was entering a whole new level of mystery.

"Like, amnesia maybe?" He offered, trying to drag the topic back from the void. Lust, unfortunately, scattered those attempts with a brisk shake of her head.

"I wish it was that simple but, no." She gazed at the floor and nervously shuffled her feet again. "It's not like there's things we cannot remember, it's that there's nothing more *to* remember." Jonathan noticed that as Lust tried to explain this to him; Envy was becoming a little more agitated than normal, twitchy and apprehensive. She looked like she had something to say but was too afraid to say it. Envy opened her diminutive mouth slightly, and then closed it again instead opting to bite her lip as Pride spoke up again.

"Like I said, unpleasant." She stated dismissively. "But regardless, this is not really the time nor place to be delving into such things. I know it's frustrating, but we cannot allow ourselves to get distracted while it's still light enough to travel." Jonathan sighed inwardly.

"Yes, I guess I agree. We can discuss history later." Everyone murmured or shrugged in agreement as Pride started to lead them into the clearing, towards the distant dwelling. Wrath passed him back the ancient helm and, after waiting for Jonathan to put the battered armour into his pack, walked beside him at the back of the group.

"Why did ya bring that with ya?" Wrath hissed quietly.

"Huh, I don't really know." Jonathan shrugged, amused at his own actions. "Souvenir?" Wrath chuckled, however he still looked troubled, so Jonathan decided to use some of his new found leadership. "What's the matter Wrath? You seem overly bothered about an old piece of metal." Wrath clenched his grey jaw, making the rust patch under his right ear flex and warp.

"Ah, I'm sorry mate. It's just got me troubled that's all." He answered.

"Because of what Lust said?" Jonathan ventured.

"Nah, that's interestin' an all, but I don't really care where I came from, only where I'm goin'" He turned to look at Jonathan, his ochre eyes filled with an uncertain concern that softened their usual burning confidence. "I shouldn't 'ave known that stuff. I've never 'eard of Hammerswell, or even seen that mark before today."

"Maybe you just read it in a book one day and forgot until now." Jonathan said, smiling reassuringly. Wrath just chuckled again, but his laugh carried nothing joyful.

"I'm many things," He replied his voice hard as flint, "But I've never been a reader." He shook his mohawked head firmly. "After Sloth's little show it all came back to me, I recognised the symbol like I'd seen it before, like it was important to me or something." He groaned and shook his head again, looking away from Jonathan. "Despite what Lust said, if there's one person I was certain of it was me-self, but now..." His voice trailed off. Jonathan raised his hand to his face and chewed on his thumb for a moment.

"You shouldn't let it bother you so much Wrath." He affirmed, "Ever since I got here you've always been steadfast and confident. Heck you even saved my life." Wrath kept looking forward but nodded ever so slightly at Jonathan's words. "What you've told me just now is fascinating, but you're still the same man you were before; solid and dependable. Don't doubt yourself Wrath, because I don't." Wrath smiled, seemingly encouraged.

"Thanks mate." He muttered.

"Not a problem, I'll always be here if you need someone to talk to." Jonathan responded warmly.

Chapter 20: The House at the Edge of the Clearing.

It was not a long journey to the opposite end of the clearing and though still rattled by Sloth's curious power, as well as the touched-on topic of the group's origins, Jonathan found himself beginning to relax slightly and once again enjoy the nature he was surrounded by. The unkempt grasses waved their tiny lime green hands at him as he crunched past, and the trees bordering the wide cutting swayed drunkenly in the mid-day winds that had been steadily gaining power, their swollen boughs bending towards the earth as if praying to the lavender sky. It had been a while since Jonathan had taken stock of the atmospherics above his head, blocked as his view was until recently by the expansive canopy of the woodlands, and now the sun had begun its ceaseless climb back toward the mountainous horizon and beamed wistful shafts of coarse white light through whatever breaks it could find in the violet haze that had gathered in the sky since the clear morning. The prickly orb's position hinted at the season being somewhere towards the tail end of Spring and entering into early Summer though the strength of the light from above made it seem more familiar with late Autumn or early Winter and Jonathan, his thoughts wandering from the short stroll, began to wonder if the strangled sunbeams ever amounted to much more over the course of the season, or if this was as good as it got for the inhabitants of this realm. Certainly, he'd not seen anyone taking advantage of the 'glorious' daylight; as it was could one even get a tan from such a poor outcast? He doubted he would ever know. Regardless, in only a handful of minutes the troupe had crossed the clearing and were brought to a halt before the curious bungalow.

It was larger than Jonathan had previously thought, however the dwelling was still fairly squat and rounded. In fact, it looked like a giant had sat upon a normal sized house and crushed it into itself to produce the bulbous stone building that slouched before them. Its wooden roof was comprised of a multitude of bunched sticks and branches, each bundle tightly wound and secured to its brothers in such a way as to give the impression that the house was wearing a giant straw sunhat, its umber surface fraying at the edges. The bulging walls of the bungalow were made up of the same kind of steel-grey stone Jonathan had seen in Anchoridge and Nox, though this particular building must have been older or at least not as well cared for as those found before as the surface was cracked and gouged in a great many places, and those stones not deformed by wear were caked in a patchy layer of dead, mint-green moss and the cream sun-bleached circles of dried lichen. Ancient windows, their glass fogged and scarred like the eyes of a blind man, dotted the wall closest to Jonathan and a half-oval door stood its ground amongst them, its paint long since peeled away and scattered to the breeze as ash from the dying embers of the house's life. There were the bottle shaped remains of a fluted chimney rising from the dwelling's left flank, though it was clearly disused as it was crowned by a concentrated halo of twigs and leaf litter; the nest of some exotic bird perhaps, and to the right stood, or more accurately slumped, the carved gazebo-like outbuilding Jonathan had noticed earlier. Before he could investigate however, Pride approached him the gathering breeze flicking the curls of her hair playfully.

"It might be prudent to stop and rest here for a little bit." She suggested.

"Yes, I think we could all do with a bite to eat before we re-enter the forest." Jonathan agreed, loosening his torn coat from around his shoulders. "Everyone take five!" He called before correcting himself, "Well more like thirty, but you know what I mean." The left corner of Pride's mouth bent in a sly smile as he said this, and she closed her eyes and shook her head a little before wandering off to find a place to prepare her lunch. Everyone else found a suitable area to drop their bags, rest and recuperate. Wrath started a fire and sat round it with Envy and Sloth, while Lust and Gluttony went in search of the building's kitchen and water supply. Wrath removed his boots and wiggled his toes, which were poking through a few holes in his thick, cotton socks. After remarking that he should have gotten them repaired before they set off, he contented himself by stretching out his legs, closing his eyes and leaning back against a nearby log, the pale sunbeams catching his rough, chiselled face and blood-red hair. Sloth, apparently spent from the recent activity, did what he always did and curled up by the fire, the flaps of his shirt ruffling gently at the touch of the wind. Envy sat, cross-legged and hunched, close to the lapping flames, her forest green eyes sparkling forlornly like forgotten gemstones in the pale snowfield of her face. Jonathan, his hunger still relatively sated from breakfast, regarded her pityingly before hitting upon an idea.

"Hey, everything ok?" He asked gently, squatting down beside her. She didn't respond so Jonathan continued with his idea. "I was going to go and look around the house a bit, and I could use some company." This caught her attention a little, and Envy, her eyes still half-lidded and sorrowful, angled her head to one side to regard him. "If you don't want to that's fine, I just thought it might be fun." Envy lowered her eyes for a second to gaze at the floor and, after a few moments, gave a diminutive nod and rose wearily to her feet. Jonathan smiled softly and led the way towards the old abode starting with the wooden structure outside.

Disappointingly there was little to see as the carved frame was mostly rotted away from many years of exposure and no maintenance. It seemed to be mostly used to store logs, firewood, and bulky gardening equipment, though Jonathan did notice a small shrine tucked away against the wall of the house. It was only a few feet tall and held the general shape of a person. There wasn't a lot left, but it was expertly hewn from a piece of black marble and had, all things considered, survived surprisingly well against the elements. At the base of the shrine there were several recesses and three of them held a coloured jewel the size of a golf ball which, though dulled by time, still clung to scraps of their original hues. Envy pointed to each in turn and noted an amethyst, an aquamarine, and a spinel.

"I didn't know you were a mineralogist." Jonathan stated jokingly. Envy however didn't take to the joke, instead simply muttering.

"Neither did I, until now."

Choosing to play it safe and not pursue her odd comment, Jonathan lead them back around the front of the house and pulled open the main entrance, which moaned on its rusted hinges and shed tears of rust as the arthritic points ground against each other.

The inside of the house was better than the outside, but not by a wide margin. It was dry but very dusty, and a thin layer of dirt and grime coated every surface. The stale air smelt musty, and minute particles of debris lazily shifted and flowed out with faint puffs under their feet. The open door allowed an uncertain aura of light to accompany them into the hallway, but still the insides of the house sat in gloomy silence, unwilling or unable to greet their new guests after being neglected for so long. Strangely the dwelling was not a proper bungalow, as directly in front of the pair was a crude staircase of faded wood led into the roof space, the well-used steps of which were bowed inward or broken and twisted, a few were missing completely leaving dark holes in their absence. Ahead was nothing but the end of the hallway and another solid oak door. To the right existed the kitchen within which Jonathan and Envy could hear the Lust and Gluttony chatting quietly as they went about their business, the odd laugh escaping from the clutches of the door and its darkened frame. To the left a door hung off its hinges, its face split in half by a massive crack so that the top segment was left ajar whilst the bottom dug its heels into the knotted boards of the floor and remained firmly shut. Peering into the room revealed it to be a sparsely decorated dining room, with the remains of a table and chairs lying in a broken heap in the muted half-light of the windows. Jonathan turned his attention upward and, being mindful of the dilapidation, carefully began to creak his way upstairs, the barren wood of the steps announcing his presence with every footfall. Envy made surprisingly little noise as she trailed at his heels, and after pulling her over a rather large gap at the staircase's height the two of them took to exploring the house's upper depths.

The roof space had only a single room coming to the right of the stairs, and odd shafts of ivory light punched in through various holes in the tangled mess of wood bundles above their heads. Jonathan had to duck slightly as he approached the door to the room and, gripping its corroded iron handle tightly, opened the door with a crunch of rust and groan of ancient timber. The space inside was a low, cramped bedroom complete with a single bed, the underlay and cotton sheets long since rotted away leaving only a malformed frame behind, next to which lived the remains of chest of drawers still half open but whose contents had ceased to exist long ago. Against the opposite wall beside the dirt blind window was thin bookcase which miraculously still held a few dust chocked tomes, aside from these meagre furnishings there was also a battered door at the far right, and at its foot the remains of a curious metallic sculpture, its form folded and crumpled, and smothered in crusty yellow rust deposits. Thinking it was an odd decorative choice but probably related to the shrine outside, Jonathan stepped over it and considered the door instead while Envy wandered over to the books to examine them. The door was nothing remarkable, in fact it mirrored every other of its kind Jonathan had seen in the dwelling. It was however different in that it, and its frame, were deeply marked and pitted with an intricate carved pattern that criss-crossed the entire surface. Though Jonathan stared at it with intense curiosity he could not make out where the pattern started, finished or repeated, in fact the only kind of consistency was that each stroke of the carving was part of three identical strokes all going in the same direction. Apart from this fact, it seemed as though the carving had been done completely at random, or it was so intricate that he could simply not understand it. Either way Jonathan resigned himself to this fact, and instead decided to investigate the interior of the space. He tried the handle but found that though it turned it was stuck tight, however determined not to be beaten by an inanimate object Jonathan put his full weight behind his grasp and pulled firmly. There was a satisfying crunch as the lock gave way and the door begrudgingly began to move, revealing the bolthole within.

Chapter 21: Lesser of the Two.

The curious door peeled away from the frame and opened outward, almost knocking into the sculpture at the end of its arc. Inside, the darkness gathered in the restrictive space like blood clotting a wound, there was an oily film to the wooden floor and the air was ever more stale and musty with a scent like old copper and decay. The feeble light from the bedroom window gradually cut a thin, fuzzy beam into the tight closet space, and Jonathan could make out a jumbled pile of twigs on the floor surrounded with scraps of cloth and a small square object. He stooped down and picked up the object with gentle fingers, wary how its age would make it fragile and turned back toward the light to better make out its details. It was a thin book with a basic brass push catch on its leather front, a kind of journal Jonathan had seen before. Gently opening it up there was not a whole lot left of the outer pages, decay and time having stolen away the paper bound there, however the central bulk of the journal was still mostly intact and, even more surprisingly, held writing in a legible script. Jonathan flipped backward through the rotten, desiccated pages till he reached the final entry. Turning back a few more times, he started to read.

202.94SC.

Day started well enough, odd chill from the Northstill. Cut more wood for the fire from the Ash banks by the river, replanting on schedule. Rymar still hasn't come back from his range up to the Ourabor. Will give it another few days, then will send resend my early query.

203.94SC.

Chill from the North still, lasted nearly half a Sun Cycle now. Checked all stores, stocks running into lower third, planning trip to Weirwood to restock. Noted unusual tracks today out by the Plomb ridge, scrape marks and several gashed Plombs from unrecognised source.

Each page for the next three was very similar in content, just noting odd markings and the cold and the slowly dwindling supplies owed to the unfavourable weather.

Jonathan skimmed along until, once he'd once again nearly reached the final entry, he read something interesting.

209.94SC.

Cold reaching new low. Found Rymar washed up on the east second bend of the Ourobor, or at least what was left of him. On way back I glimpsed something moving through the undergrowth, but I was too afraid to investigate. Feels like I'm being watched. Sent message to Weirwood reporting findings.

210.94SC.

Something is following me, I could hear it scratching around behind me, trailing me whilst I was out doing my rounds. Ran back to the house. Will double bolt doors tonight. Message to Weirwood not answered.

The pages after were scrawled with shaky, spider-like writing, as if the unknown author had been shaking with the touch of adrenaline.

211.94SC.

I don't know why I continue this journal, perhaps it is out of the need for something routine to keep me sane. I was followed today, no chased, early afternoon as I warily ventured back to the forest. I barely saw the creature, and it made no noise, but as I ran could hear the clinking of its claws on the rocks I passed but moments before. Glancing back I could only make out sunlight glinting off of...well I don't know what but it was like nothing I've ever seen in these woods before. I can only hope it is does not know how to open doors.

211.94SC. Addendum.

It got in, the outer doors did not stop it, it just broke them down. I am writing this from the closet in my bedroom as I listen to the thing scratch and claw its way through to me. I know that the heavier door will not give in, and I pray to the seven that it is just some bear driven wild by the unseasonal cold, and that it will retreat soon when it realises this.

???.94SC.

It won't leave, it just keeps up its assault at all hours, I don't even know what time it is anymore as I cannot see past the light of my candles. I don't know what I'll do once I run out of them.

???.94SC.

Please make it stop. Please make it stop. Please make it stop. So thirsty, so hungry. Please make it stop. Metal on wood. Metal on wood. Metal on wood.

The page devolved into simply scrawled markings that trailed off the bottom of the page and into the oblivion that finally followed its owner.

"Metal on wood?" Jonathan whispered, rereading the final words of a doomed man. He stopped, and his eyes widened in the gloom as he realised the simple meaning of those words and the dry twigs at his feet. Feeling a touch nauseous Jonathan rose dramatically, journal in hand, and took a lengthy stride back towards and out of the closet door. He breached the muted sunlight just in time to see Envy, who was crouched beside the of the metallic 'sculpture', attempt to touch the corroded remains.

"Stop!" He shouted, but it was too late, her fingertips already caressing the side of a rusted flower. She looked up at him then looked back down in hurried shock and astonishment as a gemstone previously hidden amongst the rust began to glow and pulse. Envy pulled back her hands and sat back in fear, the air temperature in the room plummeting and causing intricate crystals of ice to blossom into existence and hang where they formed, still and silent as death. A head struggled upward from the scrap pile and started at Envy through the remains of its helmet grill as its bottom jaw, permanently lop-sided and agape with strands of rust creaked and ground as it attempted to open and shut. The blood chilling sound of metal scrapping metal echoed round the bedroom as it pulled an arm free and made to drag itself forward towards her its opposite talons raised high to strike its cornered prey. The ancient construct made it maybe a foot before Jonathan's sword collided with the side of its armoured skull and split the brittle metal neatly in two. Jonathan struck again at the abomination, this time aiming for the gemstone heart and succeeded in shattering the core of the being and finally putting an end to its cursed existence.

Envy's eyes, the edges rimed with fear from her recent terror, slowly elevated to regard her saviour. Jonathan stood with his sword in his right hand and the journal in his left, the sunlight from the blind windows weakly surrounding him with its pale aura. The crystalline air melted as swiftly as it had formed and pattered to the wooden floor leaving only a thin sheen of moisture to whisper of its existence as Envy stood and threw herself at him, her tears adding to the watery film beneath their feet. She wrapped her arms round him tightly and buried her face into his chest as raindrops made themselves heard against the glass panes behind them. Jonathan, unable to believe his own actions and still replaying the last few moments in his head, acted on instinct and dropped the sword to more fully enclose the sobbing Envy in his protective embrace.

After what seemed like an age Envy loosened her grip and Jonathan let go of her so they could speak.

"Th-thank you..." Envy said, her trembling voice a sweet whisper above the pang of the rain.

"There's no need to thank me, I couldn't let it hurt you." Jonathan admitted, stooping to pick up his sword. As he did so he felt the delicate touch of Envy's lips and she planted a tender peck on his cheek. He stopped and leant back clumsily, the sword slipping from his bewildered fingers. "D-Did you just...?" He started to stammer but was interrupted as Lust and Gluttony burst into the room, the latter with her crossbow up and pointed out towards him.

"Ohmygosh!" Gluttony exclaimed, lowering her aim once she realised there was no immediate threat to be silenced. Lust darted forward to over to Envy, whose face was a little pinker than usual, and began to mother over her and checking to see that she was unharmed.

"It's alright." Jonathan stated, "Just a scare with some ancient soldiery, we're both fine." He retrieved his sword from the floor for the second time in as many minutes, pocketed the miniature diary, and nudged the now lifeless husk of metal with his foot. Lust, satisfied that the tiny green girl was unharmed, relaxed and rose to face him.

"We heard just below you when we heard such an awful noise." She said, smiling with relief, "So we came up as quick as we could."

"I'm just happy you're both a-ok." Gluttony chimed, shouldering her now disarmed crossbow. "What was that thing though?" She asked warily. Jonathan shrugged, and sheathed his sword in his belt.

"I'm guessing it was an older form of those Shadow People Sheol controls, but why it was here I have no idea." He sighed, "I'm just lucky it was so old and corroded." Lust frowned.

"Were there no clues at all?" She queried, but Jonathan sharply shook his head. He'd decided against mentioning the journal for now, something was off about it and until he could fully make sense of what it was telling him he didn't want to muddy the waters. Maybe he'd ask Pride about it sometime?

"Just some old bones in the closet, but we didn't really get chance to explore the room." He explained.

"There were some books, over there." Envy muttered, pointing with her sleeve at the bulky bookcase against the back wall. "They might be, um, relevant, maybe?"

Jonathan and Lust approached the case, leaving Gluttony to paw over the destroyed metal wreckage. Under closer inspection the case was made from simple slabs of wood cut and polished from a single tree truck, and although there were many spines on show the contents f the times were sadly nothing more than dust and paper scrap. Lust gave up checking after the fourth shed grey and black ash onto her shoes. However before he too retreated one book did catch Jonathan's interest as it had on its spine the same coiled symbol he'd seen upon the helmet they'd recovered earlier and, though the pages were beyond rescuing, a date printed into the front cover: *673.73SC.* Jonathan, who had something of a head for dates, made a mental note of the numbers, replaced the crusty tome and, together with a dusty, disappointed Lust, followed Gluttony and Envy back downstairs and out of the old house.

Chapter 22: Gathering the Pieces.

Back outside the weather was clearing up from the freak rainstorm that Envy had caused, though a few muddy puddles still spotted the ground here and there. Nobody seemed worse off for the unexpected shower, though Jonathan noted how all the packs and perishables were now gathered under the gazebo as opposed to out in the open as before. Wrath was crouched close by the now roaring fire, warming his hands and causing feathery trails of water vapour to leak from his outstretched arms as the rainwater evaporated from his muscled frame. Sloth is seemed had not even budged an inch and was still curled up where Jonathan had left him earlier, though he was suitably covered with the parasol to keep off the rain. Pride had resurfaced and had brought back some lunch with her in the form of a small mammal that she was meticulously roasting over the open flames, her expression a mix of disgust and grim acceptance of the nature and necessity of foraging. Jonathan, and by extension Lust, Envy, and Gluttony, marched over to re-join the troupe and partake in the reluctantly prepared food.

Jonathan settled onto the log beside Wrath, and Envy perched next to him, a little closer that comfort dictated. Lust gave a curious half smile and chose a spot opposite them both. Gluttony jogged straight over to Pride to help with the food, which Pride gladly let her take over whilst she set out a blanket, plates, and cutlery from her pack nearby. While she was getting everything ready, Jonathan leant forward to speak with Wrath.

"Wrath, do you know what the date is today?" He enquired, trying to make it seem like he was just curious. Wrath thought for a moment, puzzled.

"Erm, that's a good question mate. I ain't too sure." He admitted. "Hey Pride, what's the date today?" He called over the crackling flames.

"Come on Wrath, it was New Year's only a few weeks ago." Pride scolded him mockingly. She shook her head and sighed, false annoyance painting her face with condescension. "I think you'll find it is 23.101."

"Thanks, though I could have done without the lip." Wrath remarked playfully. He turned back to Jonathan. "Why do ya ask? Don't ya 'ave calendars in your world?"

"No, no, we do, they just work differently." Jonathan replied.

"How so?" Wrath asked, genuinely. Jonathan scratched his chin.

"Well for example before I was whisked away to this land, the date was May 15th." He stated as if that would answer all questions. He was surprised when Wrath's confusion did not abate but instead seemed to deepen.

"Ahh, what's May? Some kind of special day?"

"No, it's a month of the year." Jonathan asked, becoming a little concerned as to Wrath's lack of understanding. Was this realm detached in even the most basic was just as time?

"Ok, well I get what a year is, but what's a month?" Wrath said, continuing his distressing line of questioning. Jonathan frowned and for the first time noticed that everyone was listening intently. He studied their face for any signs of this being a trick or prank, but either they were a fantastic actors or Wrath's queries were entirely honest ones. Jonathan banked on the latter.

"In my world we divide our year into twelve sections called months." He began; trying to explain it was you would to an inquisitive child. "Each month is about four weeks long, though it's not an exact science." This produced a few shocked expressions from the attentive group.

"But that would mean your year is only 336 days long." Lust exclaimed.

"Wow that's teeny-tiny!" Commented Gluttony, as she removed the now nicely roasted spit from the fire and began carving it for the plates.

"More like 365 and a bit, but yes. Isn't yours?" Jonathan said, taking the opportunity to ask his own questions. Lust shook her head.

"Ours is 1096 days long." She announced proudly.

“1096 and two thirds actually.” Muttered Envy, though only Jonathan caught her correction. Even so Jonathan was amazed.

“So you’re telling me a year here is almost three times as long as a year back home?” He sat back, mulling over the information he’d extracted and let loose a long, impressed whistle. “That’s amazing.”

“From what I understand then, you write your dates with the month first, then the day, then I presume the year?” Pride asked her mind sharp as ever. Jonathan nodded.

“We do. Though from what I’m picking up you start with the day, and then the year or SC?” He responded, asking his own question back at her. Pride fished some bread and cheese out from her pack and, with Gluttony’s help, sliced it into equal portions for everyone to share. She then passed the loaded plates around the fire, one for each person present.

“We do indeed,” She answered him as she did so,” Though SC is not always used; it’s rather archaic and stands for Sun Cycle.” Jonathan nodded as his plate reached him.

“Thanks, both for the food and for the fascinating talk.” He smiled and made a start on the meal, his mind whirring as it processed the information. Pride eyed his suspiciously but said nothing.

The conversation for the remainder of the meal pattered back and forth between everyone, with the occasional joke and playful jibe exchanged between good friends. Lust, egged on by everyone Jonathan included, gave a wonderful solo singing performance much to her own embarrassment, Gluttony recounted her favourite inventions, with Sloth giving the more truthful details she missed, and shared her seemingly endless pouch of toffee éclairs with anyone who could guess their actual purpose, Wrath had everyone join in with a game or three round the campfire even Pride took part managing to win one of the word games by sheer stint of her impressive vocabulary. Eventually the pleasantries died down, the babble of voices simmered into a bubbling undercurrent, and the evening haze drifted down from the heavens to swaddle the land in its misty embrace.

The sparks from the fire prickled and snapped their fingers, pushing back the twilight advance and casting an eerie glow upon everything in their radius. The house, the gazebo, even the trees themselves appeared to lean in and huddle closer to the crackling embers, trying to deny the creeping darkness for as long as possible. Everyone had made themselves comfortable around the last light of the fire and were beginning to drift off into the world of dreams, everyone except for Jonathan and Pride. Jonathan was sat a little way back from the fire, his knees drawn up to shield prying eyes from the journal he was secretly staring at in the flickering light of the dying blaze. He was so intent upon its writings that he only noticed Pride creeping up towards him at the last moment.

"We stayed longer than we meant to." He stated, as he swiftly slid the diary into his sleeves, hoping she wouldn't notice.

"Seems we did." She replied, crouching next to him. "But we gained more than we lost." Her face was only ringed by the fading amber light dancing from the fire, but even so Jonathan knew her piercing crimson eyes were staring straight at him. "Why did you ask about dates today?" She challenged him, bluntly. Jonathan hesitated for a moment.

"I was just curious that's all, is that a crime?" He retorted. Pride did not react to his clumsy deflection.

"You're lying." She declared, her icy tone sending an involuntary chill through him despite the proximity of the campfire. Jonathan did not even bother to defend himself, knowing instinctively that it was meaningless.

"H-how do you know?" He acknowledged, the words falling clumsily from his mouth. Pride, the edges of a dangerous smile highlighted by the flames, lifted her right hand and caressed the jewellery clasped to her lower neck.

"My necklace gives me all the proof I need. Though even without it, you're a terrible liar." She responded, goading him. For all her charm, beauty and occasional softness, she could still exhibit a frighteningly cruel streak. "It allows me to see people's auras, or more accurately the pollution caused when secrets are being withheld." Her grin faded, "And right now your normally pure aura is thick with taint." She leant forward, a subtle yet intimidating move. "So, I'll try again. Why did you ask about dates today?" Jonathan sighed, and reached into his sleeve to retrieve the journal.

"Look for the record, I was going to talk to you about this anyway, I just hadn't found the right moment for it." He mumbled, wishing it didn't sound so much like an excuse. He flicked through the rotten pages till he reached the final few entries, and then thrust forward his hand so Pride could take ownership. A minute of silence followed, broken only by the spitting embers and the crisp chafing of parchment being carefully turned. When she'd reached the end, she, surprisingly, gave the journal back to him, her frosty demeanour gone and replaced with dark concern. "There was nothing else in there except the some incredibly old bones, and the corroded remains of one of Sheol's Shadow People." Jonathan told her.

"A little over six," Pride whispered to herself, her voice flowing like silk. "If the dates in this diary are correct, then the last entry was made a little over six years ago, or eighteen years in your time." She stopped, her fabulous mind piecing together what little she had. "Before I questioned you, I did a quick search of that bedroom," She pointed gently towards the bungalow. "That level of decay is much more than either of those numbers. We're looking at hundreds of years of decomposition and neglect." She sat back, giving Jonathan a little more breathing room, and allowing him to relax now it seemed that the suspicion had been lifted from his shoulders. "Something's not right." Pride continued. "Is there anything else? Any more pieces thus far?" She asked earnestly. Her tone betrayed her; she truly did not like this mystery and wanted to get to the bottom of it as fast as possible.

"I don't know if it's related but," Jonathan paused and removed the helmet piece from his pack, the stained surface reflecting the burnt glow like oil on water. Pride put her hands on her hips.

"The symbol of Hammerswell, yes we know that already." She murmured, her mounting frustration making her impatient. Jonathan nodded calmly.

"Yes, but what do you *know* about Hammerswell." He asked. Pride thought for a moment.

"To be frank, nothing at all. But it was Wrath that recognised the symbol, not me." She answered smoothly.

"But he knows nothing either." Jonathan explained, as he placed the helmet back where he'd got it from. "He admitted that to me as we made our way here, he'd never even seen that symbol before now but somehow once confronted with it, it became instantly familiar." Pride's features became hard as steel, but Jonathan continued unabated. "Envy also had knowledge she didn't know she had, oh and we also found this shrine round the back of the Gazebo." He pointed toward the dilapidated structure. A tense silence hung for a few minutes as Pride's piercing gaze looked out into the blackness, finally she adjusted her unblinking stare back to Jonathan.

"We need more information." She announced her voice now low and determined. "There is a library in Weirwood that could hold a few answers." Her shoulders sagged an inch, resigned to the fact that this would have to wait a few days. "For now, keep an ear to the ground, and let me know if anything else rears its head, however insignificant it might seem." Jonathan nodded his agreement before adding.

"I'm sorry I didn't come to you sooner." Pride loosened her tightly wound visage and smiled and honest smile.

"I understand you want to do this alone, but we need to trust each other so we can solve this together." She advised, "For what it's worth, I also apologise for my sledgehammer approach, you didn't really deserve that." Jonathan smiled back at her, accepting her apology. "Now, we should rest. It's going to be a tough few days walk till we reach the other side of this forest." And with that said Pride rose from in front of the fire and retreated to her original position opposite him as they both settled in for the night.

Chapter 23: Grave Secrets.

Waking uneasily, Jonathan again found himself inside the vast cathedral space, the whispering whistle of the desiccated air flowing out from the great brass door behind him as he once more stood and brushed himself down. The vault was the same as it was last time, the ribbed basalt walls leading onwards into the darkness, and the arrowhead slit windows reluctantly releasing shafts of pale, purple light into the dusty atmosphere. Jonathan began to walk into the darkness, just as before, but this time just as the trickle and scent of water was coming into focus there was another eerie layer playing along with it, the sharp scrape of ink on parchment and the chalky musk of freshly hewn rock. Jonathan froze momentarily, hoping he did not disturb the owner of these phenomenon, then moved as stealthily as he could to the cover of one of the ribs to his left. Peering out from behind the pillar and straining through the gloom Jonathan could just make out the altar podium from before, and beyond it a tall robed individual scratching notes in the tome with a crow's feather quill. The shadowy figure was mostly obscured, so Jonathan waited until it's back was turned then scurried forward to the next rib along the wall, careful to make as little noise as he could. He did this twice more till he was as close as he dared to be, his breathing shallow and tightly controlled to prevent any noise louder than the drifting, distant groans of the wind. At this range Jonathan could make out details about the robed figure; it appeared to be a human male, though ancient and withered its frame still emitted an aura of power that he found unsettling. The robes were simple but heavy and bulked out the man's body so as to not allow any clues as to its form other than the head, which poked out from the top like a bird emerging from a hole in a tree. Its long hair was the colour of quartz and hung around the shoulders giving it the appearance of a hood, it had a thick wizard's beard that was so long it almost touched the ground, and what could be seen of its pale sunken face was lined and creased with age. Two coal-black pits sat where the eyes should be, sulking and sinking into the skull giving away nothing except the eternity of the void. Two long nailed hands poked out from the ashen sleeves of the robes, each holding a quill and each painstakingly inscribing strings of runes within the tome Jonathan had seen in his earlier dream.

"I know you are there." Announced a sudden voice, deep as the void and just as formless. Its wizened depth having no outward source and resonating within Jonathan's mind. The being by the altar did not react, seeming completely enthralled by its intricate work. Jonathan hesitated, wondering if this was a ploy to get him to show himself. The voice rose again, rumbling from the very bowels of the earth. "I do not have the want to play games. You may come out from behind your pillar." Though still edgy Jonathan nevertheless obeyed and cautiously emerged, thinking that he had been given no reason to fear and that he could always run if things turned bad. Jonathan cleared his throat.

"Where am I?" He asked quietly. The man did not move, continuing his writings, however the voice boomed in answer.

"You are in a dream." It replied, in flat monotone.

"This isn't like any normal dream." Jonathan stated, climbing the few steps between him and the being.

"And you are no normal dreamer." Retorted the voice. The robed man put down the quills and looked towards Jonathan with a quick glance before turning around and approaching the granite rock face. "Why are you here?" The voice asked in a tone that suggested it knew the answer already. Jonathan swallowed; his mouth parched.

"I was brought here to help fight against a great evil." He answered. The figure began to chink at the stone, the dense metallic clinks echoing around the empty chamber. It carved a few lines into the great stone before lowering the its tools and returning to the tome, once more glancing at Jonathan as it passed him.

"Is that so?" The voice thrummed. There was a pause broken only by the renewed scratching of the dual quills, before the voice spoke again vibrating its bass through Jonathan's head. "You know so little, and yet here you are." It ruminated.

"I know enough," Jonathan said defensively. "Though I admit I wish I knew more. There is something not right." He was somewhat surprised he was being so frank with the voice, but then again Jonathan secretly hoped it might fill in a few blanks if he played his cards right.

“I applaud your perception.” The voice replied, perhaps mockingly but it was hard to tell with the deep intonations. “Perhaps this time might be different…” It continued, musing to itself as the voice petered away in Jonathan’s mind. There was another pause that only the sputtering water fountains disturbed, and Jonathan noticed that the robed man was now silently staring at him. Its shoulders raised an inch or two before sinking back down with a crease to the already heavily wrinkled brow. “…Or perhaps not.” The voice announced, matter-of-factly.

“Who are you?” Jonathan asked, a little annoyed at the voice’s aloof manner.

“I am the end of all things.” It answered.

“Death?” Jonathan guessed. For the first time the voice chuckled a deep throbbing laugh.

“If that is what you wish to call me, for I have many names.” It admitted. Jonathan considered it’s answer carefully.

“Do you know the great evil?” He asked hope lifting his voice.

“There are many evils, boy.” The voice chided, scolding his ignorance. Jonathan took the mocking in his stride, trying not to rise to the bait.

“Ok fine, do you know of Sheol?” He enquired, reinforcing his want to tease information from the being. The voice hesitated for a moment, though the robed man never stopped his eternal stare.

“The restless one.” The voice finally boomed, “Yes, I know of him.”

“What can you tell me?” Jonathan asked eagerly, perhaps a little too eagerly causing the voice to laugh again.

“He is timeless, eternal, ever-renewing.” The voice stated. “And beyond your understanding.”

“But what does he want?” Jonathan replied, getting a little desperate with the voice’s cryptic answers. The being’s gaze shifted beyond Jonathan for a moment, then shifted back as the voice’s bass rattled through Jonathan’s head.

“An end to all things.” It answered. “Now, I have said enough. Leave this place.” The man abandoned his stare and returned to his altar.

“B-bu...” Jonathan stuttered as he tried to move forward but found it was like wading through tar, his vision began to drip and melt away, and his voice caught in his throat releasing nothing more than a strangled cry. Just as he was on the edge of total blackness the voice roared one last time.

“BEGONE!”

Jonathan snapped open his eyes and awoke to a world of pure white. Slowly, his vision blearily tiptoed back into focus and the sights of morning resolved into recognisable shapes. It was a murky, misty morning, and the low cloud cover from the previous night had settled in for the long haul making even close features like the house obscure and fuzzy as ghosts. He stretched and groaned as his stiff joints resisted his attempts to move them, and once that was done he sat with his limbs sprawled and his back against the log he’d slept against. He was beginning to miss his bed, even the lumpy mattress that he’d often cursed after a bad night’s rest was downy and inviting when compared to the ground he’d had to make do with since starting this adventure. Licking his dried lips, he sipped from a water packet, the crisp air and much needed liquid steadily awakening him further, and observed the sights around him.

The fire, its enveloping warmth long since petered away with the coming of the dawn, was now nothing more than a feeble pile of ash and charred rocks sitting meekly in the middle of the camp. Surrounding it, the rest of the party all seemed to be awake and making ready to leave. A familiar face bounced into view, her jovial attitude unconsciously lightening Jonathan’s mood.

“Heyo Jonny. Hope you slept ok.” Gluttony sang and she lobbed a small cloth wrapped parcel into his lap. “I saved ya some grub from last night soooo eat up!” She grinned as Jonathan unwrapped the parcel and gingerly ate the now cold, but welcome, rations.

“Do you know anything about Weirwood?” Jonathan asked through mumbled mouthfuls. In truth, he was not too interested, and his question was more to distract himself from the chilling dreams he was having, as well as to break the unease of having her just stand there and watch him eat. Gluttony placed a mocha finger to her chin and looked pensive for a moment.

"I know it's not too far away from here, and that it's built on a big river called the Ourobor...OH! And that they have some yummy fish dishes there!" She giggled and Jonathan couldn't help but laugh too. Honestly, he felt somewhat envious of Gluttony's simple outlook on life and her ability to always remain excited about everything. "Anyway, Pride said she 'wants to get everyone moving as soon as Jonathan is awake and properly ready to lead us.'" She put on an impression of Pride with those final words that almost made Jonathan choke on the bread he was finishing. His hacking coughs and overlaid sniggers brought another figure out from the chalky gloom.

"I am glad you are in high spirits this morning Jonathan." Pride commented snidely, "But let's not overdo it before we've even had chance to set off." Jonathan stowed his laughter and, having composed himself, swallowed his final mouthful of breakfast. He picked himself up from the floor as Gluttony skipped away to gather her own things and readied himself and his belongings for the forest trek ahead.

A short time later and everyone was ready to leave. The fogs had lifted by the barest margins, burning off bit by bit with the awakening of the sun and a gentle breeze could be heard moaning overhead. Jonathan stood at the head of the troupe, a mix of emotions swirling inside him; determination to finish the quest, confusion as to the true nature of the things, hope that Weirwood would still be standing, unease at the hard walk ahead, the constant fear of the unknown ahead, but also a resolution that he was sure whatever happened they could deal with it together. Breathing the crisp morning air deeply to ground himself, he studied the map one last time before signalling everyone onwards and marching westward back into the shaded grasp of the forest, leaving the ancient dwelling and its sordid past to continue rotting behind them.

Chapter 23: Out of the Woods?

The journey back into and through the woodland had little to mark out as unusual or extraordinary. Which was both a blessing and a curse for Jonathan, who was thankful for the peaceful passage but also succumbing to the ravages of boredom during the long uninterrupted stretches of travel between the regimented breaks Pride had mapped out for the group. It was not that the forest did not hold more wonders and intrigue for the troupe; one evening the camp was host to a lively family of the tiny mammals seen gliding through the trees in the former half of the trek, they played hide and seek in, through and around everyone's legs, arms, and pockets until an unseen signal sent them scurrying away to melt back into the undergrowth. The following morning a huge flock of bone-white long necked birds were witnessed through the overhead gaps in the foliage, their swan necks and pencil thin legs held rigid as they gracefully flapped their lithe teardrop wings in unison. Halfway into the second day from the clearing the troupe halted for a rest round a narrow yet deep pool that was secreted in a grove of hanging Willow trees. Except for Wrath, whose iron body conferred a lack of buoyancy, everyone enjoyed splashing and refreshing themselves in the crystal-clear waters until Gluttony noticed that the sides of the pool were chewed from the substrate. After Pride removed a huge tooth buried in the granite walls the group hastily decided not to indulge anymore and to get a swift move on away from whatever had carved that passage.

Curiously Jonathan found his sleep to absent from the cathedral dreams that had been plaguing him since his arrival to this realm, perhaps it was the closeness of nature and the lack of Sheol's decaying influence, or perhaps they had been nothing more than the touch of imagined phantoms brought on as his brain processed the otherworldly events it had witnessed. Whatever the reasoning Jonathan found it increasingly frustrating, as he was actually looking forward to speaking with the voice again and probing it with a few more questions he had thought up. No to mention that a night void from dreams was not at all relaxing and left him feeling just a tired when day came to rear its murky head.

Early into the third day Jonathan's patience was starting to fray at the edges, he was still as determined as ever but that the constant travel was beginning to wear upon the mind as surely as it wore on the body, leaving his mood as sore as his muscles. Nobody spoke much that day, fatigue catching them all in its cloying embrace, but by late afternoon a sight emerged that lifted the spirits of all and temporarily relieved the numbness of constant travel. The troupe had just crested another of the woodland's ridges when the view ahead rapidly thinned and opened out to reveal an expansive river carving its way through from the North to the South, the water was dark and foreboding, and foamed at the edges where it met the ragged formations of toothy rocks that enclosed its banks. Jonathan took out his map and at once identified it as the mighty Ourobor River.

"Finally," Lust sighed as she pulled up beside him her face flushed from the tough climb.

"Not long now," Jonathan said encouragingly, his drive returning. He swept the map round so she could see it clearly and pointed to where the forests were cut in two by the powerful waters of the Ourobor. "My guess is that we're somewhere here, which makes Weirwood less than a few hours walk at most." He traced Northward to where the town was, nestled at the perimeter of the forests, straddling a calmer, wider portion of the river just to the South of the waterfalls that shared its name.

"Looks like we'll be there before dark." Lust agreed, a tired yet resolute smile condensing across her face.

After another short interlude to gather strength for the final push, everyone redoubled their efforts and followed Jonathan and Pride's lead northward along the shear, winding banks of the Ourobor. It was a pleasant change of scenery from the forest, which had become monotonous in its offerings and now hung its head in reverence to its watery master. The river opened up a whole new plethora of sights and sounds to be enjoyed. At thinner stretches the steep eroded sides allowed a heart stopping downward glance into the depths of the rapids, the obsidian waters spluttering and erupting into rhythmic choruses all playing in harmony as they plunged themselves against the overhanging tables of rock. At other times the powerful expanse of water opened out and its rage calmed to become almost serene and relaxing, the views this time becoming shallower and the surface more permeable to the intruding glances. Fish hung motionless or darted away when seen to avoid the lure of predators, once or twice Jonathan glimpsed the tail end of a large aquatic animal about the size of his arm as it broke the glassy surface, chasing and hunting the buzzing insect analogues that hummed and flitted across hypnotising mirror sheen of the flowing water. It was as they were traversing the third such sandy embankment that Jonathan observed a great, turquoise predator stalking the far shore. It waded through the shallows upon the knuckles of its forelimbs like the unholy cross between a gorilla and a reptile, the gnarled, pointed claws of its three fingered hands curled back towards its wrists, primed to strike. The beast's head resembled the snout of a fish-eating dinosaur, the long cone shaped muzzle and jaw sprouting from the graceful whipcord neck that undulated back and forth as the creature's golden snake-like eyes pierced the water before it. A primal crest was mounted to the predator's back, from serpentine head to the end of the stubby tail, and the ridged spines and webbing resembled the sails and rigging of an ancient junk ship, the thickly muscled belly of the beast the rolling keel of the vessel. If the creature sensed their presence it paid them no more than a passing glance, to its mind it was much too powerful and proud to bother chasing down such feeble, scrawny prey, far better instead to focus on the fat laden fish and river beasts that made for much more satisfying meal. Without so much as a twitch to telegraph the motion the beast gapped its jaw wide, and rammed its head forward making the velvet surface of the river erupt into a cascade of foam and scattered droplets. It emerged a second later, the frenzied torrent of its attack ending as quickly as it began, and held its prize high; a bulky, grey catfish impaled by the thousands of stained, ivory teeth that lined its mouth, a double row of knitting needles forged from the sharpest bone. It skulked back towards the shoreline, and as Jonathan watched with morbid fascination, tore the hapless fish to greasy shreds and swallowing the ribbons of flesh whole before stalking triumphantly back into the river to await its next victim. Before long though the beast had vanished behind them as the group continued to trudge onward, though Jonathan, his respect for such a creature marred only by his paranoia that it might just consider them a target, did keep a weather eye behind them just in case.

Just before the streaky orb of the sun settled above the mountain line that the forests were finally bid farewell to and Weirwood could be seen only a short distance upriver. It was not at first glance a particularly big town stead, though its multitude of dark wooden piers protruded into and crisscrossed the surface of the Ourobor as well as themselves gave it a very compact aesthetic. It sat buried into the river bank like a bloated tick, its timber heavy walls a hodgepodge of bulging extensions that looked strained at the seams, the tarred, black wood was studded with windows and peepholes that nosed and jostled for position and made the dome of the town look like the pockmarked shell of a tortoise. Above this the tips and tops of towers and houses could be glimpsed scraping through the thin egg-shell at the top of the walls to peek out over the fortification and leer at the landscape around the town. Boats moored to the spindly piers and quays bobbed and swayed, pulling at their weed chocked ropes like a dog establishing the boundaries of its chain, and the yawning maw of the docks could be seen just behind that the sheltered harbours strangely ominous and eerie.

It was a relief to be able to mark off another milestone in the quest, and certainly comforting to know that the detour had been a safe and worthwhile route, despite the time lost. However, the distant unease not truly felt since Nox was once more creeping back into Jonathan's skull as he led the group towards the entrance of Weirwood. The whimsical sighs of the trees faded into distant echoes, and only the harsh churning of the river accompanied them as they drew level with the wrought iron gates. The sun dipped below the craggy peaks to the west and twilight engulfed the land with its rapidly worsening violet gloom as Jonathan drew up to the gates and noticed at once that something was awry.

"They're locked." He exclaimed, pulling on the lifeless bars just to reinforce what he already knew. A sturdy chain of ice-cold steel was clamped around the iron rungs of the gate, a sadistic snake that held its grasp and jingled with an almost gleeful tone as it mocked their disbelief.

"Damn mate, ain't no way we're getting through that without a key." Wrath announced tactlessly, Pride just shook her head and started to pace back and forth searching the wall for another way in. The lavender sky started to leak a steady drizzle as Jonathan felt delicate fingers take and hold the fringes of his right hand. He looked down to see Envy, her expression downcast and her eyes on the cusp of flooding like burst pipe.

“What will we do?” She asked, her voice a timid squeak. Jonathan could do nothing except hold her hand more firmly and try to think of way through this. Gluttony approached the gates and slammed her fists against them in despair.

“Stupid! Stupid! Stupid!” She called out in frustration to nobody and everybody at once. She threw her head round frantically, searching for an idea. “You’re strong can’t you break this dumb chain?!” She shouted at Wrath almost accusatory. He just shook his head angrily.

“I already told ya, we’d need the key. Black-Ice Steel is strong stuff and I ain’t going to ‘urt myself tryin’ to smash it!” He retorted crossing his arms and huffing at Gluttony’s suggestion as rain plinked from his iron shoulders.

“Now let’s not fight, please guys.” Lust pleaded feebly. Nevertheless, they all continued to argue as Jonathan’s attention was instead drawn to Sloth who was staring at the boats chained out in the river. He murmured something that was lost in the sounds of the water bouncing off the curved flanks of the wall, before raising a bony finger and pointing wearily out into the mounting darkness. Jonathan squinted but could not see anything noteworthy, just the cavernous entry to the quayside.

He stopped and blinked as Sloth’s hinted at idea sprouted in his head.

“Of course,” He whispered. “Good idea Sloth.” Pleased that cooler heads might have prevailed, he called over Pride and, Envy in tow, wandered round the side of Weirwood to where the banks of the river met the walls and piers of the docks.

The design was obviously supposed to make gaining entry here impossible if it was properly defended, but even unguarded it was going to be tough to grip onto and shimmy around the wall especially with the layers f rain now falling in blankets from the heavens.

“What do you think?” He asked Pride, raising an eyebrow.

“It’s dubious, but what other choice do we have.” She admitted. “Let’s go get the others before a real fight breaks out.” The three of them skirted the wall back round just in time to see Gluttony storming off away from the gate, Sloth trailing after her. Lust was stood next to Wrath aghast.

"Well done." She stated sarcastically, "That was uncalled for." She added before jogging after Gluttony and Sloth. Wrath, his usual ashen face still too full of rage, did not acknowledge her instead opting to release a fiery shout and punch the true source of his frustration; the lock. He let out a strangled cry as this proved to do nothing but dent the steel box as well as Wrath's knuckles, a thin trail of burgundy weeping from the cuts and dripping to the rapidly soddening ground.

'Even metal has its cracks.' Thought Jonathan as he watched Wrath sink to the floor and sit with his back to the gate, flexing and unflexing his injured hand as he tried to calm his seething anger. He wiped the blood on his soaked top, leaving a rusted streak to match the ones dotting his arms, as he noticed Jonathan approaching.

"Look mate, I'm sorry." Wrath started sheepishly, "I didn't mean what I said, I was just angry." Jonathan raised a hand to quiet him. Jonathan understood, he'd lost his own temper before and said things he regretted, so it would be hypocritical to lampoon Wrath for doing the same thing.

"Pride, can you follow after Lust, let them know we have a way inside." He asked his crimson eyed companion who had just put up her parasol to shield herself from the downpour.

"You have a way in?" Wrath queried, watching puddles splash violently as she disappeared into the misty torrent.

"Yes, a tricky one but better than standing out here in the rain feeling sorry for ourselves." Jonathan replied. "We'll wait for everyone to return first." Wrath just nodded and watched his knuckles bleed.

Chapter 24: Thicker Than Water.

For a good while all that could be heard or felt was the deluge. Thankfully the gatehouse had a tiled lip, like the brim of a ceramic hat, so Jonathan, Envy and Wrath could at least shelter from the pouring rain that drummed out a hidden beat above their anxious heads. Jonathan found the rain to be honestly refreshing, the white noise of its orchestra soothing and the smell relaxing as it washed away the grime of his surroundings. Eventually his friends emerged out of the steaming shadows huddled under Pride's parasol, to join them. It was almost comical watching the four of them bustle about under one small canopy but the looks on their collective faces were anything but jovial, Gluttony's especially was streaked with the raw marks of recent tears. Once they were all safely under the lip of the gateway Jonathan explained the plan.

"It won't be easy, however Sloth pointed out that there is another way into Weirwood that doesn't involve the locked gate. We can use the harbour wall to skirt out way in. We'll have to cling to it and inch our way round until we reach the piers." Nobody said anything, but a few doubtful nods did appear. "I know it's not ideal but as has been pointed out to me many times, we cannot afford to waste time and we need to restock our supplies for the final leg of the journey." He concluded.

"Let us get it over with before it gets even darker." Ventured Pride to a chorus of half-hearted agreements. Jonathan took this as a sign to proceed and led everyone out and around to the river.

"Pride if you lead the way, followed by Wrath, Lust, and Envy. Sloth if you'd go before Gluttony so she can watch over you that'd be great. I'll bring up the rear." He announced. "Good luck, and don't look down." He added, then immediately cursed himself for saying as he noticed everyone glance downward into the inky, churning depths of the freezing Ourobor its beckoning motions melting into the diminishing dusk.

Hesitantly one by one the troupe, following Pride, gripped the moist flanks of the wall with tentative fingers, dug the toes of their boots and shoes into whatever nooks and crannies they could find in the gloom and edged out, step by nerve-wracking step. For the first few meters it seemed like it would easier than expected, though as the minutes ground on Jonathan's could feel a deep ache growing in his muscles and the tendons of his fingers. He kept his head firmly level so as not to glimpse the horrible conditions that awaiting him if he fell, and instead hunted for the best hand holds he could see or watched Gluttony a few feet in front of him as she did the same, her tied back curls of coffee coloured hair bobbing this way and that.

Almost halfway round and the gruelling climb added a further level of difficulty by introducing a thick layer of slimy mustard coloured algae and sickly lime river weed to the inside of the harbour's walls. This slowed everyone to a crawl and made double or triple checking your holds a necessity to prevent fingertips from sliding in the rank ooze. After a further fifteen minutes of sweating, grunting and climbing Jonathan's arms were on fire and his hands were coated in foul smelling plant matter and rotten mulch. He made another laborious few steps and looked out towards and past Gluttony. Perhaps sensing his gaze, she turned to look back at him and smiled encouragingly though her eyes and cheeks still highlighted by her teary outburst. Just beyond her Jonathan could make out their goal, the sturdy gangplanks and strong foundations of the quayside piers and upon them, Pride, Wrath, Envy and Lust, exhausted but safe at last. Jonathan smiled back at Gluttony and motioned for her to continue. As she came within a few feet of the pier Wrath strode forward and knelt down to offer her a firm hand, both in apology and to get her back upon more solid ground, however Gluttony did not take the offered hand instead opting a more independent route up the wall. Wrath questioned this with something Jonathan couldn't hear over the rain, however he did catch Gluttony's retort.

"Thanks, but no," She spat at him, "I can do this, I don't need your help." Wrath to his credit did not take the bait, still wishing to bury the hatchet from earlier, and simply retreated to give her the room she'd need to haul her own way forwards. Only a few shuffling steps away, Gluttony, her right arm outstretch to grasp the weed encrusted edge of the pier, suddenly slipped!

Jonathan could only watch as time seemed to slow down around him. Gluttony's left hand pulled away from the wall, her fingers gripping nothing but the slick, viscous detritus of the noisome algae. She fell almost silently, her mouth open in surprise and her watermelon eyes bulging wide, pleading for someone to catch her, until she hit the water with a squeal, a bone jarring crack and an explosion of jet-black fluid that swallowed her whole. She did not resurface.

The time dilation ceased at the same time as Gluttony's fall, a brief heartbeat of utter disbelief that suddenly, violently vanished as everyone exploded into movement, their chorus of cries intertwining into a barely coherent mess.

"Gluttony!" Called one.

"Oh my goodness!" Added another.

"Let me go!" Demanded a third.

Jonathan was caught, frozen to the wall in shock. He panned his head round till he caught stock of Pride stood out amongst the throng of his friends. She was holding back Wrath who was desperately trying to reach the end of the pier and leap after Gluttony.

"Gluttony can't swim!" She shouted over the incongruent mass of sounds, "And Wrath won't float, no matter how much he might want to!" Her unspoken words were the most compelling though. 'It's up to you.' Her fierce gaze pleaded with him, and in that moment, everything became clear as glass. Jonathan discarded his coat, closed his eyes, and released his grip to plunge through the smooth darkness of the night and into the frosty embrace of the Ourobor.

The rush of water overtook Jonathan almost immediately, forcing the air from his lungs as its icy hands squeezed his chest and made him gasp a burbled cry. Treading water momentarily, Jonathan took in as much air as he could manage before turning on his heels and diving down back beneath the frigid surface. Though the water was black as coal from above, it was thankfully much more transparent when submerged, the fledgling moonlight threading its dancing fingers in to help illuminate his path. It was frustratingly slow progress diving however, Jonathan not having the chance to remove his shoes or more than his coat before his heroic yet rash plummet from the wall. All his thoughts were of finding and reaching Gluttony before...well that didn't bear thinking about.

He caught sight of frantic movement below him, it was Gluttony, her features caressed by the pale aura of the moon. Her legs and left arm were kicking and swinging wildly, though her right was twisted at an unusual angle and floated by her side, unmoving save for the flow of the river water nudging in along. Thankfully the currents were not very strong, so she'd hardly drifted from her initial point of entry. She was rapidly running out of air though as her distraught flailing was gradually being more lethargic and delirious. Jonathan doubled his own efforts and brought himself alongside her, he hooked his right arm under her left and tried to swim upward however whether because of simple panic or the lack of oxygen diluting her thoughts Gluttony started to fight him and gave one last burst of chaotic motion, knocking Jonathan away and dazing him slightly with a frenetic kick to the head.

Jonathan shook his head, casting away the stars in his vision from Gluttony's unintentional blow. He was quickly running out of time and his own lungs were beginning to burn as they longed for air. He tossed his head back and forth one more time as he regained sight on her and ploughed through the freezing depths to attempt another rescue. By this time Gluttony had gone completely slack and, more worryingly, her eyes glassy and unfocused so he had little trouble in once again hooking an arm around her and swimming for the surface with all his remaining might, his chest now screaming at him to reach air soon or suffer the consequences.

The same panic that overwhelmed Gluttony now started to infuse itself into Jonathan as a horrific truth slowly dawned upon him; he wasn't going to make it. Had she been conscious Gluttony's buoyancy would have helped to mitigate her weight at least partially, however now that she'd lost consciousness and was essentially a dead weight, one Jonathan hoped was not literal, she was severely hindering his upward progress. So much so that he knew he'd not return to the surface of the river before being forced to gulp in the freezing water that surrounded him. Jonathan gritted his teeth as he teetered on the edge of his endurance, his vision tunnelling and his world fading into a blurred nightmare of airless death.

Chapter 25: Pièce de Resistance.

Suddenly he felt a pressure on his waist, and something powerful yet frigidly cold wrapped around him and whisk both him and Gluttony up towards the petals of moonlight. Jonathan, Gluttony, and the unseen saviour broke the surface with a fierce crash, air greeting Jonathan as he spluttered and sucked in oxygen with hoarse, ugly gasps. He looked around but his vision, still fuzzy from before, could only make out the form of Gluttony floating face up next to him, broken and unmoving. He realised the grip around his waist was gone, though it had left a crust of rime across his middle, and he was bobbing under his own power.

"Hey!" Jonathan shouted, before coughing up a few wayward drops of water. He wasn't sure who or what he was calling too but he didn't know what else to do. He heard something heavy bounce off the rippling waves behind him. It was a floatation device, a sturdy ring the colour of off milk with a thick piece of industrial rope tied around it.

"Grab hold!" Demanded an unfamiliar voice, though Jonathan didn't need telling twice. He nestled Gluttony securely through the middle of the ring before clinging on with all his strength as it rose methodically and plucked the sodden pair from the glacial grasp of the Ourobor. The bumpy, jumpy ride continued as Jonathan stared up into the all-encompassing blackness of the docks, hoping beyond hope that whoever was tugging on the rope was an agreeable soul. As the dangling pair crested the edge of the pier, he could finally see who or what it was that had helped them. He could see Wrath, Lust, Pride, Envy and Sloth, but there were also now three unknown figures, their features caught stark in the flicking umber glow of a bladed torch-glaive held upright by the left most individual.

The flame bearer was a short creature with the body of a fennec fox, its slim build covered in silky blonde fur with zig-zagging stripes the shade of an overcast sky, though its belly and chest were a pleasing snowy white. It stood upright upon its hindlegs, a bushy balance assisting tail flowed behind it, and Jonathan could see that from the knees down the legs were not like a canid's at all but more avian with black scales and three claw tipped toes, two pointing towards him and one sprouting from the heel. Looking more closely Jonathan noted that the arms matched this aesthetic too and were reptilian from the elbow down with two fingers and thumb on each hand, tipped with midnight black talons. The creatures head was also not entirely in keeping with its initial image as, though akin to a fennec fox in shape, the eyes were those of a spider, huge black orbs that caught the light with their moist sheen. Six identical tiny spider eyes also lined the muzzle, three in a line on each side of the padded nose, and below them a half dozen or so fangs peeked out from under the top lip. It wore no clothing, Jonathan reasoning that its thick downy fur probably did a good enough job for warmth's sake, but it did have several belts wrapped round its person, the surfaces of which were studded with bullet sized punches each containing a tiny vial or corked tube.

The tall, right most figure, the one hoisting the rope, gave Jonathan the most pause with its initial appearance, looking too much like a Stalker for his comfort, but as Jonathan watched there were many differences that reassured him. For one this individual was much more like a crustacean than a mantis, its broad flat head the shape and size of a horseshoe crab's carapace and the same glossy hue of river mud, the entire body in fact was ridged with armoured plates that creaked as the being shifted its considerable weight around. Its face was hidden behind an undulating mask of thick, double jointed bristles folded inward from the underside of the mantle. The arms were asymmetrical; the thick right arm capped with an impressive lobster pincer, and the whipcord thin left much shorter and terminating in coiled mass of puckered fingers, like the tubular feet of a starfish. It approached him upon pair of robust plated legs that were remarkably human when compared to the upper body and stooped to retrieve Jonathan and the unconscious Gluttony from their rubbery swing. The weighty pincer firmly plucked them up and, with a surprisingly delicate touch, deposited them gently upon the decking. Jonathan gazed upward at his saviour.

"Thank you." He whispered breathlessly, as he caught a glimpse of two eyes shining back at him with the watery lustre of a pair of polished onyxes. Their owner chittered its mantle bristles as the third figure, who was initially stood back and shrouded in shadow, came forth into the dancing torchlight.

It was even stranger than the other two and clinked its way forward upon a quad set of pointed, stilt-like legs, the skin of which was a sickly, mint green and looked slick and oily in the gloom. Where the legs met and connected sat its torso; an emaciated husk of twisted olive flesh that might have once been comparable to a human's but now looked more like the remains of an ancient mummy or desiccated corpse. There were no limbs except for a single bony arm that jutted from the solar-plexus, its wiry six-digit hand reaching up to remove a pair of coiled glasses from the creature's bald earless skull, the face of which looked stretched and as horrendously dry as the body with a single reptilian eye and a thin human mouth whose upper and lower lips were split vertically.

"You are quite welcome," It moaned. Its voice sounded like someone very old breathing in while they spoke, and the ends of its words whistling slightly as they brushed passed its pointed teeth. "You are lucky we found you." The creature, clearly the leader of this group, continued.

"Who are you?" Asked Jonathan, try to raise himself unsteadily to his feet. The crab-man scooped up Gluttony and cradled her upon its claw and the fox-spider gracefully jogged forward to tend her as the corpse-leader scuttled to Jonathan's aid.

"We," It breathed, its stick-thin fingers grasping his forearm firmly and drawing him up to stand face to face. "Are the Resistance."

Chapter 26: Never Laid to Rest.

The corpse-leader ushered everybody deeper into the docks of Weirwood and beyond, explaining the situation as it went. The interior of the great domed roof was far removed from the sparse, spread out nature of Nox. Even Anchoridge felt less claustrophobic than Weirwood, but even so the latter matched the former with its whitewashed walls and oaken beams, its cobbled streets and thatched roofs. The differences were subtle but pervasive; things were gloomier, dirtier, and generally more dilapidated. Steel was a more common material than in Anchoridge, and was used to reinforce the chunky, patchwork shell forever above their heads, but it too was rusted in places, missing a few spars here or a bolt or two there. The town sat in partial shadow and twilight, with only a jagged oval of sky sat dead centre of the roof, the meek moonlight filtering through to reflect from the grime flecked windows and tiles of the high towers that clawed up toward the sky. Even if it were daytime Jonathan did not think there would be much more light available to strike down at them and the only think more subversive than the darkness was the odour of neglect seeped out of every pore of the buildings, and with it the feeling of great depression and subconscious dread. Oblivious to it all, the corpse-leader dropped back to stroll spiderlike next to Jonathan.

"My name is Chyssmire, and I am sorry we did not intervene sooner." He wheezed.

"I'm Jonathan. What do you mean 'sooner'? Were you watching us?" Jonathan asked.

"Of course they were," Chided Pride, "We were mostly likely being observed as soon as we left the forest." Chyssmire chuckled, a dry rasp of breath.

"In actual fact we learnt of your journey far before that." He responded, taking them single file down a particularly brooding street. They were travelling beyond the quayside now and into the bowels of Weirwood, past empty boarded shops and dusty stained-glass display windows, through moss and algae caked gunnels, and along a veritable maze of dingy side-streets and alleyways. All the while a subdued murmur of voices flowed from the troupe, most worryingly from Lust and the fennec-fox who were fussing over Gluttony, still carried in the lobster-man's 'arms'. Chyssmire continued speaking over his shoulder at Jonathan as they went, the points of his four feet tip tapping of the cobbles like fingernails drumming impatiently on a tabletop.

"As I said we would have intervened earlier, but we had to be sure you were not a threat."

"And I'm guessing we proved not to be...somehow?" Jonathan asked.

"You selflessly tried to rescue your friend." Chyssmire stated, ignoring the rhetorical nature of Jonathan's question. "No servant of Sheol would do that." The way opened up into a central plaza, small and surrounded on all sides by the looming bulk of thick timbered residences and steel flanked warehouses with only the way they'd come as an entrance or exit. Chyssmire wandered towards the low stone well that sulked in the far-left corner. He drummed his sharpened points upon the floor in a rapid flurry of blows. After a few seconds the well began to rise from the ground and Jonathan could see that it was actually the top of an ornate steel caged elevator, large enough for maybe five people at a time to travel.

"Emilee, take our wounded guests to the hospital, I will take everyone else for some refreshment." Announced Chyssmire. The fox-spider nodded curtly.

"Come with me." She said quietly, her voice tinged with a vague lisp due to the fangs lining her jaw. "This one should be fine, but she will require much rest and care to make it so." Her words were very carefully pronounced, almost over-pronounced with the speaker making sure to hit every syllable exactly giving the whole tone a very laboured feel and a curious Russian sounding accent. Jonathan found it reassuring, and honest which helped him to deal with the unsettling spider eyed stare and sideways blink. They entered the elevator, followed by the lobster-man and his charge. Emilee yanked the chain to her left and the whole apparatus vibrated and shook as it lowered them into the pits beneath the streets of Weirwood. Solid rock and clotted earth swept by at alarming speed and Jonathan leant in closer to the metal bars, anxious to see if he could see the end of the shaft.

"Looking to lose your nose?" Enquired a crackly, bubbling voice, deep as the ocean. Jonathan turned to see the lobster-man watching him from behind his twitching bristles.

"Ignore Kross, he has odd sense of humour." Explain Emilee.

"Not as odd as your grammar." Retorted Kross. Emilee just shrugged.

"At least I can learn other language. I don't hear you making effort to speak mine." She responded.

"I could if I wanted to," Answered Kross, froth dripping from his bristles. "I just don't want to." Emilee laughed like she'd just made the winning play in a game of chess.

"Exactly, no drive." She said mockingly. "All muscle, no brain." She tapped Kross's massive claw, baiting him.

"At least I have muscle, sparrow leg." Kross replied jokingly, making Emilee laugh harder than before.

"What be you, five? Not heard that name since was little cub." She exclaimed, smiling at Kross.

"Just keeping the past alive." Kross stated warmly, releasing a burbled snicker. Jonathan relaxed, the playful banter helping to ease and adjust him to this new turn of events, as well as his unusual new friends.

"Whilst I appreciate the levity, is Gluttony going to be ok?" He asked, the elevator's descent slowing down as it reached the lowest levels and crunched to a stop. Unseen chains rattled, and the cage door swung open, its hinges whining.

"Your friend?" Answered Emilee, stepping off the rickety contraption. "She's badly injured her arm, but other than that she is stable, and is just requiring rest." Jonathan huffed, knowingly.

"Good luck with that, once she's awake I doubt she'll sit still for very long." He warned Emilee as he followed her and Kross down into the tunnels.

The area resembled a huge trench complex, the kind Jonathan had seen in old World War One photographs, except it was enclosed with an earthen roof and strengthening beams of pale wood, their faces crudely tarred to prevent weathering and damp. Oil lamps hung at every junction, illuminating crisscross bundles of signs that looking more confusing than helpful. The occasional voice could be heard echoing along from the other sections, but nobody came into view. Still Emilee and Kross did not break pace as they deftly navigated towards the Hospital entrance; a low-ceilinged doorway framed by a dense log of chipped oak and two supporting pillars co-opted from a set of lead pipes strung with a multicoloured bead curtain. Everyone ducked inside, Kross having to almost revert to all fours to haul his massive frame through the entrance, and into a long spacious hall dug from the ground and filled with row upon row of mismatched hospital beds, screens, trolleys, stretchers, and other miscellaneous equipment. One corner was devoted to a spiralling set of glass tubes, steaming and frothing as they distilled their mysterious contents, and another corner was closed off behind a thick set of drawn woollen curtains, perhaps for surgery or simply perhaps somewhere for the on duty to doctor to speak with patients privately. The acrid bite of antiseptic and bitter copper hung in the stale air like a malaise.

While Emilee jogged to retrieve clean equipment from a trolley, Kross took Gluttony across to one of the, thankfully many, empty beds, his dense frame raising hollow thunks from the duckboards that concealed the drains built into the hospital floor. Jonathan tried not to notice the rusted stains that streaked along the gutters. Kross tenderly lay Gluttony down, her short stature exaggerated by his massive asymmetrical form and giving her the impression of an exhausted child being laid to rest, he then stepped back and made for the exit.

“I'll meet ya upstairs, just give the chain two pulls.” He mentioned to Jonathan as he passed by and vanished back through the jiggling sheet of beads. Emilee returned and wasted no time immediately making notes and re-checking vital signs for her report. Jonathan was surprised to see such intensive and diligent medical care from somewhere that was frankly rather medieval in appearance, but then again, he was constantly learning to re-evaluate what he thought he knew since beginning this quest over a week ago. He walked over to the opposite side of his friend's bed and gazed sadly at her prone form as Emilee completed her required inspection. Gluttony seemed so peaceful, well as peaceful as she could be considering the circumstances, though her clothes were still soaked with river water. Her dark, chestnut hair was stuck to her mocha skin though it seemed to be beginning to dry out and regain its trademark curls, her shallow breathes flicking the ends close to her mouth. He wished she was awake; it didn't seem natural for her to be so calm and still. A sharp scratching sound etched its way into Jonathan's ears as Emilee made a few final observations.

"Subject stable; water extraction completed above ground." She murmured. "Right upper limb; possible dislocation, no other complications noted." Emilee slide the notepad and pencil into her belt. "Are you trained for medical?" She asked Jonathan.

"I'm afraid not," He replied, he was a little embarrassed to admit that he'd never gotten around to renewing his first aid training, there's never been any need, so he'd kept putting it off. Now that hesitation seemed lazy and irresponsible. "I knew a little about this stuff but that was a while ago." He admitted sheepishly. Emilee smiled gently.

"It is no matter. Just follow my instructions, we need to reset shoulder joint." She explained. Jonathan nodded as Emilee unbuttoned the top straps of Gluttony's dungarees to give them better access to her wounded arm. Which her arms up the sleeve, Emilee felt the injured shoulder with expert fingers. "Give firm support to chest." Emilee pointed out where to hold Gluttony as she straightened the loose arm. "When ready, will attempt joint relocation." She grasped the limb securely and scrunched up her nose with concentration.

"Ok, I'm ready I guess." Jonathan announced, quietly dreading what was about to happen.

"On three," Emilee began, "One, two," Jonathan tightened his grip. "Three." Jonathan braced himself as Emilee applied force to the arm, pulling it away from the body. After a few seconds there was a wet clunk as the joint slipped back into its usual position, Jonathan could feel the reapplication as he held onto Gluttony and a subtle wave of nausea swept over him as he imagined the socket reconnecting.

"Is that it?" He asked, trying to distract himself.

"Joint is relocated," Emilee nodded, "Further preventative measures will be applied, but if she is being careful, she will be fine." Jonathan smiled with relief as Emilee removed the notepad, scribbled down a few sentences then took out several vials from her belt. "Drink this, it will help you with exposure, then I begin with topic agents for this one." She stated after thrusting a tiny crystal vial into his palm, then seemingly awaiting a response from Jonathan, who just sat there nodding dumbly. "Which means, I am needing to remove her clothes now. Would you be giving us privacy please?" She asked.

"Oh? OH!" Jonathan exclaimed, the edges of a blush rushing to his cheeks. "O-Of course." He hastily stood and left the bedside as Emilee laughed quietly and pulled a screen round for modesty. She paused for a brief moment and called out to him.

"You should be changing your clothes too, or you will catch a death of cold!" She indicated toward the curtained off corner of the hospital. "There is storeroom beyond curtains. Go, and find yourself something you like, I will make sure old clothes are returned to you when dry." Jonathan, still blushing, nodded his thanks as Emilee and Gluttony vanished from view, and swiftly ran over and brushed by the dense woollen blackout curtains. Once inside he found that it was not a cramped cubby hole but a whole other hall, albeit a smaller one that the hospital, filled with crates and supplies all neatly arranged and labelled alphabetically. He picked his way down the rows of shelving till he came across the clothing aisle and set about rummaging through the dozen or more boxes till he found something that was both his size and species.

A good fifteen minutes later and Jonathan was now dressed in mismatched collection of articles, old, patched, and slightly musty perhaps but at least no longer waterlogged. He's picked out a pair of worn yet solid brown leather shin-high boots to wear over a pair of khaki cotton trousers with that were baggy from the knee up and thinner from the knee down. He'd located a breezy white cotton shirt for an underlayer and padded it out with a sleeveless ivory shade arming jacket with frayed leather cords down the front. I'd also managed to locate, with some amazement, a replacement waxed coat in dark olive-green with a black inside layer that turned outward at the cuffs. As an afterthought he also purloined a suitably lengthy knitted scarf in criss-cross hues of emerald and ruby, but he just stuffed it into his pack for later. Not entirely sure what to do with his old, sodden clothing he neatly folded it and left it at the foot of the aisle for Emilee to collect, then he rearranged the crates and scattered items that were of no use and removed himself from the storeroom back the way he'd come.

Chapter 27: Keeping Your Friends Close.

Jonathan quickly exited the hospital, so as not to disturb the screened off bed, and retraced his footsteps back through the grim halls to the elevator. Once there he did as Kross told him and pulled the chain twice. The pulley systems immediately got to work, and the enclosed birdcage sank once more. Jonathan looked at the Emilee's vial clenched in his fist, it was nothing remarkable just a cold cylinder of frosted glass, the liquid inside a crisp, apple red. He removed the wax stopper to sniff the contents and was greeted with the warming scent of cinnamon. Blinking in pleasant surprise he drank the vial's meagre offer, which had a semi-sweet flavour like liquorice, and felt a balmy heat spread through his system, the comforting tendrils making him giggle uncontrollably as they restored a modicum of strength and an aura of wellbeing. The joyous feeling persisted until he reached the second level and the elevator squealed to a stop. The bars on the door swung open with a high-pitched moan like untuned violin and Jonathan stepped out into another spacious hall. This time the architecture was more like an amphitheatre with the centre of the hexagonal room sunken in the middle and the raised sides acting as rows of pews for the audience to surround whoever was addressing them. A basic chandelier was suspended from the ceiling, a simple inverted diamond of glass filled with thousands of dancing lights, each a different shade of yellow from sun-bleached sand to radiant daisy. The flowing, undulating light source made the whole room feel like it was underwater, and lent an unknown, yet calming atmosphere.

Kross was sat next across from the gates of the cage, next to Wrath, and he waved to Jonathan vigorously as soon as he noticed him leave the elevator's embrace. Jonathan walked briskly towards them and climbed the stair seats to take his place next to his new acquaintance. Scattered around him he saw the rest of his friends, plus a dozen or so resistance members with varying traits and a myriad of appearances.

"Hey mate, nice threads. You've already met Kross then?" Asked Wrath, leaning forward to greet Jonathan.

"We have yes, I presume you have too?" Replied Jonathan. Wrath grinned and slapped Kross's back.

"It's bin a while but me an' Kross are old mates," He stated enthusiastically.

"I used to live in Anchoridge till I moved to Weirwood." Bubbled Kross, "I'm construction by trade."

"Not that that's surprisin'!" Laughed Wrath.

"Hah I know I know," Continued Kross, "But that's how I met Wrath, we were quite a building team back in the day." Wrath grinned happily, reminiscing as Kross changed the subject. "Anyway, he was telling me about you Jonathan. Quite a long way to come, aye." Jonathan smiled nervously, not knowing where to begin.

"I'm just here to do my part." He said.

"Well we're happy to have you." Kross burbled. "Must be a change from the ordinary."

"You've got that right, but to be honest it's a welcome one." Admitted Jonathan. "I just hope I can do some good." Kross nodded and patted him on the shoulder with his claw.

"You'll do fine; besides you've got this geezer to keep you safe." He said encouragingly, jerking his tube-thumb in Wrath's direction. Wrath laughed out loud.

"Currently it stands at one-nil on the safety front." He teased playfully, but before Jonathan could offer a retort a figure ambled its way into the middle of the circle. It was Chyssmire, the flitting lights catching the sickly sheen of his skin and making him seem even paler than normal. He removed his single lensed glasses from his cyclops eye and balanced them between his stick-thin fingers as he wiped them with a cloth on his thumb, before placing them back upon his sunken face. He wheezed a threadbare cough to gather everyone's attention and the murmur of background voices dropped away.

"My friends, my colleagues, today is a great day." He exposited, his frail voice reverberating from the walls and somehow filling the cavernous space with ease.

"The time we have long waited for is almost here, the reason we have hung on so tightly and everything we have prepared and trained for will soon be upon us. We have in our company tonight those who would see the end of the great daemon we call Sheol, they have within them the means to depose of the mad god forever!" A brief cheer rose from the resistance members and Chyssmire paused as it petered out, not wanting to quash their high spirits. "Our military commanders and reconnaissance advisors have formulated a plan to help this intrepid group achieve their goals. Spymaster Doorn?" He gestured to the shadows and a new figure evolved from them, flowing like smoke and settling into view. She was a tall, lithe individual, humanoid but with unnaturally thin and long arms and legs. She was clad in a grey bodysuit that seemed to generate its own shadow and made her seem permanently out of focus if you weren't completely concentrating on her. Over that she wore a floor length leather coat that looked like it was made from darkness woven together. Her face was old but not weak in any way, more lined with experience and hard-edged wisdom than the fragility of age, and she wore her streaky straw-blonde hair tied back in a practical bob. A lengthy scar creased her right cheek and ended below the jawline, the only blemish to an ancient visage that command respect with its sheer presence.

"We have identified a two-prong approach," Her voice buzzed like it was being projected straight into the mind through an old radio, and had a clipped knowledgeable tone, like a teacher schooling her pupils. "By coordinating with our brother cells to the west we will strike at key points along the borders to Sheol's sanctum. I must stress that these attacks are not designed to be anything other than a diversion allowing our new compatriots to infiltrate and enact their own plan. Therefore, we must fight well, but do not sacrifice yourselves unnecessarily." She stared round the room. "The attack begins in four days' time; you should seek out your squad leaders if you have further questions." With her piece finished she nodded at Chyssmire and folding back into the darkness, melting away as if she was never there. Chyssmire coughed again and waved his hand to lower the rumble of conversation that had been sprouted from Doorn's announcement.

"I don't need to re-tread old ground, but we have a lot to thank our new friends for and we will make sure the Resistance is more than passive in their moment of need. Now, get some rest, and good luck for the future." He scuttled off to converse with a few important looking figures as the rumbles of conversation reasserted themselves, and the various groups began to break up and head away to heed his order to get some rest.

"I trust Gluttony is alright then?" Asked Wrath, standing from his seat.

"Yeah it seems that way, she'd hurt her shoulder but otherwise seemed ok. Emilee's taking care of her." Jonathan replied, smiling.

"That's grand mate." Wrath said, nodding. "I was so worried for her."

"It wasn't your fault Wrath." Stated Jonathan gently. "Anyway, we have Kross to thank for taking us to the surface." Kross cocked his armoured head curiously.

"I didn't do that, I just pulled you up. I'm actually not a very good swimmer." He admitted. "No, it was one of your lot that helped you out there." His words slurped forth, froth bubbling up from behind his mask of bristles. Kross raised his meaty claw to wipe it away.

"Aye you've got Envy to thank mate. Used 'er ice powers she did." Wrath explained, a proud smile erupting across his grey face. Jonathan also smiled warmly and looked round to find her amongst the huddles of milling resistance members. He eventually spotted her holding Lust's hand, whose bright pink hair stood out even amongst such a varied crowd.

"She's down there, come on!" Jonathan cried as he leapt up and bounded down the steps, Wrath and Kross chasing his newly booted heels. Once at the bottom he led them to where Lust and Envy were conversing with a six armed bat-person, and curious lumpy shadow.

"Excuse me ladies," Kross announced as he lumbered over to them. Lust sighed with relief when she saw Jonathan, and even Envy allowed a puny smile to crease her face as she stared at him from under her forest green fringe.

"Jonathan," Lust said, her motherly tones floating across the gap between them, "I'm so glad you're ok. We were just describing your heroic dive to our new friends."

"I'm g-glad too." Stammered Envy her voice brittle as glass.

"It was nothing," Dismissed Jonathan, waving away their praise modestly, "Besides it would have all been for wasted if I hadn't been helped out in the end." He cleared his throat, as Envy blushed a little and tried to hide away behind her fringe. "Thank you Envy," Jonathan said, trying to look her in the eye. Lust grinned down at her tiny friend and gave her a reassuring hug whilst Wrath shot her a thumbs up.

"You're welcome." Envy muttered from inside Lust's embrace; her face now pinker than the latter's hair.

"How's Gluttony is she ok?" Asked Lust, as she released Envy.

"She'll be alright, she's being treated as we speak. Maybe we could-" Jonathan began.

"Jonathan!" Cried a tuneless woodwind voice, suddenly interrupting them. There was a clacking of bone on wood as Chyssmire hobbled over to them, his hand extended to greet everyone he came across as he traversed the relatively short distance over to them. For all his hideous looks Jonathan was warming to Chyssmire, he had a wizened charm to him, and Jonathan could see he cared deeply about each member of his beloved resistance, old and new. Wrath, Kross, and Jonathan waiting patiently for him to join them.

"I am glad you could attend." Chyssmire wheezed happily. "It is a mighty burden you bear for us my boy." He creaked a cracked smile across his broken lips, his needle teeth peeking through the cross shaped gap.

"Thank you Chyssmire, but as I keep saying I'm just here to do my part. I'm really not that special, I just want to help." Jonathan couldn't help himself; he'd never been comfortable accepting praise especially from people he'd only just met.

"Nonsense, nonsense." Chided Chyssmire, his smile turning wry. "You're more important than you realise. We formulated our plan around that very sentiment."

"Yeah about that, it seems extremely dangerous, who came up with it?" Jonathan asked him. Chyssmire's desiccated features contorted to a look of thoughtfulness.

"As luck would have it I was about to introduce you." He turned and waved forward another new figure, who strode into view, his hands clasped behind his back. "This is..." Chyssmire started to say before Jonathan stopped him with a gasp.

"I know who this is." He stated.

"Y-you do?" Stammered Chyssmire.

"Yes, and his name," Replied Jonathan, a smile blossoming across his face. "Is Greed."

Chapter 28: What Once Was Lost.

There was a veritable explosion of noise as Jonathan and the rest of the Sins gathered around their old leader. Lust was the first to reach Greed and could not help but throw her arms round his stiff shoulders and force an embrace upon him that was barely reciprocated with more than a nod that would have been awkward had the emotion from Lust not been so genuine, the tears streaming down her face attesting to that. Envy shuffled around Greed and Lust's heels, awkwardly trying to usher a greeting before giving up and slinking back towards Jonathan. Pride was the next to reach Greed, gracefully descending the stairs to his left, and peeled Lust off him while hushing words of comfort before turning to greet Greed herself with a brisk, yet firm handshake. Though as she turned away to give others the chance to say hello Jonathan noticed her wipe away a few tears of her own from around the rims of her crimson eyes. Sloth smiled a fatigued smile and greeted Greed with a yawn and a nod, whereas Wrath strode right up to Greed and placed a metallic hand on his old friend's shoulder, an unrestrained grin of pure relief plastered across his face. Though being the first to see Greed, Jonathan was the last to properly greet him, and had to push his way through the ring the troupe had assembled before coming face to face with his lost friend.

"Mr Rhodes." Greed announced, his flat, dry gravel voice a welcome sound despite its raspy nature. Jonathan nodded; his smile still broad.

"Greed, I...I can't believe you're alive. What happened to you?" Jonathan demanded with forceful wonder.

"After you fled Nox, as per my instructions, I immobilised the initial Stalker by collapsing the fireplace upon it. I then made my own escape through the mine to the North and used the cloud and darkness to cover my tracks. The altercation took longer than I had anticipated, and by the time I had navigated away from Nox, you had all vanished into the wastes. So, I made my way to Weirwood where I knew the resistance was based." Greed explained, apparently having lost none of his aloof frankness. "It is odd we did not cross paths before."

"Yeah we went a slightly different route to the original plan." Jonathan admitted.

"So I see, you went through the forest. I difficult route, though I admit an ingenious one." Greed stated.

"Well I wasn't sure what to do to be honest." Jonathan said, somewhat sheepishly. "But I knew we had to continue onwards, and I didn't want to go a predictable way." Greed stared at Jonathan for a few heartbeats, his skull mask impossible to read. He shifted his weight onto his heels and nodded smoothly.

"I knew I had made a good choice." He declared, a smug edge to his gritty words. However, he did not continue his train of thought and instead looked round slowly, searching the gathered faces. "I am not usually remiss, but I do not see Gluttony's face amongst you."

"She fell into the river, and Jonathan rescued her." Lust announced, her face still slick with tears.

"Really." Greed said, though it was hard to judge if he was concerned or not. "You have grown into quite the hero in my absence." Pride, who was stood behind Greed, smiled slyly.

"Hero, leader, and investigator." She quipped. "We've learnt some very fascinating things whilst you've been away." Pride's tone surprised Jonathan, as it was more aggressive than he'd have thought considering she'd only just found out he was not dead. Had she figured something out, something accusatory? Greed did not even bristle, her sharp words slipping away like water off a duck's back.

"That is good. The more we know of Sheol the better." He declared, disarmingly. "I look forward to discussing your ideas at a later time." Greed turned and gestured towards Chyssmire, who was watching everything with fascination. "However, I believe we have had rooms prepared?" He queried.

"Yes, yes, let me show you to them." Chyssmire wheezed happily.

He led everyone out the back of the amphitheatre and down a flight of rickety stairs till they reached a long branching tunnel marked with the signpost 'Barracks'.

"They may not be much, but these are our dormitories. I had the liberty of having everybody's things moved to the rooms next to Mr Greed's. I'm sure he can lead the way, as I regret I have many other matters to attend to before the day is over." Chyssmire smiled wearily and returned the way he'd come, his pointed quad legs clinking like a typewriter on the duckboard steps. Greed took over and the group wandered down the winding hallway, passing by ranks of spartan dormitory rooms, each capable of holding two to four occupants depending on the beds. Most of the twenty or so rooms on the level were occupied, the welcome sounds of activity and preparation renewing a sense of determined pride, however several rooms were completely vacant, and these stood silent, their furnishings drab and atmospheres hanging low as if in mourning. Finally, at the end of the dusty trench tunnel there was a set of four rooms, two on each side, and it was here that Greed stopped and turned.

"Though we won't be here for long, I have already divided up our belongings into appropriate pairs for the rooms." He declared, taking charge as if he had never been away. "Wrath, you and I occupy the room to my left, Lust and Envy the room to my right if you please. Sloth, you and Gluttony are in the top left room, and Pride, you and Mr Rhodes are set up in the top right." Everyone nodded as their places were designated and accommodation checked out. Jonathan and Pride's room was a sparse bunker with little in the way of comfortable furnishings. There was a squat, battered desk and chair to the right of the door, and to the left slumped an open wardrobe wit hooks for clothing and a wooden case for weapons and the like. A steel bunk bed that had clearly been salvaged from scrap metal and hastily bolted together sat rusting opposite the doorway on a carpet that might have been maroon at one point but was in dire need of either deep cleaning or burning. There was a pervasive musty scent, and a paper-thin layer of dust coated everything, but to Jonathan it was a thousand times better than the hard ground and bedroll, and was more welcoming than its ramshackle nature should have made it. Pride's things were already neatly arranged on the bottom bunk, so Jonathan set his own bag beside the ladder. He was just about to sort through his things when Sloth's sickly face slunk round the side of the door.

"I was going...to go see...Gluttony...if you wanted...to come?" He asked, his voice lazy yet still layered with concern for his symbiote. Pride shook her head.

“Not yet, I’m going to find some decent showering facilities and finally refresh myself.” Her typical fierce gaze softened gently, “Then I will join you at Gluttony’s side.” She said with a smile. Jonathan thought for a moment as Sloth rotated his neck to ask him the same question with a curious, half-lidded stare.

“Everyone else…is going…” Sloth announced, perhaps hoping this might convince Jonathan to tag along too.

“Actually, I was hoping to catch a quick nap,” Jonathan admitted. “And if everyone else is going I don’t want to overwhelm her while she’s recovering.” Sloth looked visibly disappointed, which considering his usual gloomy visage was quite a feat. Jonathan felt guilt sweep through him. “But I guess I could tag along too and see how she’s doing.” He declared, changing his mind to not wound his friend. “I’ll come along with Pride, so she doesn’t get lost.” This seemed to cheer up Sloth and his face slackened back to its standard, fatigued droop.

“Okay then…see you both…later…” He said as happily as he could manage before creeping away.

“I don’t ‘get lost’” Pride muttered defensively. Though her objections were more joking than in actual offense.

“Sure, but also you don’t know the way.” Jonathan said as he hoisted himself up onto the top bunk and settled down on his back for a quick rest.

“Touché” She replied, smiling. She rummaged around in her bags for a while, arranging and sorting out her towels, spare clothes, and making sure her rapier was properly stored in the weapon rack. After ten minutes or so, as Jonathan was starting to drift off to sleep, she sighed. “Now it’s time for a well-deserved shower. I’ll come collect you afterward.” She announced to him as she left the dreary room.

“Good luck.” Jonathan called after, barely conscious.

“I don’t need luck.” She replied jokingly, popping her head round the door. But Jonathan was already asleep.

Chapter 29: Amity of My Enemy.

Jonathan's eyelids flickered and creaked open, revealing that which had been hidden from him for the past few nights; the ancient cathedral and its cavernous hall. Once again Jonathan sat up, and once again he was greeted with the stale caress of bone-dry air and the distant corpse groan of the wind finding cracks far above him in the carcass of the vault. He stood but did not bother to brush himself down, instead walking with determination towards what he knew awaited in the gloom, towards the altar and its lonely occupant.

Jonathan felt a rigid strength reinforcing him, it had been too long since I had last been here, and he wanted to make full use of whatever time the being allowed him. He had questions that needed answers, and answers that required questions, the puzzles were starting to fill themselves in and Jonathan was certain that the voice had at least some of the pieces. As the fountain's sombre trickling once more tickled his ears and the desiccated air turned bitter with the chalky bite of chiselled stone, the altar unveiled itself from the darkness and robed man stood where Jonathan ad left him many moons ago, twin quills in hand.

"Hello!" Called Jonathan, but the man ignored him and continued his writings. "I was hoping we could talk, I have more questions." He continued, his words echoing outward into the clutches of the shadows that watched like predators from above. Still the robed man paid him no mind, turning a page with a rasp of dry parchment. Jonathan was somewhat wrong footed, though he had only briefly spoken to the voice before he was at least expecting more that to be ignored. Jonathan decided to climb the steps onto the vast pedestal that supported the altar and its carved rock face.

"I said, I have questions." He repeated, now no more than a few feet away from the robed man who continued to scratch runes into the book with an almost mechanical precision. Unexpectedly, a low rumble erupted into Jonathan's mind.

"And what makes you think you are deserving of answers?" The voice rasped with a dangerous tone.

"I, um, I mean," Jonathan swallowed, intimidated but nevertheless determined to hold his ground. "You said Sheol was beyond my understanding, so help me to understand." He pleaded.

"Why should I do that?" The voice replied.

"Be-because I want to help, I need to help, and to do that I need to know more." Jonathan stated. "So please, tell me what you know."

"You? You are nothing, just another soul amongst the billions that have come and gone." The voice rattled.

"You're wrong." Declared Jonathan, his fire returning. "You said yourself I was no normal dreamer."

"Ahhhhh," The voice thrummed, echoing through Jonathan's veins. "And you believe that?" It asked.

"Honestly, I don't know." Jonathan replied. "Does it really matter? I have only your word that this is even a dream at all." There was a bone shaking rumble that Jonathan interpreted as a thoughtful laugh.

"Go, ask your questions, that your brief existence may find some solace in their answers." The voice declared. The robed man lifted his gaze to watch Jonathan, listening and waiting. Jonathan licked his parched lips and asked the first question on his list.

"What is this place, and why do I keep coming back to it?"

"You are linked to this place, as you are linked to me. We are both born of the same realm and are drawn to each other through this link." The voice explained.

"Wait, so I'm the only one who has these dreams?" Jonathan asked, surprised at this revelation. The voice purred with a low vibrating tone.

"Indeed. These halls have been vacant for over three hundred years." It boomed. There was a lingering silence as Jonathan thought over this new information, he decided to change the topic.

"Who is Sheol?" He queried.

"This has already been answered." The voice said. "But again; he is eternal, ever renewing, and without rest."

"I know, but what *is* he?" Jonathan reiterated.

"The result of an imperfect system, the spawn of an imperfect world." The voice boomed in response.

"What does he want?" Jonathan asked.

"Again, an end to all things." The voice stated, echoing their last meeting. Jonathan thought about his next question at length before asking, afraid that he already knew the implication but hoped he was wrong.

"And why do you want that?" He whispered, tendrils of dread snaking their icy fingers into his chest. The world vibrated, low and ominous like it was in the outermost grasp of an earthquake.

"So that I may finally rest." The voice whispered back, drowning out the trickling fountains with its bass. Jonathan swallowed again; his throat drained of moisture was quickly as his face drained of blood. There was a lengthy pause as Jonathan considered the scope of the situation, this was Sheol, this was the great eternal evil that he had been brought to this realm to defeat. Could he do it, he wondered, could he strike this being down and end everything here? Jonathan felt a sudden familiar weight on his hip and lowered his hand tentatively to grasp the pommel and handle of his sword. The robed man's hollow eyes drifted towards Jonathan's hand anticipating a sudden drawing of the weapon, but Jonathan relaxed his grip on the sword and instead let his arm naturally fall back by his side once more.

"Are you not afraid boy?" Boomed the voice.

"No." Replied Jonathan.

"You lie," The voice stated, "Your other hand trembles as you stand before me." It was right and useless to try and deceive it, Jonathan was alone and terrified.

"I figured it out, I know who you are." He called out, attempting to conquer his fear.

"So?" Rumbled the voice.

"Aren't you going to kill me or something?" Jonathan blurted, inwardly cursing his stupidity in suggesting the very thing he didn't want to happen. "I could end this right here." The robed man shuffled forward a step, his vacant void stare locked with Jonathan's own eyes. A deep flowing rumble bounced round Jonathan's mind.

"Is that truly the answer? For you would soon waste away, as all mortals do, whereas I and my children would eventually return to begin this cycle again, and again, again." The voice shifted in tone. "That is my curse." Jonathan ground his teeth as he considered the information.

"You'll let me go?" He queried hopefully.

"You may leave whenever you wish." The voice boomed dismissively. The robed man turned away and went back to his writings as Jonathan began to cautiously back away, feeling his way down the paved steps of the plinth with his feet. When he reached the bottom he swiftly turned and ran. "Until we meet again," The voice rumbled through his joints as he hastily reached the brass doors and grasped their frame with outstretched fingers.

Chapter 30: Not as it Seems.

Jonathan awoke violently, lurching forward with a jerk that slammed his face into the ceiling banishing his panic into a world of stars and impact trauma. Sitting back with a startled cry Jonathan threw up his hands to protect his now bruised forehead. Blinking back tears of pain, he turned towards the door to see a lone figure silhouetted against the glowing torchlight of the tunnel hall.

"That looked painful. I'm sorry if I startled you." Pride's voice whispered to him as she entered the room and approached the bunk bed. Jonathan shook his head, more to release the plaguing stars than to dismiss her concerns, but regardless he assured her no permanent harm was done.

"Were you having a bad dream?" She enquired, "You were murmuring something about 'answers'." Jonathan crawled his way over to the ladder and carefully started to descend it.

"It was nothing." He sighed. Pride however was not convinced, and she ran a finger over his temple which came away slick with sweat.

"Please Jonathan, all things have a meaning. Even innocent dreams." She stated, with genuine concern. Jonathan cast his eyes downward.

"It was about our mission, and our enemy." Jonathan admitted.

"Sheol." Pride said, disgust blanketing her words. Jonathan brought his gaze up to lock eye contact with her.

"I've met him Pride, talked with him, via my dreams." He explained. Something in his voice, in his demeanour made Pride second guess her immediate doubt. Rather than questioning the claim, she believed him.

"Wh-what did he say." She demanded, with a rare stumble. This was new territory for her, and it scared her.

"Many things, some more worrisome than others." Jonathan paused for a second, remembering something. "Pride you said that there's a library around here yes?" He asked.

"Yes, though the original would have been on the surface, I believe I saw a sign for one earlier." She replied, making Jonathan smile.

"That would make sense, they must have moved the content down here to protect them." He stated, pleased. "We should go there. I have a hunch I'd like to reinforce. Then I promise I'll tell you more about my dream." Pride considered his proposal before grabbing her bag and nodding in agreement as the pair of them ventured out into the dimly lit corridors.

The library was at the far end of the sub-level, behind a thin cloak of speckled silk that twitched occasionally, inviting passers-by to enter its world of knowledge, as ventilation from the surface brushed aside its folds. Pride and Jonathan gingerly stepped inside the dark library and were engulfed by the musty scent of old books, heady aroma aside the library was a fantastical place filled to the brim with tomes, scrolls, and manuscripts of all kinds. It reminded Jonathan of Greed's tree-house back in Anchoridge, a place that now seemed to be so far behind him in both the literal and metaphorical sense. A lot of care and attention had gone into organising the many bookcase and stands that lined the double rooms, each room devoted to either fiction or non-fiction, and each case clearly marked off for the appropriate genre. Jonathan was surprised that there was no librarian or guard on duty to protect the artfully arranged and sorted collection, but he did crack a bemused smile at the signage declaring a 'Take a book, leave a book' policy that was pinned to the inside of the library door above a drab steel trolley.

"Where do you want to begin?" Enquired Pride in a low whisper. It wasn't that there was any actual need to be quiet, but apparently a healthy respect for the sanctity of libraries was something all realms shared. Jonathan cast his eyes round the cosy shelves till he located the one marked 'History'.

"Over there," He whispered back, pointing a finger toward a surprisingly small case that did not seem to contain nearly as many volumes as the ones around it. Once face to face with the diminutive case, Jonathan started to scour the spines and bindings of the books entombed there, he was not entirely sure what he was looking for, but he knew he would know it when it reared its head. After several minutes of searching Pride, having had nothing to do but kick her heels, leant over to question if she could help him find what he was after.

"Yes, see if you can find anything about Hammerswell, or anything a hundred years before." He replied. Pride was intrigued and set to work gracefully pulling out tomes with her index finger and flipping through the first few paragraphs before replacing them.

A further twenty minutes ticked by before Jonathan excitedly removed a large and ancient volume from the shelf, releasing a shower of dust from its worn pages.

"Aha!" He cried triumphantly. Pride shot him a questioning look and he beckoned her over. "*673.73SC.*" He announced to her, whilst also pointing out the coiled symbol on the spine. "I found a book just like this back at that old house in the woods. It was pretty far gone, but I was hoping to locate a more usable copy here." Jonathan glanced at Pride's empty hands sadly. "Nothing?" He asked.

"Nothing." She replied.

"Not to worry," He said reassuring her. "I didn't think you'd find much. Now let's take this back to the room." He suggested, making for the exit.

"Just a moment." Pride cried before he could cross the threshold. He looked back at her and watched as she removed a small book of her own from her bag and dusted it off before placing it very precisely on the trolley to his right. "Take one, leave one." She decreed quietly.

Back in the gloomy dormitory room Jonathan and Pride bent low over the lower bunk, their prize spread out before them. They spend a good while trawling through the bulky book which contained a wealth of knowledge about Hammerswell, their feudal leadership, military, and economic systems, as well as their allies and the surrounding countries. Halfway through the third reading, Pride abruptly stood up and stretched.

"Are you going to enlighten me as to why we've just spent so much time dragging ourselves through this old tome?" She enquired, her patience starting to fray.

"I'm surprised I have to point it out to you." Jonathan announced. It was his turn to play the smart one, and he would be lying if he said he was not enjoying it. Pride yawned, trying to play off his smugness.

"What does it contain that is so important then?" She asked, weary of his game already.

"It's not what it contains, but what it does not." Jonathan answered cryptically causing Pride to roll her eyes.

"What do you mean?" She groaned. Jonathan flipped through the ancient book, its pages cracking and rasping their joints, until he came to the section entitled 'Topography of Hammerswell.' There he found a drawing of a very familiar landscape.

"Look like someplace you know?" He asked rhetorically. He stood up, opened his pack, which was laying where he'd discarded it on the top bunk, and removed the map from within its grasp. He unfolded the stained torn parchment and flattened it out side by side with the tome's open page, they matched up perfectly. Pride's eyes widened a fraction, but she was not immediately taken with his idea.

"Yes, it's the same place," She said dismissively, "But that's to be expected is it not?" Jonathan grinned and wigged his finger at her, thoroughly getting into character. "Get on with it!" She laughed, brushing his hand aside.

"Sorry," He joked, "But yes, you are correct, however look at the place names." He ran his finger back and forth between the current map and the old one. "There's no mention of Anchorridge, Nox, Weirwood, Mesaton, even the capital Bitterbark is missing."

"While I admit that's odd, if our world is built upon Hammerswell then it's expected that names would change." Pride suggested, crossing her arms. Jonathan nodded, but still a frown wandered across his brow as he closed the old tome and held it so the spine caught the flickering torch light from the hallway.

"But look at the date Pride. It's *673.73SC*, and what did you say the current date was?" He asked, finally getting to the crux of his argument.

"23..." She paused as the pin finally dropped. "...101. Wait." Jonathan's frown deepened.

"Exactly, how can this book describe a whole other culture, one that all this is currently built over," He gestured around the room, "And yet be dated just thirty years prior to now?!" Pride sat back, shocked to her core.

"What are you suggesting Jonathan?" She asked darkly, looking towards the floor as she digested his words. "What does this have to do with your dreams?"

"When I spoke with Sheol, he eluded to the fact that he was ever-renewing, and that simply destroying him was a wasted effort because he would eventually rejuvenate." Pride's eyes floated North and she stared at him through her black lashes, looking simultaneously dangerous and yet so vulnerable.

"You think this has all happened before." She whispered, voicing his idea with a lining of fear. Jonathan nodded solemnly.

"I do." He declared, wishing he did not have to.

Chapter 31: Preaching to the Choir.

"We must inform Greed." Decided Pride. "This changes everything about his plan."

"Inform me of what?" A gravel-laden voice echoed from the doorway, and Greed strode in from the hallway the candlelight shining from atop his naked skull.

"Greed!" Cried Pride, taken by surprise. "What are you doing there?" She asked as she stood abruptly.

"Calm yourself Pride," Greed said softly, raising a single hand to quiet her. "We were wondering why you had not come along to Gluttony's side yet, and I volunteered to find you." He ran his vacant gaze around the room. "I trust I am not interrupting anything?" He asked.

"No, not at all." Jonathan stated, also standing. "In fact, we found something we think you should know."

"So I gather, what is it you wish to tell me?" Greed enquired.

Jonathan and Pride calmly explained everything that had happened and that had been explored during Greed's absence, and right up until he had entered the dormitory room. Greed listened with growing interest and uttered nothing more the occasional verification so as to link everything together. It was at times like these that Jonathan wished Greed had an actual face with which to gauge his reactions, as it was a black skull gave nothing in the way of determining Greed's feelings on the information he was receiving. When they had finished Greed slowly raised a gloved hand to his chin and rubbed his lower jaw while he thought things over. Pride and Jonathan waited with bated breath while he considered what they had told him. Finally, after what seemed like an age, Greed lowered his hand and clasped it once more behind his back.

"Firstly, I must commend you both for piecing this all together." He grumbled, his sandpaper tone barely scraping the air. "However, this is not something that troubles me, in fact I have known all this from the beginning." Jonathan was stunned, though admittedly he harboured doubts that anything would unseat Greed from his plinth of superior knowledge.

"You knew we could never kill Sheol?!" Exclaimed Pride. "Then what was the point of all this?" She sounded extremely hurt by this revelation, she clearly put a lot of faith into Greed and here it was being abused. Greed gave a brisk shrug, a cold and dismissive gesture to his friend's questions.

"I never stated that our goal was to kill or destroy." He stated calmly. Jonathan put a supportive hand on Pride's shoulder.

"Then what is our goal Greed?" He asked, trying to wrestle with his twisting emotions.

"As you have correctly managed to deduce, using physical force is pointless. Eventually the emotional flow from his source would rejuvenate him and we would be forced to undergo the whole process again." He stared at Jonathan, not shifting an inch. "But we do not need to destroy this...thing, in fact there is a better and more permanent solution." Greed slowly raised his right hand and pointed towards Jonathan's wrist, where dwelt the amulet he had been wearing since setting out from Anchoridge. Jonathan's head snapped to the amulet and he drew his hand away from Pride's shoulder and held it up to better view the glistening gemstone that twinkled with rainbow colour like a prism.

"I thought this was to protect us from Sheol's influence?" Jonathan said quietly.

"And it is." Replied Greed, "But only so much as it amplifies the wearer's innate abilities."

"Like Jonathan's so called 'nullness'." Pride stated, regaining a little of her composure. Greed nodded.

"Indeed, if this amulet were to make contact with our great foe then Mr Rhode's ability to resist its power would in effect trap it within the amulet itself." He explained.

"Like a soul stone..." Pride gasped, however her face quickly grew sour once more as a nagging doubt wiggled to the surface of her mind. "But why did you not tell us this from the beginning?" She asked.

"I told you all you needed to know, would have made other choices had you been included to a greater degree?" Greed announced, with almost rehearsed precision.

'Was this something he'd been expecting to happen?' Jonathan thought. Pride however shook her head and glowered at Greed.

"Had you spouted that line five days ago I might have believed you." She declared, "But now, I know there's a greater reason so tell us Greed." She gazed into his deep sockets, hurt plainly observable from her body language. "Please, tell *me*." She pleaded.

"I..." Greed lowered his head and grounded his teeth together, perhaps with frustration, but Jonathan was sensing a much deeper conflict within him. After a few seconds Greed let out a long, sorrowful sigh that escaped his mouth like steam from a boiler. "There is an, unpleasant complication with this route." He said, carefully choosing his words. "To imprison one being, something else of equal value must be lost." Jonathan nodded, tiny pieces, scraps of information and understanding slotting together to produce a grim picture.

"Equal and opposite energy exchange." He whispered.

"You mean this journey..." Began Pride.

"Would claim my life." Jonathan finished. There was an almost audible snap as the puzzle within Jonathan's mind became something tangible at last. He was surprised that he did not feel as shocked as he felt he should, maybe he's always expected something like this from the get-go but until now had managed to distract himself from it by exploring this new realm. Now it was in the open there was little he could do to distance himself from it. Pride on the other hand was rocked to her core.

"How could you Greed, how could you deceive him like this?!" She cried, fire flaring as red hot as her crimson eyes.

“I had no choice.” Greed tried to explain but Pride was having none of it.

“No choice!” She roared, “There’s always a choice, we don’t need to lie to let alone kill innocent people to save our own skins!”

“When viewed logically…” Greed started to say but Pride was not finished. She balled up her fists and Jonathan was afraid she might actually strike Greed.

“Logically?! LOGICALLY!?” She shouted, completely overcome by rage. Jonathan sensed that there was a dam within Pride that was just about to burst. “I’m sick of your damn logic Greed, you think you’re so high and mighty because you have no need for emotions? Well some of us do!” Wet flecks began to appear in Pride’s eyes as the floodgates opened and released their untold years of bottled fear, sadness, and despair that until now Jonathan had only extremely briefly glimpsed.

“I don’t understand.” Greed murmured, his gravel voice now flat and lifeless.

“Of course you don’t,” Pride continued, her voice slightly quieter but her tone no less angry or filled with grief. “You never could, where was your logic when we needed you most Greed? Where was your logic when you removed your emotions to become this?” She gestured at him wildly, “Where was your logic when you abandoned the people that cared about you to pursue some unknown goal, leaving us behind, leaving me behind, leaving Lust to weep, and spend so many nights cold and alone because you could no longer see that which was once so precious to you both?”

“I didn’t…” Greed mumbled, an inner pain layering his tone.

“No, you never did, you just left me to pick up the pieces and try to rekindle what was so violently snuffed out. Left me to attempt the impossible task of explaining love to someone how no longer knew such a thing existed.” Pride’s trembling voice wavered, her anger spent, as true tears welled and started to gather on her lashes. “Now you want us me to sacrifice a good person to accomplish your twisted idea of justice.” She approached Greed threateningly, her manner hunched and low like a coiled trap ready to spring. “Something I feel like you’re in league with Sheol.” She grumbled. Jonathan, who had been busy processing all of this, step forward and, again, placed a comforting hand on Pride's shoulder. He gently pulled her back, his mind clear as glass.

"It's ok," He said calmly, his voice full of resolve. He levelled his gaze at Greed. "I accept this 'complication'." Pride froze and her face dropped causing the few remaining gathered tears to dampen onto the dormitory floor.

"Y-you, what?" She stammered.

"I've never had much of a life back in my world, I live alone, and no one visits." He chuckled humourlessly, "I even lost my job recently so in truth, even if I lived, what reason do I have to go back."

"But you're friends, and family." Pride said, her energy all but spent and Jonathan's cold acceptance having smothered what was left of her anger. Jonathan just shrugged.

"I haven't spoken to my parents in years and as for friends," He smiled warmly at her, "I have those right here."

"B-but you can't just..." Stuttered Pride.

"But I can," Jonathan replied with a shake of his head. "I've never done much during my life, but perhaps I can do something great with the end of it."

"Jonathan." Pride muttered, her fierceness all but spent and a look of great sadness draining her features.

"Mr Rhodes. I...was wrong." Admitted Greed. "I apologise for my perceived misdirection." Jonathan laughed softly, amused at the fragility of Greed's apology. He straightened up and once against became the Greed they all knew.

"Let's not dwell on it, Pride we should go to the hospital before people start to wonder what's happened to us." Jonathan stated. Pride said nothing but nodded sadly and wiped her eyes.

"I shall go back ahead of you and inform them that you are on the way." Greed announced before stepping silently out of the dormitory and disappearing into the murky torchlight of the corridor, Pride let him go without a word but watched him leave from the edges of her vision. Jonathan was concerned for her and asked if she would be okay.

"I'll be fine," She said, a little shakily. "I'm sorry you had to see that." For the first time Jonathan felt a great wave of sadness overtake him, for all her veneer and demeanour Pride was far more broken than she wanted to ever admit or appear. He took a brief step forward, and gently hugged her. Pride reflexively brought her arms up parallel to her body but amazingly did not resist his comforting embrace, instead she surrendered to it, resting her head against his neck and closing her eyes. Jonathan put a hand upon the back of her jet-black hair and just stood with her as he felt tears wet his neck and flow unbidden from Pride's silently weeping eyes.

Chapter 32: Preparing the Ground.

A short while later, once she had reaffirmed her image, Jonathan and Pride wandered down to the hospital to see if Gluttony had recovered from her near drowning.

"Should we tell the others?" Pride asked quietly as they traversed the now deserted amphitheatre and reached the lift to the hospital.

"Though I don't like leaving people out. I can't see it doing any good." Jonathan admitted as they stepped inside and slammed the door closed with a rattle of cast iron. Pride's eyes wandered round the floor as she thought about it, and Jonathan gave the chain a single firm tug.

"I guess I agree." She said. Jonathan turned his head towards her as the lift started to ascend to the upper level, the clacking of its oil starved gears grating against Jonathan's mind.

"How come you didn't know he was withholding information?" Jonathan asked, his voice raised against the tempo of the elevator. "I thought your necklace thing gave you that power."

"No, it gives me the power to see people's auras," Pride re-explained, smiling at his ignorance. "Which I can use to help make informed deductions. I was...am a prosecutor after all." Jonathan looked at her quizzically, urging her to answer his real question. Pride sighed. "But Greed, ever since his incident I've been getting no reading at all from him. So, I just had to trust he had our best interests at heart." Jonathan smiled.

"He does, in his own way." He stated hoping to reassure her.

"We shall see." Pride said her gaze steely and determined. "Regardless of how this turns out, I am glad to have met you Jonathan." Jonathan nodded and smiled more.

"And I am glad to have met all of you." He replied.

The lift's drumbeat of gears and pulleys wound down and the ornate iron door wailed as it creaked open to reveal the familiar corridor to the hospital and storage rooms. Jonathan lead Pride the short distance to the hospital, where the welcome and joyous sounds of conversation could be heard emanating from the beaded doorway. Holding aside the threaded curtain Jonathan let Pride enter before him.

"Pride, Jonny!" Shouted a bubbly voice joyously. Jonathan smiled and looked over to Gluttony's bed where he could see everyone had gathered, Wrath was stood over her, almost protectively, with his arms crossed and a wide grin on his face, Lust and Envy were perched on the end of the bed and had plainly been chatting away, Gluttony herself was sat up with a sling on her arm and a thick robes wrapped round her body, though her shoulders were exposed, Sloth's head could just be made out poking over the bed from its opposite side, and Greed was stood away from the group and as impassive as ever.

"Sorry we took so long, I fell asleep." Jonathan announced, feigning embarrassment. He wandered over to join Wrath as Pride went to stand next to Lust, trying not to make eye contact with Greed.

"Thank you so much for saving me Jonny!" Gluttony cried, trying to throw her arms wide so she could hug him. "Ah-OW!" She yelped and pulled her recently re-located arm back sharply. She pouted and looked at Jonathan with a pathetically sad gaze. He tutted and bent down to hug her, careful not to touch her injury.

"You shouldn't move it Gluttony, not for a few days at least." Jonathan explained.

"I know, I know." Gluttony replied, still pouting. "Emi explained, but it's so boring cooped up here and I feel perfectly fine!"

"Be giving it one more day, then I can see about discharging you." Declared Emilee as she entered from the storeroom. She was carrying a tray of freshly sterilised instruments and went about sorting them onto a trolley. Jonathan left the bedside as the murmur of chatter rose once more and walked over to her.

"Hey, I just wanted to thank you again for helping Gluttony and me." He said warmly.

"You are welcome." Emilee huffed, not tearing her eyes away from her task. Jonathan was puzzled.

"Are you ok?" He asked. Emilee scrunched her foxy nose up at his question.

"Is not my place to comment." She answered. She finished her sorting as quickly as she could, then sighed before relaxing her shoulders and looking at him finally. "And anyway, is not your fault."

"What?" Jonathan asked.

"I am just not thinking we should be wasting all our strengths on this one hope." She said as fast as she could, as if she wanted to get it off her chest quickly and painlessly.

"You mean the mission?" Jonathan said.

"Yes that." Emilee replied quietly. "When it begins beds will quickly fill, I do not want to witness such things for a second time." She looked round the room as she spoke, painful memories floating to the surface. "Anyways, have said too much. Will be seeing you later." Jonathan said nothing as she gathered a few things and hastily left the hospital, gracefully trotting on her avian feet.

Everyone spent the better part of the night at Gluttony's side, retouching friendships and passing a few stories and jokes to help bond the team back together. For the most part Greed kept his distance, brushing off the comments levelled his way, and even remaining unmoved by Gluttony's retelling of her amazement with his survival and how much she'd missed him. Finally, in the early hours of the morning, which could only be guessed at from the magically dimmed torches now which started to rekindle and mirror the approaching sun, Emilee and another doctor, who resembled a human but with four eyes and a bark like crown and arm coverings, willed everybody out so that the patient could in theory get some rest. Reluctantly everyone made their temporary goodbyes and left, apart from Sloth who was in a deep sleep and was allowed to stay due to Gluttony's protests. Jonathan and Greed were the last two to leave.

“Hey, Greed.” Jonathan called to his skull-headed friend as he ducked through the bead curtain and jogged up the passageway to join him.

“Mr Rhodes.” Greed replied, not breaking stride. “You wish to speak with me?” He asked.

“How long are we staying here?” Jonathan asked, breaking even with Greed’s pace.

“Gluttony’s injury will require no more than three days of rest and careful manipulation. I believe we can best utilise that time to prepare for the final phase of our journey.” Jonathan nodded as they reached the lift. The pair turned and closed the squealing gate before Greed tugged the chain twice.

“Greed forgive me if I’m being silly here, but I don’t want you to think I’ve taken your place or anything.” Jonathan stated, the rattle of chains echoing along the lift shaft.

“We are very different beings Mr Rhodes,” Greed responded, “However, we are not mutually exclusive and indeed it may be possible for us to both benefit from dual leadership.”

“I agree,” Announced Jonathan, eager to smooth things over.

“Excellent,” Greed declared, his gravel voice still flat and emotionless. He reached into his pocket, pulled out a neatly folded square of paper and handed it to Jonathan all the while facing the trembling iron gate and the rushing earth beyond it. “That is my…suggestion as to how we can best prepare and equip ourselves during this pause. I would…value your thoughts.” Jonathan smiled and put the paper into his own pocket.

‘It must be difficult for Greed to share the reins like this.’ He thought. ‘But I am grateful and, in a way, honoured that he is trying to include me.’

“Thanks.” Jonathan said, “I’ll look it over and get back to you later today.” Greed simply nodded as the lift stopped with a lurching thump, and the protesting gate once more creaked open back at the amphitheatre level and the dormitories beyond.

After crossing the amphitheatre, Jonathan and Greed went their separate ways. Jonathan walked to the washing room to refresh himself, after which he went back to the shared dorm room where Pride was laid on her bunk reading. She exchanged the wish of a pleasant night's rest as Jonathan climbed back onto the top and settled down for a lengthier sleep.

Chapter 33: Second to Last.

The next few days were a blur of fevered activity and numbing sleep. Jonathan divided most of his time between sparring and planning the final leg of the quest with Greed, the former task was overseen mainly by Pride, who had taken a new interest in Jonathan's survival and reversed her initial contempt of him learning swordplay in favour of being a personal tutor. He took to the swordplay hesitantly at first, but Pride's harsh yet fair teaching methods, as well as the pain of being slapped with the flat of a wooden blade, soon gave him a firm grasp of the basics such as blocking, footwork, and striking a single target. When the final days were up Pride commented proudly that while he might not be a fantastic swordsman, he had all the makings of a good defensive fighter. The latter task, the planning of the route, was a much more calm and studious undertaking. Greed and Jonathan conversed mostly in Greed's dormitory room, though occasionally they utilised the silence of the library to their advantage as well as the compendium of maps and other books available. Jonathan was wonderfully surprised at how open Greed was to his suggestions and advice, he'd expected more opposition from the de-facto leader of the troupe, but it seemed like Greed was willing to expand the leadership role to accommodate both of them equally. Jonathan's dreams however took a more placid tone, with him opting to observe and try to learn about Sheol rather than directly engage with him. Jonathan was still of two minds as to Sheol's real goal and the truth behind his apparent disinterest in the person specifically recruited to end his reign. Was Sheol so eternal that he had lost interest in the lives of those before him, or was he playing a game of ruse so tall that Jonathan could scarcely see the top and had no hope of understanding? He had no answers, yet, so he contented himself with observation, and speculation as to Sheol's true purpose. The lack of night-time activity actually had a more subtle and benign affect in that Jonathan's sleep was more wholesome, aided by the rickety bunk that was much more welcome than the dank, dusty ground, and over the course of the three days he started to feel much more himself again.

Everybody else did what they did best and prepared how they saw fit. Wrath also spent at least part of his time sparring, and even shared a few sessions with

Jonathan, but was for the most part either hanging out with Kross or working away in the resistance foundry, creating or repairing arms and armour. Lust and Emilee got along like a house on fire, each having an affinity for working with patients, and were often found together taking care of those unfortunate few that found themselves in need of medical attention. Envy found a quiet spot in the library to claim as her own, rarely leaving unless it was for meals but even then, she would usually take half her food back with her to her hiding spot to read. Jonathan and Lust managed to coax her out a few times, and even started a training regime to help her have greater focus over her weather powers. After being discharged from the hospital Gluttony, and by extension Sloth, took to training together at the archery range and racked up an impressive accuracy score with the crossbow, she even learnt how best to aim and fire the weapon while using only one hand. This joy was short lived however when Gluttony was caught, and subsequently thrown out of, the kitchen where she'd snuck in to 'improve the food'. Jonathan tried to explain that she was actually quite a good cook, but the pig nosed chief took the attempt rather personally. Eventually the vast compass of time ticked over, the three days of preparation were over, and the group gathered once more in a far corner of the amphitheatre for the final briefing.

Greed and Jonathan stood side by side before the assembled troupe, who sat on and around one of the upper rows Emilee, Kross and a trio of Resistance members amongst them, before them was laid out an annotated map of the world which was referred to heavily during the meeting. The route outlined would coincide with the movements of the Resistance and would rely upon their distraction to draw away any of Sheol's troops that were lying in wait around, and past, Weirwood Falls. The Falls themselves had two main paths of traversal; the primary arterial road was a zigzagged passageway to the immediate west of the actual waterfalls wide enough for to accommodate the movements of a sizeable force, and open enough that any such force would be noticed fairly quickly by those occupying the Falls and the scrublands they led into. Tactically the approach was a nightmare awaiting to happen, however as outlined by Doorne the Resistance plan was not to win a victory here but to draw out as much opposition as possible and lessen the risk and burden to Greed and Jonathan's group. The strike from Weirwood would also coincide with an attack from the combined north-western forces from Bitterbark and Mesaton.

Greed and Jonathan would lead their party along the more arduous eastern passage; a tiny, hidden path cut into the mountain.

"What if we encounter the Shadow People?" Inquired a concerned Pride.

"A good question." Answered Jonathan, "But that is precisely why we have back up coming with us." He waved his hand out before him. "Emilee and Kross have both volunteered to join us on this last, and most important, leg of the journey." Kross gave a casual salute in Jonathan's direction, whereas Emilee simply nodded firmly. "In the event of a confrontation we cannot avoid, these two are to engage the foe and enable us to retreat." Greed said, continuing where Jonathan left off. "It pains me to say it," He began, which raised an eyebrow or two of doubt. "But we must be prepared to leave them behind, it is something I believe they have both volunteered for and know the risks of."

"Not that we be wanting it to happen of course." Interjected Emilee, which raised a few chuckles from the group.

Greed raised a hand to quiet everyone and the briefing continued. The specifics of the plan were outlined, including the advance round Snake's Head Lake, the source of the Ourobur, and into the ancient ruins that held Sheol's core. Jonathan noticed that Greed left out the plan of attack once they reached the ruins, but as only him and Pride knew the truth, he kept his mouth shut. Pride simply glared at Greed throughout the remaining time but also said nothing that might lead to unpleasant lines of questioning. The meeting, which had been going on since the later quarter of the day, finally finished with Jonathan wishing everyone luck and Greed advising a good night's rest. Most of the troupe wandered back towards the dormitories, Jonathan included, and settled in for the night. Pride was not in the dorm, but Jonathan reckoned she was probably taking another of her, now famously, long showers so he paid it no mind, and stripped down to his trousers before climbing into the bunk for another night by Sheol's side. As his eyelids grew heavier, Jonathan's thoughts drifted between the immediate future, is nagging guilt about Gluttony, and the whirlwind of events and discoveries that culminated with him offering, willingly, to sacrificing himself for the good of a foreign realm. He fell asleep without so much as a murmur, surrendering to the cacophony of his mind in hopes that the tempest would blow itself out.

He awoke to the now familiar fuzzy vision of the cavernous, ribbed cathedral that beckoned him forth like a long-lost friend. Once more made his way from the brass double-doors to the altar and rock where he knew Sheol would be located. He was strangely happy to see that everything was still the same, which given the current record of the quest was a luxury that had thus far not made itself known and approached Sheol's altar to a respectful distance. Jonathan felt oddly as ease these past few nights, the initial shock of the old man's identity having been worn away to ashes when the hostility he might have bestowed was never exercised, he brushed off a section of fallen pillar and quietly took a seat slightly to the left of the altar so he could observe both the book and the rockface behind where the robed man currently stood, not looking at him but Jonathan was sure observing him all the same.

"I sense the end of your journey is drawing near." The distinctive voice of Sheol boomed gently. He was probably speaking rather quietly, but Jonathan doubted that could ever be the literal case, but nevertheless it was somewhat fascinating to have Sheol mark the beginnings of a conversation instead of the other way around, which had been the norm until now.

"Does that matter to you?" Jonathan asked, neither confirming nor denying Sheol's assertion.

"It was simple observation. Nothing more." Sheol purred deeply.

"Then what happens?" Asked Jonathan. He was reluctant to mention or even think about the amulet, which curiously did not manifest itself in the dreams as did almost everything else about Jonathan's person.

"I care not how you wish to throw away your life." Sheol responded, "You have made for an, interesting, diversion nothing more." He admitted.

"Another's life much mean so little to you." Jonathan surmised.

"Do you question the setting of the sun?" Asked Sheol rhetorically, the bass drum of his voice rising slightly. "The curse will continue, as it has and forever will."

"I take each day as a blessing." Jonathan stated.

“Then you are a short, lived fool.” Sheol announced, though there was little malice in his thrumming voice. Jonathan had found that his statements were always conducted with a more matter of fact tone, as if he wasn’t being insulting just stating a universal truth. “I have witnessed countless billions of mortal kind ebb and flow throughout the many millennia of this cursed dance. What value should I place upon the life of one more, when so many have come and gone?” Jonathan thought on this for a moment, would he feel any different were he in Sheol’s position?

“But how many of those lives are ones you have chosen to take?” He asked, trying not to sound too provocative, but Sheol released a sigh that sounded like it could erode mountains.

“Do not seek to understand my curse.” He said, “There is little choice if I wish to truly rest, while both realms exist, I am bound to forever be connect to the flow and forever renew, even against my own will.”

“Have you never tried to negotiate, to explain your curse?” Jonathan replied, frowning as he stood. There was a low rumble, Sheol was starting to get annoyed so Jonathan carefully sat back down to give off an aura of calm.

“You mortals presume too much even while your lives are too short to question things that you believe you have mastery over.” Sheol said. “Eons ago, when I too was young, I attempted to communicate but every time, every age it was the same and I was branded as the ultimate evil to be destroyed rather than trusted.” The simmering tremors settled down and Jonathan felt Sheol’s annoyance pass. “You cannot be reasoned with while you think you know the truth.” There was silence for a while as Jonathan considered what had been said. Though he did not agree with Sheol, he did feel a pang of sympathy.

“I’m reasoning with you.” Jonathan announced eventually as he got up from his carved slab. The robed man paused for a second in his scratched writings and gazed through hollow eyes over the top of the altar as Jonathan made for the exit and slowly dissolved into nothing more than mist.

Chapter 34: Scratching at the Surface.

Jonathan awoke back to the real world with a clarity and calmness he had rarely experienced since setting foot in this realm. The dawning of the new day was met with a palpable feeling interpretation, as in only two days' time the fate of worlds would be decided and everything that everybody had fought for would either lay in ruins or be lit in the glorious fires of victory. Even though it still felt early to Jonathan, the Resistance base was a hive of activity, with members running, trotting, or even flying back and forth to finish last minute tasks and make themselves ready to march out a short time after Jonathan and Greed's party had left. It had been rigorously decided that the main Resistance force would stagger their advance with the that of the task force, the reasoning being that the tiny strike group would be able to use the extra half day of pacing ahead to secrete itself as far into the mountain, or even possibly scrubland, as possible before the diversionary attack began, and thus have a shorter distance to their eventual goal and lower chance of discovery.

Greed, Jonathan and the rest gathered back on the surface, in the decaying courtyard that cradled the entrance to the Resistance base. From there they quickly and quietly scurried through the deserted streets and back alleys led by Emilee and Kross who knew this city like the back of their hand, or in Kross's case claw, and made a beeline back to the harbour that they had originally entered through four days ago. Light from the surface broke through the haze and thick shell of Weirwood at the jaws of the docks and bathed the party with the first golden-purple rays of sunlight they'd seen in days. The moist scent of the river water, mixed with the tang of weed and algae, greeted them as they approached the quayside and its vast outstretched piers, like the cracked jointed legs of a giant insect, that splayed across the open water. Gluttony was visibly disturbed to be back where she so nearly met her maker, but Jonathan reassured her that there would be a marked absence of wall climbing this time around. In truth their immediate goal was to find a vessel that could accommodate them all, and safely transport them to the other side of the vast Ourobor. The party split into rough groups of three to pick through the abandoned remains of the watercourse, and as they swept through the damp docks Jonathan could see a varied abundance of smaller water craft, mainly tiny fishing boats thick with netting and looking like floating, tangled spider webs, as well as a few cargo tugs and barges that were too conspicuous for a stealthy exit from Weirwood. Eventually There was a loud, high pitched whistle from Emilee; she'd found something that could be of use.

The vessel was old, very old, the flaked paint and rusty side railing were evidence enough of that and it seemed to be a small personal transport rather than a fishing vessel with robust twin paddlewheels on the port and starboard sides that made the whole thing look like an upturned helmet. The vessel rocked uneasily, and the wooden boards of its topside creaked and groaned like they could give was at any time, however despite its dilapidated appearance Wrath and Kross, the only members of the troupe to have some knowledge of boat construction, insisted that it would be watertight enough to transport them across the river. Gluttony was not so sure however and although she hesitantly climbed aboard with the rest, she asserted that she would spend the entire voyage atop the bulky wheelhouse as far away from the water as possible. Jonathan was the last the clamber over the steep sides of the boat and, once he had found firm enough footing upon the swaying, slippery decking, made his way to the middle where a wide, squat cargo hatch had been requisitioned to serve as a square bench with enough room for the majority of the group to perch along its rim. After figuring out how to untie the rope from the pier, which culminated with Pride impatiently hacking at it with her rapier, it still took a while for things to get started, as none of the group had any actual knowledge on how to pilot a boat. Sloth's power however proved to be instrumental in this regard and, having probed the past owners of the vessel, he could glean enough information on the boat's basic workings to get the intricate mechanisms of its engine turning. Or at least he would if the boat's engine, which to Jonathan seemed like it ran on a primitive form of steam power, was not completely out of usable fuel. It was, surprisingly, Lust who came to the rescue next and she suggested that Greed could use his telekinetic powers to turn the water paddles in lieu of an engine, Greed was intrigued and, with Sloth at the steering wheel, took a forward position and assumed a strong, braced stance with his gloved hands outstretched, primed and ready. Sloth traversed the spoked wheel completely to the right as Greed's head started its signature clotted blood glow, which spread along his arms to the very tips of his grasping fingers. Jonathan crossed his fingers as, extremely slowly, the radiant rays of maroon from Greed crept along the broad paddles of the drive wheels until they had completely cocooned the hefty mechanisms, then steadily, and with much protesting from their tortured gears that had sat idle for far too long, they began to turn and drag the boat with its nervous crew out of the docks and away from the gaping maw of Weirwood.

The journey was relatively short, and rather pleasant, or at least Jonathan thought so. There was a delightful breeze that flowed around and over the boat, and the spray from the now turning wheels was refreshing and revitalising after spending so long underground. Jonathan moved from the cargo hatch to the front of the boat to see where they were going, and to fully appreciate the vast violet sunrise that was forming a halo over the mountains before them and a rainbow behind them where the light caught the droplets kicked up by their passing. The hypnotic swishing of the boat's mechanisms drifted across the strangely tranquil river, blanketing everything with its foaming mass of noise like static from a radio.

The far bank of the Ourobor rapidly loomed into view as the boat chugged closer, a broken collection of jagged, obsidian teeth. As they drew closer Sloth steered the boat Northward to bring them parallel to the shoreline with hopes of finding a suitable place to disembark. It took a good many minutes of searching during which time the river, which had been wide and calm, started to narrow again and its waters become agitated, churning against the invading hull of the boat and rocking it with their protests.

"We must find somewhere to set down soon!" Called Pride from the hatch, her voice raised above the liquid swirling of the paddles.

"I know!" Jonathan yelled back before turning and jogging back to the wheelhouse where Sloth and Gluttony were scanning for a landing sight, the latter with a weathered brass telescope the size of her forearm. "It's starting to get rough, do you see anywhere yet?" Jonathan asked them calmly. Sloth shook his head.

"It's too spikey," Gluttony replied, not tearing her eyes away from the nearby shore. "There's teeny-weeny patches of sand and dirt, but nothing we big enough to safely ground this boat." Jonathan frowned.

“Can I borrow your eyeglass?” He asked Gluttony. She shrugged and passed him the dented tube before swiftly pulling another from the bulging bag round her waist. “Thanks.” Jonathan said and lifted the device to his right eye, closing his left in the process. It took a second for the lines of craggy rocks to come into focus but when they did Jonathan could see that Gluttony was, annoyingly, correct. The dark crown had little in the way of a safe harbour for their vessel and, more distressingly, the bank walls were becoming steeper and steeper with each passing metre. Jonathan kept scanning with the scope as his mind churned, looking for an answer, when suddenly he caught sight of a low, broad pyramid of granite jutting from the frothing flowing water. “Sloth, bring us round, aim for that rock and keep her steady I have an idea.” He stated sternly. Sloth turned the wheel firmly and held his grip as Jonathan bolted from the wheelhouse and ran over to Greed who was still powering the paddles.

“Mr Rhodes?” He questioned as Jonathan pulled up beside him. His dry voice was strained with the effort of moving the wheels, and Jonathan could tell he was starting to become tired from the effort.

“Sloth is turning us towards that outcropping there,” Jonathan pointed at the rocks he’d seen earlier, “I need as much power as you can give Greed, we only get one shot at this.” Greed did not verbally respond, but instead nodded his understanding and ground his teeth as he assumed a lower, stronger stance. Jonathan jogged back to the hatch where the anxious faces of his friends were waiting. “I don’t have time to explain but hang on...tightly.” He shouted as the boat started to accelerate, the thick paddles now spinning and whirling with a thick mist of kicked up water clouding the deck. Everyone scrambled to grasp onto whatever they could; the railings, the hatch, each other, as the craft shuddered and rocked violently before hitting the solid, natural ramp of rock and its bow, followed by its keel and then its stern, lifted from the water and travelled along the length of the pyramid with a crunch of shredded timber. There were a few startled cries, as well as an involuntary wail or two, as the water craft briefly became an extremely heavy, and not at all aerodynamic, air craft, sailing through the air with all the grace of a catapulted hippopotamus, shards of wood and thick watery spray catching the violet light of its flight.

There was a moment of purity for Jonathan, a single second that was stretched out to ten times its length, something that he would remember until his death, where he could see everything as it hung in the air. Everything from the decking of the boat, to the assorted faces of its occupants stood out in sharp, slow focus, and burned themselves into his mind. Then it was all over, viciously whisked away like it had never existed as the boat's hull met the shore, and its cargo was vigorously thrown around and tossed back and forth with the tempest of its lumbering landing, and the end of its career both as a boat and a plane. Jonathan felt his feet lose their fragile grip in the decking, then something solid impacted his head and the world dissolved into swirling darkness.

Chapter 35: Pit Stop.

Mumbling shadows clouded Jonathan's visions as he slowly came to, his hearing and touch numb and his mind swimming through the murky, treacle-like remains of his last memories before the blackout. He flexed his hands and feet in sequence and found nothing missing, however he no longer felt thick, tarred planks beneath his feet and under his hands, but instead dust, dirt, and sand. He tried to sit up as a tall blob, shrouded with the haze of his half functioning vision, slunk into view and offered a tendril of support.

"Hurmurmur." It murmured, though its voice lost was to him like his was being spoken to from underwater. "Hurrmur murmur?" It asked. Jonathan fumbled and grasped for the words, but they floated just out of reach. With the phantom's help however, he managed to sit up and raised his tingling hands to his throbbing head and grimaced immediately as he felt hot liquid coat his fingertips.

"Am I dead?" He whispered, his own words sounding hollow and echoey, like they were being spoken by someone else. The figure murmured a few more words that were indistinct from the background waves of pain Jonathan was experiencing, he shook his head slowly then sat back again as a torrent of nausea overwhelmed him and forced his vision to tunnel into dark-rimmed pinpricks of light before he passed out again.

He awoke a second time feeling remarkably better, though the throbbing in his temple was still achingly present, his eyes seemed to be able to correctly focus, and he no longer felt like his ears were full of cloying wax. Everything felt calm, and clearer, he could see the whisked purple sky, hear the beating of the river on the rocks, and feel the grittiness of the ground between his outstretched fingers. Jonathan closed his eyes and carefully pushed himself up with a gently grunt of effort. He felt a hand on his shoulder, helping him, and Wrath's warm, familiar voice fill his ears.

“'Ow you doin' there mate? You feelin' better now?” He asked. Jonathan opened his eyes and gazed at his friend, all blurriness now forgotten. He nodded his sore head.

“What happened?” He enquired.

“We made it ashore is what ‘appened. Some farther than others.” Wrath said, grinning. He hauled Jonathan to his feet, careful to fully support him in case his legs gave out, then pointed down the shore to where the wreckage of the boat could be seen nestled forlornly between the pitted fingers of rock that lined the shore. Jonathan could see the rest of the group scattered about the place, every seemed to be present and correct.

“We flew.” Jonathan stated. Wrath let out a chuckle.

“We didn't ‘alf mate, a little rough on the landin' but thanks to Gluttony's healin' we're all pretty much in one piece.” He explained. “In fact, we were all worried for a bit, you took quite a blow before we lost ya over the side of the boat.”

“Y-yes, I remember something hitting me just after we became airborne.” Jonathan admitted, rubbing his bruised temple.

“Ahh yeah, that would have been me,” Wrath stated sheepishly, he turned away a little embarrassed, “Sorry about that.” Jonathan laughed, then wished he hadn't as a dull throb travelled from his skull down his neck.

“No permanent harm done, I think.” He told Wrath as the duo started the short walk to regroup with the others.

Once everybody was accounted for the troupe climbed the damp, craggy slope of rock and scattered scree that made up the banks of the Ourobor and, whilst keeping a weather eye out for anything that might be stalking them, continued to follow the great river northward towards the distant falls.

Now that he was above the level of the water Jonathan could actually make out the distant waterfalls through the dream-like mists that surrounded them, mists that were generated by the turbulent waters themselves and ejected from the frothing liquid streams in swirling plumes of cloud, and even though the group was still a few hundred meters from Weirwood Falls the air was quickly succumbing to the vast droplets thrown up and was rapidly getting clogged with moisture.

It didn't take long for the visibility to swiftly dropped to only several meters, causing the group to huddle closer together as they delved deeper into the perpetual fog. Walking two by two so as to not lose sight of each other, the group wandered tentatively through the cloying mists towards the yawning roar of the waterfall basin as Jonathan's eyes clawed at the swirling white fog for anything of substance. It only took a few minutes for the watery applause of the waterfall to become deafening and for its immense, scimitar shape to proudly wade into view. Jonathan shook his head to rid himself of the droplets of water that had begun to condense on any exposed surface and stared at the towering monstrosity of a water feature.

Weirwood Falls was composed of several great gouts of rushing, charcoal coloured liquid. The humped-back surges of water snaked, and leap frogged their way down from the gloom of the mountain peaks above, carving a frenzied path through the rock and strata before ending their descend violently at the last and largest hurdle, plunging down to form the starting point of the mighty Ourobur. The scent of ruptured moisture was ripe in the air as Greed dissolved from the mist, and although Jonathan could not hear him he did recognise this gesture for them to follow closely.

'He must have found our secret passage' Jonathan mused, his thoughts struggling to surface under the torrent of white-noise thrown up by the crashing water. His suspicion was proven correct moments later when the group discovered a deep crag cut into the side of the ragged rockface, a crag that looked to lead them upward and into the grasp of the mountainside. Greed stood beside it and waved everyone forward to duck through the crumbling entrance, Jonathan was the last one to enter and was relieved to find the enveloping darkness free from the suffocating mists outside. He rubbed his sodden face to free it from its blanket of moisture and ran his damp fingertips over the rubble thick walls of the passageway whose rough texture and mottled grey colouration dredged up long forgotten memories of his parent's house from his youth. He chuckled quietly to himself and considered that, if he were to somehow survive this suicide mission and make it home, he would have to at least attempt to re-establish ties with them. He pulled his damp hand away from the dusty surface, leaving four long black smudges in its wake, and trotted after the rest of the troupe who had swiftly ventured deeper into the crag and away from the diminishing rumble of the waterfalls outside.

Though the winding rocky cove was hidden away from the rapturous deluge of the falls, it was not immune to the oppressive effects of the rushing waters, which made the air hang heavy and saturated with moisture. The twisted pathway snake back and forth as it travelled up the side of the cliff to such a degree that Jonathan feared they were all stuck in a perpetual loop, the lack of any definable features other than the crusty, slate grey walls that repeated endlessly did little to ease his worries, however soon enough the way opened out into a slightly wider, more circular crevasse whose crown of pointed canine-like stones brought to mind images of medieval fighting pits. The group shuffled from the dank tunnel exit and into the chamber, squinting slightly at the violet daylight that, while sparse, was still a veritable flood when compared to the dark, dust choked glimpses of sun offered by the caves they were leaving behind them. The vibration and turmoil of the waterfalls had almost faded into the background by this point, and with its departure Jonathan started to notice there was an undercurrent of scraping disturbance that remained behind. Unsure of the exact nature of the noise, but keenly aware of its familiarity, Jonathan decided to keep his eyes and ears open for any threat that might emerge now they were in a more open and vulnerable area.

“We are past the halfway mark with regards to this cave.” Greed announced quietly from the front of the party. Jonathan, taking advantage of the wider passageway, sidled up next to him.

“We should keep moving.” Jonathan suggested with an air of nervous impatience. “I’m not sure we’re alone here. I keep hearing...unsettling noises.” He continued.

“Unsettling how?” Pride asked from over his shoulder.

“Familiar, and not in a pleasant way.” He answered, “But I can’t place my finger on it.” Greed nodded thoughtfully.

"Mr Rhodes is right, we should keep moving. By now the Resistance should have begun their own atta..." Suddenly there was a long, deep, burbled cry from the rear of the group; the horrific noise of someone taking a most terrible wound. Everybody threw their heads round in shock and morbid wonder, everyone except for Kross who just stood there, his bulky form awkwardly hanging an inch or two off the ground. Emilee, who was immediately in front of him, stumbled back a few paces in surprise at her friend's sudden condition.

"Kross!" She shouted urgently, "What is going on?!" He did not answer her instead emitting a long frothy string of bubbles from beneath his hood-like head, a string of bubbles tinged an unpleasant shade of ruby red. Emilee was about to answer again when there was a sickening scrape of metal through organic tissue and Kross's body slumped forward and pitched face first onto the cold, grainy floor. The talons that had wounded him could now be seen poking from the shadows, their burnished chrome surfaces slick with Kross's blood. They retracted, and their owner crept into view, its armour creaking like chitin and its movements twitchy and alien. Jonathan's eyes widened as he immediately recognised the creature's six crimson almond shaped eyes, its pair of whip-like antennae, the powerful armoured body, insectoid legs, and lethal armament as belonging to one of the most feared and mysterious of Sheol's creations.

"Stalkers..." He whispered under his breath, as his blood ran cold and the memory scars of his last encounter flared red hot along his arms.

Chapter 36: Line in the Sand.

There was an eerie double-thumps that echoed through the chamber as two more of the terrifying creatures descended from the from jagged crack of a hole in the ceiling and, with surprising grace given their size, impacted the floor amongst the surprised party. One of them landed to the right of Gluttony and Sloth, who were in the middle of the group, causing the former to yelp in fear and reflexively raise her crossbow, whilst the other mechanical mantis landed just behind Jonathan, who had turned at the sound of Kross's demise, causing a foetid halo of chalky dust to billow from the rocky ground beneath its metallic insectoid feet. The first Stalker, to the rear of the group, stared silently at Emilee, who had started to regain her wits. It spread its bloody talons wide and advanced with long purposeful strides, the claws on its feet kicking up flurries of tiny stone shards. Emilee, with a look of determined resignation on her canine face, stood her ground and brought her torch-glaive up into a defensive stance as the mantis bared down on her. Just before it reached her however there was a loud gruff battle-cry as Wrath charged in from the side swinging his hammer and causing the Stalker to stumble back a few steps as it was forced to check its advance against this new threat. Wrath made an impressive swing, but it was effortlessly deflected by the Stalker who crossed its twin talons like a pair of enormous scissors, the blow ringing off the metal skeleton, it then advanced once again in a rushing stride that broke through Emilee's guard and threw her to the floor, her glaive cast aside as if it were merely a toothpick.

While this was transpiring the second Stalker began its own leering advance deeper into the group, not that it went unchecked for Gluttony unloaded several bolts its way, her crossbow singing its twanging tune into the stale cavernous air. However, the bolts proved to be little more than an irritation to the mighty metallic insect who swatted them from the air with its lethal claws, their passage making only the tiniest dents to its chrome shell. The Stalker reared up seeming to gloat at the uselessness of Gluttony's attacks, but before it could begin its chittering charge an unearthly chill filled the air and Envy advanced the from shadows, her tear-stained and previously fearful face now hard and sharp as flint, determination and raw fury swirling around her as hard, biting blizzards of ice streaming from out of the air and enveloping the chitinous horror.

The Stalker behind Jonathan, conscious at the fragility of surprise, did not wait to study its prey instead it lunged forward in an attempt to grab and skewer the hapless human before it, however there was a blinding flash of crimson corpse-light as the Stalker was blanketed with a corona of fizzing energy, its momentum halted and its position left hanging in the swirling, dusty air. Just as in Nox, Greed stepped forth his hands raised defensively, and his now trademark powers at work to hold the Stalker in place, though he was still plainly tired from the boat trip and with a gritty shout urged his allies to action lest his hold on the creature fail. Jonathan gathered his senses and drew his broadsword from its scabbard with a hiss of steel, he flanked round the stricken foe to its right, and noticed how Pride did the same to its left, so that it was trapped between the two swordsmen in a deadly crossfire. The ruby stasis field stuttered and died, and Greed retreated from the Stalker as Pride and Jonathan launched a simultaneous assault from both angles, their combined shouts of battle echoing around the cramped chamber.

Emilee gritted her teeth as she struck the coarse ground the Stalker's shadow towering over her, scarcely having time to think she rolled to her right just as the first of its cruel talons speared downward spitting chunks of dark rock as it chiselled into the granite below. The creature tracked her movement however and, with a split-second strike, thrust forth its second talon at the apex of her roll. Emilee screamed in pain as it made contact and sheared through fur, skin, and flesh, pinning her right arm to the floor. The Stalker chittered and cackled at its victim's pain, but before it could deliver the killing blow Wrath lunged into view, raw fury plastered across his face and his hammer raised high. With a roar that split the very mountains he brought his weapon down in a vertical arc and planted it between the insect's shoulder plates, the impact rippled out from the head of the hammer and along Wrath's muscled arms, the sound of the impact ringing clear round the chamber. The Stalker wrenched its claws free and tried to turn to face this renewed threat, however the cracked plates in its back slowed its response and gave Wrath another opening to attack, who, with a grunt of effort, swung his hammer round again horizontal this time, and in line with the monster's chest.

Envy's ice field blossomed forth, but the Stalker did not cease its relentless advance towards them. Though sheets of frozen liquid formed around the creature's joints its beating core remained unscathed and reduced any of the frigid ice that touched it to little more than pools of meltwater at its feet, leaving a prominent trail to mark its stubborn path. Gluttony, having recovered partially from her initial terror, continued to sink ammunition into the menace the *thwang* of her crossbow playing in time with her frantic heartbeats. At first glance it seemed as though the bolts were having as much success as before, however Envy's cold front had begun to work its insidious magic and the frame of the Stalker was becoming more and more brittle with each passing second. With the Stalker almost upon them Gluttony hastily reloaded and pulled the trigger to her device, her eyes shut and a high-pitch cry escaping her lips. The first bolt glanced off the insect's lower face, bending its mandible, the second punctured the socket of its middle left eye, the third sparked from the side of its armoured head and buried itself into the chrome collars that made up its neck vertebra, the fourth and fifth rounds impacted squarely with the Stalker's chest and, with the help of Envy's blizzard, punched clean through the now fragile armour and cleaved the gemstone that sat behind nestled at its core, shattering its beautiful diamond shape into a million radiant shards. The Stalker spasmed and thrashed as the strings that controlled it were severed, and the twisted, broken form fell lifeless to the floor, inky black smoke leaking from the neat holes in its chest plate.

Jonathan and Pride's desperate fight with their own assailant was having trouble evolving past a stalemate. Though they were both keen combatants, their weapons were not suited to cutting through the thick plating that covered the Stalker's body, and it was all the pair could do to hold back the beast as they probed for weak points. Their two-sided approach was, for the moment, working to their advantage and holding their enemy off balance and on the back-foot, however Jonathan could feel himself tiring as he continued the barrage of swings and lunges that Pride had drilled into him the days before. Even Pride was beginning to feel the effects of constant combat, and Jonathan could see she was starting to slow down ever so slightly in her moves. The Stalker however moved just as cleanly and with purpose as it had when the fight had begun, it was if it was toying with them, waiting for them to lapse in focus and make a mistake that it could capitalise on, a lethal misstep that it could push to the fullest and end the bout as quickly as it began.

Greed, who had slunk back from exhaustion, was knelt on one knee nearby, overseeing the fight and gathering his strength, and raised his head and hands to ready himself and assist his embattled companions. Jonathan caught himself being distracted by his friend's movements from the corner of his eye, this hesitation was all the Stalker needed to break Jonathan's slowed and clumsy guard with a rising back blow from its claws, and power forward towards the seemingly helpless Greed. Jonathan stumbled back, the half-blocked blow jarring his sword arm and twisting his shoulder joint painfully, he shouted for Pride to do something just as he witnessed Greed rise form the ground in anticipation of the metallic fiend's attacks. The Stalker swung outward for Greed, looking to smother him with its deadly embrace, but the its skull headed target nimbly dodged backward away from the scything talons. The Stalker swung again and again for a third time, each strike slicing the air just out of reach of Greed who continued to gracefully step back and away. However, Greed was rapidly running out of room to manoeuvre and as the creature swept its claws round again his heels and back clipped the boundary of the chamber. Suddenly there was a surge of pink hair as Lust leapt from seemingly nowhere and, with a forceful shove, knocked Greed to the floor. The fiend's razor sharp claws swung downward where its skull-headed prey had been standing a mere second ago, but now instead connected with Lust who fell with a chilling scream as the talon scythed down her middle leaving a spattering of spilt blood in its wake.

Wrath had no time to catch his breath as he fought tooth and nail with the badly damaged yet still deadly Stalker before him, now it was fully upon him he was having trouble in creating an opportunity to strike, his hammer requiring time to fully bring to bear and finding none. Emilee had managed to drag herself away from the conflict but was now lent against the back wall of the cave, woozy and leaking blood at an alarming rate, while Gluttony, who had rushed Emilee's side after slaying her own adversary, tried to stem the flow from her friend's severe injuries with her healing magic. Sloth stood back from the scene and watched over them both, his usually doleful eyes scanning back and forth for additional threats should they appear, he had no weapon of his own and could not assist with Wrath's battle except to study the baleful creature he was locked in combat with, and try to find a way to end the conflict quickly before Wrath succumbed to the Stalker's assaults. Suddenly he watched with intense focus at the way the wounded metal beast would was reluctant to fully extending its right talon to take advantage of Wrath's slow defensive movements, scratching his head Sloth slunk he way over to Gluttony's abandoned crossbow and scooped it up from where she'd dropped it to tend to Emilee's wounds. Carefully, as if they weren't all in terrible danger, he took aim at the Stalker and waited for it to attempt another lethal swipe, when it finally did so he gently squeezed the bulky trigger and unleashed a single black steel bolt that buzzed through the air as it flew towards the grappling pair. The bolt cut through the air like a knife through silk and slammed into the Stalker's right shoulder joint jamming the upper part of the limb and making its owner wheel round in surprise and anger. Wrath, who had finally been given the chance he needed, swung his hammer round in a wide diagonal arc and slammed it home under the Stalker's armpit, the blow was monumental and almost completely crumpled in the side of the creature's chest, demolishing its beating gemstone heart, and scattering the remnants of its souls to the wind.

Jonathan stared in horror was Lust's form crumpled to the ground, he felt a strange anger rise within him, something that he had never felt before. The feeling blazed outward from his heart and along his arms, igniting his brain into action. He pulled his sword up and across his chest in a middling guard and charged the Stalker responsible as the feeling continued its rapid ascent, bubbling up through his chest, until it was finally released from his lips in the form of a ferocious cry that seemed to quake the very foundations of the cave around him. Pride looked on in astonishment but found herself joining his advance despite herself, adding her own voice to his rallying call. The pair of them collided with the menacing Stalker before it could lay another claw upon his friends, their weapons clattering and ringing off its armoured back and sides, chips of chrome scattering far and wide. A cleaving strike from Jonathan bent the fiend's faceplate, a sideways swipe from Pride removed a back leg, another blow bent its left talon almost in two, whilst a further stabbing thrust cracked several ribs. The Stalker almost seemed to dissolve under the barrage of hits that rained down upon it from the furious duo, blows that had previously been deflected or defended against cut deep and sheared through the monster's blocks and within a minute the Stalker had been reduced to little more than a smoking pile of scrap and metal chunks. Pride and Jonathan stood over their fallen foe, breathing heavily and gathering themselves from the dizzying adrenaline rush now that the danger had been temporarily silenced.

Chapter 37: Parting of Ways.

Still panting slightly Jonathan knelt by his fallen comrades.

"Greed! Lust!" He called, "Are you alright?!" Jonathan lay his sword to one side and tried to prop Greed up.

"I am...fine, Mr Rhodes." Greed protested as Jonathan clawed at the splattered front of Greed's shirt, until Jonathan noticed that Greed's chest was surprisingly unhurt. Relieved, but now doubly concerned about Lust, Jonathan pulled Greed to his feet.

"Pride give me a hand here." He ordered, as Pride jogged up beside him. Gluttony at her heels, who immediately began to try and treat her pink haired friend.

"I found these in your pack." Pride whispered calmly, as they both knelt back down. She placed several rolls of bandages into Jonathan's lap, away from the dusty floor, then started to assist in applying pressure to Lust's grievous wound. Jonathan nodded his thanks but his overwhelming worry for Lust's health was plastered plainly upon his face.

Agonising minutes crept by, but it did not seem like Gluttony was having much success in treating so deep and lethal a blow.

"It...it won't stay closed!" She panted through clenched teeth. She was right, the azure worm of her magic worked its silken way back and forth across the laceration but no sooner had it sealed one section then the opposite end of the lengthy cut reopen to expose its grisly innards.

"You are doing great." Emilee's trembling voice sudden stated as she appeared beside Jonathan. Her skewered arm was held tightly to her chest, but the deep ruby stain of blood was still plainly visibly against her white fur. She crouched next to him.

"Emilee you're injured too!" Jonathan replied, trying his best not to betray his inner worry about Greed's condition. "Let me help." He started to unpack some of the bandages, but Emilee shook her head.

"I already told Gluttony to leave me." She announced through gritted fangs, "Lust is needing your help more than I."

"We can't just abandon you dummy!" Gluttony snapped, her tone very much on the edge of panic. "I know I can fix this I just need more time, th-then I can work on you again."

"No." Emilee stated, raising her foxy form shakily to stand back up. "There is no time." She cocked her head slightly and flicked her ears round to the direction of the exit. "I am hearing more abominations approaching, you must stabilise her and flee up the side passage before they arrive." She gave Gluttony a reassuring pat on the head, before grasping her torch-glaive, which had been placed by her side. Using the weapon's haft as a crutch she struggled uneasily to her feet and hobbled over to where Wrath was knelt next to Kross's lifeless body. "You must all be moving!"

"Why?" Asked Wrath bitterly.

"This tunnel is being very small, enough for me to hold them back...for a while." Emilee said softly, but just loud enough for Jonathan to hear her. "And anyways, the enemy is not aware of your presence so if I am having luck on my side," She gestured to Kross's vast fallen bulk sadly. "They will be thinking it was just the two of us." Everyone was motionless for a second as Jonathan thought over Emilee's plan, he hated to admit it, but she was right, with the enemy rapidly approaching he could not save everyone, and he needed to remain undetected for as long as possible. With a sorrowful nod Jonathan reluctantly gave the plan his blessing.

"I...a...I'mma try my best but..." Gluttony announced before closing her eyes more tightly than before and thrusting both her hands towards Lust's prone body. After around ten very tense seconds most of the terrible gash had been reduced to a slightly thinner cut that, while still nasty and swollen, at least allowed did not immediately put Lust at risk of bleeding to death. Gluttony opened her eyes, and the azure worm of healing withdrew. “That’s all I can muster for now.” She whispered, somewhat breathlessly.

“You’ve done great.” Jonathan reassured her before turning to Pride. “Help me with these bandages, please.” He asked her.

Soon the pair of them had Lust’s torso firmly wrapped in clean, white bandages though how long they would remain so was something neither of them wanted to think about. Sloth stepped forth to carry her, so Jonathan and Pride helped him to get a suitable grip. Jonathan risked a brief glance at the young woman but instantly regretted seeing her pale, defeated form whereas Pride meanwhile moved to scout the obscure stairway Emilee had mentioned earlier.

“Do you know where it leads?” She asked Greed.

“It is a longer and more perilous route, but if what I have read is true it will take us directly to the heart of our destination.” Greed called back to her, his gritty vocals tinged with an odd element as he approached to also gaze at the stricken Lust. He gingerly place a gloved hand to her bandaged side, which was steadily beginning to seep ruby beads into its snowy surface, and for a second Jonathan could have sworn Greed as about to say something, but alas he remain silent and instead swiftly withdrew his arm as if stung before turning on his heels and proceeding after Pride who had begun to tentatively climb the forgotten passageway. Jonathan made sure everyone else entered the cramped tunnel after them.

“We must move Wrath!” He cried as loud as he dared given the proximity of their foe. Wrath stood from his mourning and faced Emilee who gazed at him sadly with her beady spider eyes.

“Ya real brave, ya know that?” He stated flatly as he held out his right hand. Emilee took it and the pair shook a final goodbye. “He mentioned you a lot ya know. Wish I’d have gotten to know ya better!” Wrath continued as the two broke their hold on each other. Emilee smiled a pained yet genuine smile.

“I’ll be seeing him again soon.” She replied faintly, a fondness for her fallen friend layering her words.

“Tell ‘im I said hi.” Wrath responded as he turned and made his way towards the rear of the cavern where everyone was being their ascent into the hidden stairway.

Emilee watched them vanish one by one into the hazy blackness. Once they were out of sight she stooped next to her dearest friend’s body and silently she lay a clawed hand upon the carapace of his back. With her eyes closed she uttered a few words of benediction for his lost soul, before taking a moment to gather herself for her own final act. The terrible metallic scraping sounds of the approaching Shadow People reverberated from the entranceway, the collective screech of a thousand nails down a vast board of slate, Emilee opened her spider eyes and rose from her prayer, steeling herself. Using her functioning arm, she picked up her torch-glaive, readied it into a guarded stance and took a few stoic, determined steps forward to greet her end, fearless and resolute. There was a heartbeat pause where time seemed to dilate and stop, then the first of the abominations erupted from the tunnel and Emilee’s throat began a final, defiant scream that it would never finish.

Chapter 38: Stairway to the Grave.

The lonely staircase of blackened stone wound its way deep into the body and bowels of the mountains. It brought back unpleasant memories of Anchoridge's catacombs, memories which now seemed to long ago but were in truth far closer than Jonathan would have liked to admit. Perhaps urged on by the numbing darkness of the cramped passageways Jonathan's mind began to think back through the many days that had passed by since he had first arrived in this realm that he now almost considered home. How far had he come? How much had he changed? How much was he still to change before it would be over? Would he have any regrets at the end of the quest, any lingering misgivings about everything that had unfolded during this long trek into the truly unknown? He hoped not. So far, he mused that he had enjoyed his unexpected adventure and foray into this realm. He'd done things that he'd never thought he'd do back on earth, he'd fought for and been tested in ways that he would not have thought he was ready for had he been told about them before Greed had appeared that sad, rainy night in his apartment. He recalled meeting his new and strange companions, people he was very unsure about initially but now counted amongst his closest friends. Jonathan smiled as he dredged up the meal they'd shared at Greed's house, the flight through the caves, their discovery of Nox and all that had followed since. He recalled the mysteries that had arisen, the confrontations overcome and how he and worked with his new compatriots to uncover truths behind everything, even if those revelations brought unhappy tidings, and had landed him into making the ultimate decision for the betterment of a realm he had no real connection to. A decision that would pit his life in exchange for the lives of everyone he'd ever known and countless more besides. Jonathan's mind fell silent for a moment as it toyed with that final notion, he sighed, for better or worse he was determined to finish what he had reluctantly started.

The winding tunnel continued its slow march onward. It was almost impossible to measure the passage of time though Jonathan suspected that even if he could it would be maddeningly unwise to record this part of the journey in seconds and minutes, and it was better to simply focus on putting on foot securely in front of the other. The corridor of stale stone snaked back and forth through its mountainous host, rarely leaving a straight stretch long enough to look back into, and this ceaseless twisting, which verged on the insane, seemed to heighten everyone's paranoia and nervousness. There were hushed cries as party members tried to push each other onward deeper into the choking gloom, and twice Jonathan had to call a stop and give people a chance to rest briefly and calm their nerves that were as fractured as the stone that surrounded them. Eventually, after the fifth such stop, the pathway's usual stuffy air started to slowly become cooler and fresher, and Jonathan could taste a sharp unpleasant tint within it that reviled him on an almost instinctual level. It was the tang of corruption and magic, which meant they were drawing dangerously close to the end. A simple doorway leered into view as the party rounded the final corner of the now accursed stairway. A foetid wind touched their faces mockingly as they one by one passed under the unmarked archway and out into the cold grasp of the barren lands outside.

Before them lay the desolate ruins that contained the essence of Sheol, ancient decrepit structures that may have once been elegant towers lay rotting and broken around a wide circular pit that oozed an almost visible stench of corruption, the remains seemed curiously out of place for although their surfaces were blighted by taint Jonathan could still make out the original pearlescent marble underneath, a touch of colour that was mostly absence from this world. Scattered out toward the north there was a thick blanket of navy-blue spines, the long dead corpses of needless pine trees that made up the now deceased Boreale Forest, their charcoal tips reaching futility toward a sky that they would never again witness. Around the edge of the wretched chasm Jonathan could see yet more stairs, their obsidian shapes sprouting from the gums of the earth like the needle teeth of a colossal daemon. The case itself was devoid of guards, which was something Jonathan gave silent thanks to the Resistance for arranging, and so the troupe had little trouble in picking their way over the cracked and broken ground towards this final decent into the pit. Pride insisted on heading down first but Jonathan superseded her and took charge, to his mind the quest was entering its final phase, and it was a part that was wholly his own, just as Greed had described all those many days ago the Sins had done their job now it was time for him to do his.

The polished steps of the chasm both reflected and devoured light, an impossible feat that made their smooth colouration seem to ripple as Jonathan's eyes cast their gaze along them, casting distorted faces from deep within their internal blackness. Despite his initial fears the stairs were not slippery and were instead his feet found amble purchase upon their silently screaming surfaces, his boots making muted thuds that were quickly swallowed by the rapidly enveloping void that inhabited the pit. Time seemed to dilate the deeper the party went, its eternal touch stretching out before them into the liquid night that surround them, and soon the very act of walking became a leaden trudge that sapped strength. Even with the very essence of the world being strung out around him, it was not long before Jonathan could make out a platform materialising from the ink that clouded his vision. Grateful that the shadow encased staircase was at an end Jonathan and party dismounted from the steps and huddled together in awe of what lay before them; a huge set of burnished brass doors sunk into the side of the pit, more grown than carved, a set of doors that to Jonathan at least were frighteningly familiar.

"So, this is it then." Pride whispered, her rapier twitching in her grip. Greed stepped forth and nodded.

"It is difficult to believe that everything has led to this moment." He stated, his usual gritty voice wrapped in the shroud of anticipation. "All the planning now comes down to this." Greed turned towards Jonathan and, in an uncharacteristic display, grasped his shoulder tightly with his gloved hand. "Are you ready?" He asked quietly.

"I am." Replied Jonathan simply. With that Pride, Greed, and Jonathan walked side by side towards the bastion doors, the group parting to let them pass by, a revered silence hanging in the void around them. Before they reached the doors however Greed stopped in front of Sloth and Wrath, who had lowered the deathly pale Lust to the floor and were now standing guard over her frail-looking body. Without a word he removed his suit jacket and tenderly he placed the stylish article over her broken form so as to shield her from the cold of the pit, before returning to Jonathan's side once more. Jonathan took a longer hesitant look over at Lust, whose bandages looked like they'd been soaked in rust, before stepping up towards the great brass entrance to Sheol's tomb.

"Everyone else is to remain here and guard this entrance." Pride demanded. "We do not know what will happen when we finish this, but I would like our escape route to be clear." There was a quiet chorus of confirmations that was quickly drowned out by the creaking of the enormous doors as they slowly parted of their own accord, allowing the trio inside their cavernous tomb before closing shut behind them with an immense metallic boom that, even with the dampening effects of the darkness, still echoed around and out of the pit like the death toll from a graveside church.

Pride, Greed, and Jonathan stood silently for a few moments as they absorbed the sight in front of them. To Jonathan of course this was like waking into one of the many dreams he'd spent in this ancient cathedral, but for Pride and Greed is was a truly awe inspiring and yet terrifying locale, for this was the heart of the being that had caused so much pain and misery, the tyrant that had to be deposed to save not only their own realm but all realms connected to the great flow of energy. The space itself was just as Jonathan's visions had portrayed it; the granite brick walls were coarse, carved examples of otherworldly architecture, the stone pillars that supported the bulk of the room like ashen ribs towered before them remaining noble and humbling even as some of them lay broken, their husks visible through the haze. The narrow arrow-slit windows vented their withered shafts of violet light that exposed the desiccated clouds of dust that flowed from hidden drafts and gaps from between the chipped flagstones beneath the trio's feet. Jonathan lead Pride and Greed deeper into the cavernous space careful to make as little noise as possible though secretly he was sure that Sheol already knew they were there.

After several meters they came to a fallen pillar, its cracked surface sneering at the three trespassers, and Jonathan held up his hand to stop them from going any further. He turned towards his friends and smiled sadly.

"I feel that this is where we must part ways." He whispered, his voice betraying not a note of fear for truthfully there was none, only unspoken regrets and a resolution to finish what he was brought here to do.

"Very well." Greed replied, his sandpaper voice growling in the darkness. "All you must do is have that...thing, touch the amulet. Then it will all be over." He explained.

“It has a name Greed.” Pride quipped quietly, causing Jonathan to chuckle quietly at the way things had changed yet still remained oh so similar.

“Is it painful?” Jonathan asked. “For him I mean?” Greed cocked his head at the odd question but answered without delay.

“It is doubtful, as soon as contact is made the amulet should draw upon your life essence to reduce...Sheol...to its base form and store such energy within itself. Whatever consciousness it had would cease to exist.”

“Why do you care anyway?” Pride asked, “It’s about time this came to an end.” Though she had adopted her usual haughty tone Jonathan could see through her act and into the cracked veneer as she raised her eyes to look at him. Knowing this was to be the last time they’d see each other, she let her demeanour slip just an inch and leaned forward to hug him gently. “It’s been an honour.” She whispered with a slight tremble in her clipped voice. “The honour’s mine.” He responded calmly. “Thank you, Pride. Thank you, Greed, for everything.” Greed said nothing and simply nodded, his empty sockets betraying not a word as to his thoughts. Not wishing to waste any more time, Jonathan turned and swiftly walked his way onward towards the altar and its master that he knew was waiting for him, leaving the final pair of sins alone together in the shadows.

Chapter 39: The Final Resting Place.

Jonathan's lonely footsteps crunched and echoed softly as he approached the raised plinth at the centre of the chamber, in many ways reminding him of the silent strolls he used to endure on return to his home after a long shift, back when he had a job. Not that that mattered anymore because soon he'd no longer exist and his empty apartment would forever be locked, gathering dust against the passage of time, a testament to the average and bleak life he'd lived back on earth. He smiled strangely content with the outcome that even if no one back home knew what he'd done, he'd at least he remembered here perhaps.

The altar, the rock and its master all loomed into view as the veil of shadows was peeled back. The hollow-eyed man, Sheol in all his 'glory', gazed at Jonathan with disinterest from over the top of the reading podium. Jonathan could hear the curl of parchments as the man's ancient withered fingers turned the worn pages of the tome before him, quickly followed by the sharp scratching of the quills he held in both hands. Sheol wrote without breaking eye contact with Jonathan, transcribing runes with a slow and deliberate manner as if he had all the time in the world to complete his work.

"We finally meet." His voice boomed, its presence erupting from all around Jonathan. "Are you here to slay me?" He asked. Jonathan stopped his advance at the foot of the plinth, his confident stare radiating upward towards Sheol.

"I am here to help you." He replied his voice steady and strong. Sheol scoffed.

"Help me? You barely know anything about anything." He responded with mocking truth.

"I know enough." Jonathan said, smiling softly, "I know this cycle cannot continue Sheol, it must end here, but also I know destroying you isn't the answer." He paused and started to climb the steps towards Sheol's altar, "It isn't the peace you seek." Sheol said nothing, watching Jonathan through his lidless eyes, his shrivelled expression remaining a blank and placid as ever, until Jonathan was standing by his side his head level with Shoel's own.

"And yet you bring a weapon." Sheol stated, his rumbling tones sounding. The wizened man pointed a single gnarled finger towards Jonathan's hip and the sword that resided there. Jonathan glanced down at his broadsword, the weight of which was now so familiar that he'd forgotten he was even carrying it. Jonathan took a careful step back and slowly, so as not to alarm Sheol, drew the blade from its sheath with a timid hiss of metal. Sheol started to raise his arms as if welcoming a blow from the sword but after a few seconds Jonathan instead threw the weapon to one side, its solid steel blade clattering loudly against the granite floor. For the first time since Jonathan's many visits to his sanctum, Sheol's time ravaged form creaked an expression onto its ancient face; he frowned contemplatively, studying this unexpected reaction. "What is the meaning of this?" The voice thrummed.

"I have learnt a lot since arriving here, much of which I have you to thank for actually." Jonathan said. "It doesn't have to be this way Sheol, I have a way for you to finally be at rest, and for the peoples of these realms to live out their lives in peace, without being thrown again and again into this maelstrom of destruction." Sheol stared back at Jonathan, his arms lowered to his sides. There was another look on Sheol's face now, an expression of concern but also a faint glimmer of hope perhaps?

"What would you have me do?" Sheol asked, lines of age creasing his words as uncertainty slithered forth, the first of its kind in aeons. Jonathan, careful to keep the amulet on his wrist hidden, brought forth his hand and offered it to Sheol as a gesture of peace.

"I need you to trust me." He announced.

"A mortal?!" Sheol stated, his officious voice swathed in a cloak of disgust.

"A friend." Jonathan replied calmly, extending is arm more to reinforce his words. In truth he felt as though arrows of guilt were raining down upon him, here he was trying to get this poor creature to trust him when in truth the slightest touch of the amulet would consume them both and leave nothing but energy behind, trapped within the prison of the amulet. Heedless to Jonathan's inner conflict Sheol considered the proposal silently, his hollow cavernous eyes staring at Jonathan's offered palm. Slowly like the very passage of time itself Sheol lifted an ashen hand to stare blankly at it for a moment.

"I..." He began, the weight of the implication and the unknown still tentatively holding him back from making the leap, so long had he existed in his own realm, safe in the knowledge that the torturous cycle would forever continue and that mortals would never change.

"Please." Said Jonathan, knowing that feeling all too well. Sheol did not verbally respond but instead, the movement as fragile as a dying gasp, extended his own bony hand to reach for Jonathan's fingers. Jonathan smiled a sad smile and adjusted his wrist so that the amulet could be flicked towards his hand as soon as contact was made, sealing the deal was well as their combined fate.

It was just as Sheol's chalky fingertips, with their pointed nails, brushed his own that there was a sudden scrapping of light foot falls to Jonathan's right, which was swiftly accompanied by a slam of movement as a be-shirted figure, its head alive with a bubbling maroon glow, careened into his side. Jonathan felt the wind being forced from his chest as the figure's shoulder was planted with expert precision, forcing him away from Sheol. Simultaneously he also experienced the heart stopping feeling of the amulet slipping from around his wrist and out into the stale air, a corona of burgundy surrounding the object as it tumbled away. Just before Jonathan impacted the ground, he felt something small yet dense bounce off his lap and saw through blurred, tear lined eyes the figure gracefully pluck the bracelet from the air. With one gloved hand grasping Sheol's forearm the man firmly rammed the artefact onto the old man's wrist, causing a dazzling halo of pure white light to bath everyone.

"We meet at least, Father." Greed stated, his voice as dry as sandpaper. The words flowed outward, smooth and clear, and Jonathan just had time to recognise them and his friend before the Greed and Sheol both vanished in a blinding flash that caused Jonathan's vision to spin and his mind to black out completely, leaving him sprawled upon the cathedral's dusty stone floor.

Jonathan awoke what seemed like only moments later to Pride's worry streaked face and she shook him by the shoulders and shouted his name anxiously. With her help he sat up and surveyed the scene around him.

"What happened?" He asked groggily, as his eyes registered his surroundings. He was still in Sheol's sanctuary, though it was now deathly quiet as it seemed that even the statue fountains had ceased their trickling flow of water, replaced only with the silent passage of dust and stone dust that forever marked the air.

"I was going to ask you the same thing." Pride replied to his query, as she helped pull Jonathan to his feet. "Greed ran forward just after you'd vanished into the darkness, then there was a blinding flash of light." She continued, brushing some of the filth from his shoulders and back. "By the time I'd recovered and run over, Greed was gone and you flat on your back." Jonathan approached the alter once more, his sheepish footsteps echoing with dull knocks. The great stone monolith that had once been so intricately carved was smooth and featureless, its crisp face as fresh as the day it was quarried free from the countless layered runes that had once crowded it. The ancient tome that Sheol had been writing in was also still there but its withered form was now torn roughly in two the dual halves of the book now sat dejected looking as dull and lifeless as the plinth they were resting upon, and in front of that there was something new upon the ground where Greed and Sheol had stood before vanishing, there was a charred ring a few feet in diameter. Jonathan slowly approached the blackened marks, their spreading arms resembling a sunburst but in negative, and reached down to touch them but he flinched back almost immediately as the marks stung his fingertips with sharp pricks of static. Shaking his shocked hand to sooth it, he turned back to Pride who had now joined him up on the raised platform.

"Did he not say anything to you?" Jonathan asked her quietly, anguish cracking his voice with wavering folds.

"Not a word." She stated, shaking her head. "I don't understand why...why did he...?" Jonathan felt his own remorse mirrored in Pride and he stumbled over to her, his legs still a little shaky from the blast.

"I don't think any of us ever understood him." He said as he put his arm around her. "But that doesn't mean we won't miss him dearly." Pride nodded.

"We mourned him once, we can do so again." She relented bitterly.

"I just wish I could have known what he was thinking, what his plan real was." Jonathan stated softly, gazing at the scorched star before him, the only remains of his friend and ally. Pride turned her back on the scene, however her gaze dropped as she noticed something half-hidden in the rock dust on the floor. Stooping down for a second, she picked it up and, a look of curiosity upon her face, turned it over in her hands.

Maybe we won't ever know what he was thinking, but maybe this will answer some queries." She held out her hand and Jonathan could see nestled in her palm a curious black book, its non-descript face clad in unblemished velvet and a single bootlace like string holding the pages shut with a neat double knot.

"Where did you find this?" Jonathan enquired as he gently removed the item from Pride's grasp.

"It was just lying in the dust, next to where I found you." She answered with a soft shrug, "But I've never seen it before."

"Neither have I." Jonathan admitted. He turned the diminutive object over in his hands, studying it closely, though after a thorough stare there was little to suggest the book's purpose. Timidly, that it might fall apart in his grip or otherwise be damaged, he undid the string that so tightly hide the book's secrets and pulled the twine away, before opening the compact tomb between his thumb and middle finger. Flipping through the pages revealed many paragraphs of neat yet scratchy writing, as if the owner of the book had been in a hurry to note everything down as quickly as they could lest it be forgotten. Pride peered over his shoulder as he skimmed.

"It looks like a journal." She said confidently.

"Yeeeaaah." Replied Jonathan slowly, "But whose?" His hasty run through the pages had failed to turn up any marks of ownership. A single idea struck to two of them and they both barked the answer in unison.

"Greed." Their dual voices echoed the name round the deathly quiet hall.

"I think you should be the one to read it Jonathan." Pride shook her head, "I've had just about enough of this quest, and I'm happy to leave the final pieces to you." She began to walk toward the cavern's great brass doors but stopped for a moment. "At least it will give you a something to do on the journey home." She sighed, "Speaking of which, we should tell the others what happened here." Jonathan nodded and followed her as she led the way back towards the entrance of Sheol's cathedral, his fingers clamped firmly around the mysterious notebook.

Chapter 40: The Truth Without.

Back outside the gloomy cavern and once more engulfed by an atmosphere that, while morose, was at least not as stale as the one they had left, Pride and Jonathan faced the weary group who stared at them with eyes dripping with anticipation. Wrath approached the pair the journey's trials finally creasing his iron hard features.

"Is it over?" He asked quietly, his booming voice unusually quiet.

"It is," Replied Pride, "But..." She hesitated as a mournful whistle of corrupted air wailed up from the depths below. "It was not without loss." Jonathan tore his attention away from the journal.

"Greed, he..." He announced softly, swallowing, the truth making his throat stick with dryness.

"What's wrong?" Gluttony asked as she too trotted to confront him and Pride.

"We've lost Greed." Wrath stated flatly, before bringing his hands up to his forehead as disbelief crept through his system.

"For real?" Asked Gluttony, "Then that makes...that makes two of us..." Tears began to well from the corner of her bubble-gum eyes like water from a spring, she hastily wiped her face on her sleeves but the drops continued unabated and started to create dirty black stains in the dust at her feet. Pride stepped forth to comfort her as Jonathan looked on puzzled and concerned.

"Two of us?" he asked, "You don't mean?" Wrath nodded, looking paler and greyer than normal.

"I'm afraid so mate, Lust she..." He ground his teeth, "She held on as long as she could but..." A pair of grief filled tears streaked down Wrath's rugged chin and buried themselves into the front of his spark stained vest. Jonathan slide passed his friend, his feet moving of their own volition, and knelt beside two crumpled forms to the left of the obsidian stairs. Lust's lifeless body looked so peaceful that were not for his prior knowledge, nor the blood-soaked bandages around her chest,

Jonathan thought that you could be mistaken for thinking she were just in a deep sleep. It left him feeling numb and detached, he'd never seen a body before and though in many ways it was less grisly than he'd imagined it was still horrified him to his core. To his right the other turned her head silently to gaze at him; Envy, her dejected face surprisingly absent of tears. Wordlessly she shuffled round an lent her head against his shoulder in a shared moment of wordless feeling, as a soft flurry of snowflakes pattered down from the heavens far above to gently coat the mourning pair.

Eventually the time came for them to begin the long trip back home to Anchoridge. Pride cautiously placed her right hand upon Jonathan's frost coated shoulder so as not to make him jump, and helped him to his feet, Envy rising along with him.

"Are you ok?" She asked with genuine concern. "We have to leave." Jonathan looked into her crimson spheres.

"I'll be ok, I think." He said, though in truth he felt hollow and sour, the victory against Sheol was hanging bittersweet. 'It's funny,' He thought, 'These kind of things are always so much easier in the books, so more clear cut. The evil is gone, so why do I feel so rotten?' Pride smiled sadly, perhaps reading his mind but saying nothing, her silence offered in solidarity with his inner musings.

Sloth gingerly picked up Lust and Wrath helped to wrap her in blankets from his pack.

"We'll bury 'er safely, and I'll make 'er a proper marker back in Anchoridge." Wrath announced, eliciting sorrowful nods from the troupe.

The journey back to Anchoridge did not seem to take as long as the one to the ruins, the travel back did not consist of the same route but rather a reverse of the original plan, with a stop off in Mesaton to rest and restock their strained supplies. This was mostly due to Sheol's forces no longer being a threat, the expulsion of their master's influence having weakened the bonds of their bound souls and robbed them of a sizeable chunk of their power as well as destroyed the means by which they could repropagate themselves. The valiant Resistance, having fought hard to draw Sheol's minions away and open a hole for Jonathan and the Sins, had lost a good many of their brave number, but with Sheol's demise felt a renewed sense of victory and drove forward, crushing the shattered waves of minions before them. Chyssmire, who had led the southern Resistance cells, had been wounded in the battle and relocated to Mesaton where he met with the drained troupe a few days after they'd set off from the ruins.

The meeting was heartfelt, but the weight of loss detracted from its wellbeing, a drain felt on both sides. Chyssmire showed them round Mesaton, which consisted of a vast city of huge canvas tents, strengthened with wood and weather resistant coverings. Jonathan vaguely remembered being told about the history of the place, that the city was preserved in this way as a memorial to the early settlers and those that gave their lives to secure the northern provinces in some ancient war. Mesaton was not the capital, that honour went to Bitterbark, however it was the centre of culture and tradition for this land and it certainly showed it. The party stopped in Mesaton for a few nights to properly rest and to gather themselves physically and mentally, not that the locals gave them much chance as everyone seemed intent on treating them like heroes by throwing parties, celebrations, and all wanting to meet the legendary group that put a stop to the 'mad god'. Jonathan, and to a lesser degree the rest of the Sins, did not feel much like the revered souls they were being portrayed as, but he and they obediently went through the motions during the day, greeting people, shaking hands, even saying a few speeches here and there always retreating back into themselves during the nights, either basking in each other's company or in spending the hours alone in solitude; which for Jonathan meant he could finally study Greed's journal in peace.

Most of the opening chapters, which covered the first third or so of the journal, were simply a catalogue of the day to day musings and lists of items gathered and archived by Greed. From the more organic and colourful style of writing, as well as the date which placed the texts way before Jonathan had entered the picture, he guessed that these initial entries were from far into Greed's past, probably even before he'd become the skull-headed logical analyser that Jonathan had known. It was somewhat depressing to relive Greed's old self through his writings, as this individual clearly had a sense of humour and a passion for this magical in nature that, though bordering on the obsessive, gave past Greed an energetic life missing from his future self. Still Jonathan decided not to dwell too long on this lest his pain and regret at not knowing and then losing his friend dug too deeply.

A decent chunk of the way into the diminutive book Jonathan noticed a steady change in Greed's handwriting and style. The cheerful lines about unlocking old knowledge were replaced with chilling recollections of disturbing dreams, and nightmares that haunted the corners of Greed's mind but could not be recalled once awake. It was not a sudden thing, but it was noticeable however and it left a lingering coldness in Jonathan's mind as he read through the passages.

Once again, Greed wrote, *I find myself pulled back into the land of the living, my own disembodied screams lingering in the shadows. I grasp at the straws of the waking mind but only empty air slips through my fingers. This has gone on long enough and is most troubling, as well as frustrating. With all this knowledge at my disposal there must be some possessed piece that can unravel this riddle of shade that dances and weaves beyond my vision?*

The next page's scribblings were more hastily written as if Greed had been in an excited rush to get everything down.

It took much searching, though I knew it not to be in vain, and I am glad my past self embarked upon such a rigorous method of archival. But enough self-congratulation, I must now make haste and prepare what I believe to be an oral tonic of some kind, the properties of which should allow me to retain control over my dreams, and perhaps even shed some light on their true meaning and content. We begin in approximately seven moons.

Jonathan, his heart starting to beat loudly in his ears with intrigue, skipped ahead a week's worth of pages, and scanned with his finger until he found the outcome of the potion. The black spidery ink letters had a subtle yet unmistakable stutter in their form, were Greed's hands shaking? Was he afraid of what he had seen?

I write within these pages and accuse my past self of what I now know him to be most firmly; a cursed fool. They say ignorance is bliss, and I can concur that that saying is indeed most apt. What I have seen, is no dream but a vision, something that I feel creeping through my very bones as the truth and the end of all things as it has been before. The double-edged sword of my conscience and this circumstance now drives me to find a solution to this coming doom, an ending that is already here and is growing like a cancer. Thus far I know only its name; Sheol.

Jonathan swallowed and folded the top corner of the stained page, before closing the book. He found that he was breathing hard, and he closed his eyes to steady his nerves.

<u>Chapter 41: Stranger than Fiction.</u>

It was several days before Jonathan reopened Greed's journal and continued reading through his many scribbled notes. By this time the troupe had almost returned to Anchoridge, though their trip had to be waylaid somewhat by unfavourable weather that had forced them to spend the better part of two and a half days curled up and encamped beneath the ragged remains of a cave. Overall though, despite the pouring rain, the party's mood had begun to improve somewhat after the shock of losing two of their close friends, as that now they were detached from the jubilations of the realm's inhabitants they could begin to properly process everything that they had been forced to set aside beneath a veneer of triumph. There was time or tears, and laughter, mutterings of regret, but also whispers of golden memories that time would not be able to erase. Jonathan joined in as if he'd never once not been a part of their world, his role as group leader cementing him closer to the group and the losses, strange as it was, tightening their bonds of friendship.

The storm soon passed, and it was as Jonathan was repacking his things for the final leg that he found the journal stuffed into his pocket, and the waves of good feeling started to be stripped away and replaced with a burning mix of curiosity and fear. Upon continuing the final leg of the trek, he opened the curled pages and continued his reading.

It has been a few moons since I last wrote within this journal, though Lust has convinced me to continue my logs. I find all my time is frittered away as I search for more information about this force that has spawned. I am discovering things that should have probably been left buried, for no-one should have to burden themselves with the truths I have witnessed. For the sake of my sanity I will list the facts here: This being, previously named as Sheol, has been born from the flow of emotional energy that our realm shares with its twin. It is formed from the coalescence of negative energy, and projects an aura related to this ancestry. Curiously I have found evidence that this process has been repeated countless times over a fairly consistent intervals, but why such evidence is so hard to acquire as well as mostly unknown to the 'common man' is another mystery. I have yet to find documentation as to this force's goals, and to how it was bested in ages past. It disturbs me however that I am still plagued by the shade choked dreams from before, and I have this unpleasant feeling that there is more to myself, my friends, and this being than meets the eye.

The next few pages detailed the resources Greed had exhausted in his search for fresh knowledge. Eventually, after a good chunk of papers had been flipped, there was another gap in Greed's writings just after he had returned from a trip to Weirwood to access the public library. This paragraph was accompanied by a sketch of a timeline accounting for all of Sheol's appearances that Greed had found evidence for.

I write with a heart full of regret, not that even my love for Lust can shake. I wish I did not have to search for this knowledge, but it appears I actually have little choice. I have found records that tell of there being seven beings, not dissimilar to ourselves, that appear on the eve of Sheol's formation. The beings…we…are the harbingers of his rise, and also the means of his temporary destruction. If it were not obvious already Sheol cannot be permanently destroyed, for he eventually return and reform. This thus far has been done by reintroducing our forms to our 'parent', our combined magical presence breaks up Sheol's energy in a similar way to how the negative energy is usually dispersed and converted. This however is not an acceptable solution, not least because it results in the death of my friends, and of my beloved. I will now focus my studies on finding an end to this that does not involved such an unsavoury process.

The next several sheets held rough ideas for defeating Sheol, but all were crossed out or scribbled through, and Greed's writings seemed to get more frantic with each flip of a corner.

I am getting desperate, and I cannot take this strain for much longer. What am I if I exist only to act as a living key for this unholy lock. There can be no end I can find that does not involved unnecessary risk to my friends or the people of this world. I have sparks for more unethical plans however my logic is overpowered by my feelings…

The writing stopped suddenly, clearly Greed had had a revelation as the next section showed.

This is perhaps to be the last entry I make as a complete individual. My thought processes have revealed to me that the linking feature of us all, and our worlds, and even Sheol, is feeling i.e. emotions. It seems so obvious to me now, but everything about me and my friends is to do with negative emotion, even down to our names, and it is this that breaks down Sheol not our physical forms. Thus I have devised a way, with the aid of my arcane collections, to split away my emotions and to bind them to a special Soul Stone of rainbow colours, thus allowing me, and then by extension the others, to survive the process. I do not know how much I shall remember once the process is done, will I even know what emotions are? I do not know, and it breaks my heart that I will most likely have to leave behind my devoted partner, however I hope she understands that I do this for the good of everybody in both realms. Goodbye my dear Lust, and if you ever read this know that I will always love you.

Jonathan closed his eyes, a lump in his throat. He slipped the journal back into his pocket, and it was a few hours before he had the strength to continue but eventually he felt that, for Greed's memory, he had to finish what he had written. The following entries were scrawled in a very different style, it was cold, sharp, bold, and logical...much like the being that Greed had become by this point.

This new form is fascinating, it is hard for me to fully recall myself, however I do not have time for such trifling thoughts. My mind is clearer than it has been for some time, and I find that new ideas to this problem are flowing better than ever before. I have some more areas to explore research wise before I settle on plan A, and I shall begin with the study of the other realms. Perhaps a solution can be gleaned from that.

Jonathan carefully turned the page.

Pride is becoming troubling, she has been trying lately to insist that there is something about me that I, in her words, 'missing'. I know that something is different however I fail to see how whatever it was that was removed was as important as she is making it out to be. Regardless, for now I shall ignore her and report on my promising findings. I have found a way to utilise my artefacts to tunnel my way into another realm, and not just any realm but a third realm that might just contain the very thing we need to put a stop to the great foe. I shall go on a few trips to this world, gather some initial findings, and record them here.

By this point Jonathan had nearly reached the end of the journal, much to his dual relief and sadness. The overleaf had a description of the items and ritual needed to travel to Jonathan's realm. Jonathan, excited that he'd finally found the way home, showed it to Pride who told him to fold over the top corner so that he could access the page later. By now the troupe had rounded the mountains and had travelled through the Northern Pass and into the final stretch of wasteland before Anchoridge. Jonathan, feeling that the end was very much near, vowed to finish the tiny book before crossing Anchoridge's boundaries.

I have formulated a plan based around the facts I have established following my travels to this curious third realm. It seems that this world does not fully exist as our realm does, hence the extra steps needed to access it, and that its inhabitants do not register in the emotional flow. That is to say, they actively reject its influence, even as they feed off of it like a parasite and exhibit enormous emotional responses as a by-product. This quality has one enormous benefit to me, and that is that we can substitute these inhabitants for ourselves and use their vibrant life-force as the catalyst for a reaction that can be used against Sheol. I will use the curious multi-hued stone I found by my fireplace as the prison to trap the mad god, Wrath already has the amulet created and awaiting the gem. This will of course terminate the life form I bring here, however such a loss is trivial. The many will survive. I shall initiate the plan tonight, and only refer to my journal should I have any developments that fall outside of this plan.

There were barely a few pages left in the thin leather book, however they were well worn and slightly frayed around the edges, and Jonathan could not help but envisage them being frequently visited and flipped through. His mind brimming with anticipation as to why these final entries would have been so fascinating to the late Greed, he ploughed on with his reading. Each of the five entries was interlaid with rushed markings and scribbled fragments of sentences, it was a messy and unrefined final section that spoke to Jonathan as being perhaps the true face of Greed's final inner thoughts and their troubling meaning.

The journey is well underway, though there have been complications resulting in my separation from the group. I can only hope that Jonathan sticks close to the others and survives the trip to Weirwood where I shall re-join with them.

I have safely arrived in Weirwood, though it seems I have beaten my companions here. I am sure they will appear in due course through I find my mind frequently occupied by illogical thoughts concerning their well-being. I cannot allow myself to be distracted, and I am attributing such wastes of my energy as merely the result of a lack of proper sleep.

The group arrived last night and I found myself the centre of much jubilation. Lust's reaction was the most curious and I admit I even felt a tingle of something deep within my soul, it remains however now elusive. It turns out that Gluttony was injured, and I find such news to be troubling. I...worry for her recovery.

The quest is becoming more difficult the more a interact with Mr Rhodes, perhaps it was foolish to even learn of his name? I do not know if I wish to fully commit to the final phase of the plan but I cannot alter this course now, we must push forward and deliver Jonathan and the amulet to the monster's core. I hope the others will understand why this must be so. I hope Lust can forgive me.

We are nearly there, the end is within sight and I am becoming torn apart. I doubt that I can do it, that I can fulfil this last section and sacrifice this being...this friend, a man who possesses something I lack, something I can almost taste on the edges of my mind. As I listen to him speak, and I imagine living free of oppression, and even as I look in Lust's dying eyes I cannot help but be drawn towards a field of some strange feeling. The latter example being something that has ripped a chunk of me open, a gash that I am helpless to close. When we face Sheol, I do not know what I shall do. I hope it is the right thing.

With those final words, and as they approached the shattered gates of the township, Jonathan closed the now completed journal. He felt a strange connection with his late friend, his own feelings echoed those written within the pages, and he felt that he now understood a little better the strange soul that was Greed. He palmed the jet-black book and swore that he would value it and its contents for as long as he lived.

Chapter 42: Our Tales Ends...

Anchoridge was a literal ghost, a husk now devoid of life, withering away in the middle of the grey and dusty wasteland. The town was deserted, and nothing moved save those scraps of debris touched by the rise and fall of the wind. The air's wounding moans were unsettling, and Jonathan did jump once or twice at worryingly mantis-eske shadows that brought back one too many unpleasant memories and fears. Having instructed his friends about what he had found within the journal Jonathan led them through the tangled streets, across plazas that were heartbreakingly empty and robbed of life, and towards Greed's old abode that he prayed to whatever being might be listening, was still in one piece. Finally, they emerged from the slumped opening of an alleyway into the circular space that contained the only vestige of life to be found within the bones of the decaying township.

Greed's house sat, entrenched into the grey soil, just as they'd hurriedly left in what seemed to Jonathan to have been another life. The lonely tree solemnly awaited the return of the master now lost to it, the wind creaking through the barren airways of its structure, expanding and contracting in the breeze like the immense breath of a slumbering giant. The old oak was surprisingly untouched by the forces that had ravaged the rest of the town and its crimson door stood stalwart in the morning haze, the single porthole eye glistening slightly with the dew that collected along the cast-iron rim. Jonathan approached the dwelling in respectful silence, and pressed his palm against the cool, damp wood. He frowned in contemplative reverence and gently pushed outward to open the door, which responded with a long, creaking yawn from its stagnant hinges. As its arms opened wide to admit the sickly fingers of morning sun Jonathan hesitantly stepped inside, followed closely by the rest of the group, and closed the door behind him to banish the invasive shafts of light.

The inside of the house was, much like its exterior, just as could be remembered from the blurred vision of haste that accompanied the retreat from Anchoridge. The books, scrolls, and other knowledgeable artefacts were all still tucked away into the correct and proper places, their contents catalogue, studied, and stored all according to Greed's own personal machinations. Enclosed by rustic, carved walls of the tree which were now, to Jonathan at least, as dreary and confined as those of an immense coffin, holding the life's work of by a man who had taken all contained secrets to his untimely grave. He walked further inside, brushing his fingers along the length of a nearby shelf, his boots dislodging miniature clouds of puffy dust, and pulled out the journal to review the instructions once more. With help from Wrath, Gluttony, and Envy they found the three necessary items and arranged them neatly on a bookstand that hid nearby; first the cracked leather tome, then the magic infused chalk, and finally the chimera engraved stone that would grant him safe passage. Meanwhile Pride and Sloth helped to clear the floor space of dust and debris, as it would probably not be conducive to have stray matter interrupting the delicate process of inter-realm travel. Jonathan couldn't help but his comfortableness with the situation somewhat amusing, he had grown so used to the weird and wonderful happenings of this realm that the thought of leaving it behind brought up twinges of regret and sadness. But alas he could not stay forever, he had family and a life of his own, and it would not do to simply abandon those responsibilities any longer than he already had done. He grasped the chalk between his fingers, the tips of which tingled slightly at the residual power held within, and squatted down to draw the wide, initial circle upon the dry, knotted wood surrounding his feet. Once that was done, he stepped out of the circle and, with some guidance from Pride, completed the northern facing arrow that sat at the heart of the symbol. Jonathan at Pride's shoulder and smiled at the simple elegance of it all, he'd miss that aspect of life here for sure.

"Are you ready?" Pride asked quietly.

"Do I want to leave you mean?" Jonathan responded, "No, I don't. However," And he flicked over the journal page to where the final instructions lay. "I am ready to read my final words."

Pride simply hummed her agreement as Jonathan turned to the ancient tome and pried apart its time-stained pages to the appropriate passage. He traced his finger along the correct line, and silently mouthed the alien words a few times until he was happy he could repeat them without stuttering. Then he picked up the talisman in his left hand, turned back around, and placed himself in the centre of the chalk pictogram as his troupe gathered around to say their goodbyes. Surprisingly Sloth was the first to offer up his emaciated hand to Jonathan, who took it lightly shook it twice.

"It has...been an...honour...thank...you..." Sloth stated blandly, his words as thick and heavy as ever but with a weight of honest respect mixed into their usual treacle denseness that made Jonathan smile as they washed over him.

"The honour was mine Sloth." Jonathan replied. Sloth nodded slowly and slunk away to allow Gluttony to take his place. With tears in her eyes she practically threw herself at Jonathan and embraced him with the sincerest hug he'd ever received in his life.

"Goodbye Jonny!" She cried as she buried her face into his chest. Jonathan hugged her back, his usual reserved nature lost, and after a moment she pried herself away and looked up at him with red rimmed eyes. "I...I'll bake lots and lots of sweets for when you come back!" She exclaimed, her sing-song voice a warbled mix of joy and despair. Jonathan, who didn't have the stomach to correct her that this was likely a one-way trip, chuckled and simply said.

"And I look forward to tasting them all!" Causing Gluttony to beam and wander away to join her symbiotic partner.

Envy was next, her pale skin catching the lazy morning sunlight and highlighting the meandering trail of silver tears that were moving unbidden down her cheeks. She said nothing and instead opened her jumper draped arms so as to welcome him forward for a hug. Jonathan took her cue and knelt on one knee as he embraced her and felt fresh drops escape her eyes and soak into his neck. Jonathan noted that he could not hear the usual sodden downpour that accompany such feelings, and he found himself inwardly smiling despite the sadness of the moment, perhaps out of all the Sins Envy had grown the most. After a few moments the hug ended, and Envy delivered a final, delicate peck on Jonathan's cheek before wiping her eyes on her jumper sleeves and stepping back to allow Wrath to take her place.

The barrel-chested man strode into Jonathan's field of view and thrust forward a powerful arm to vigorously shake his hand.

“You take care of ya’self mate.” Wrath announced cheerily, “I ain’t a soppy type but, you’re a good guy, and I’ll miss ya!” He added quickly before Jonathan could respond.

“Me too Wrath,” Jonathan said, nodding firmly. Wrath released Jonathan’s slightly crushed hand, patted him on the shoulder, gave him a nod of admiration, and finally joined Envy at the edges of the circle.

Pride was the last and final friend to bid him goodbyes and she as she melted from the shadows to approach, Jonathan could not help but crease his face with a bitter-sweet smile. If he was ultimately forced to pick, Jonathan felt that he would miss her the most. Though he had been initially put off by her sharpness and bristling venom of superiority, she had in time grown to become a solid, trusted ally, and had even allowed Jonathan to see past her graceful, spider-like veneer and to truly bond with the woman behind the mask.

“It is time.” She said bluntly, her words conveying a plethora of hidden meaning, as she extended her hand.

“It is indeed.” Jonathan replied, his own response silently reinforcing her own initial words. He confidently took her palm with his own as the pair of them half-embraced for moment.

“Be safe Jonathan.” Pride whispered in his ear as her lips drew parallel with the side of his head.

“I will.” He said back quietly as the closeness ended and Pride drew back to allow him the space to complete the ritual.

With the farewells complete Jonathan closed his eyes and raised his arms, repeating the words again and again in his head for a minute as he summoned up the courage to speak them aloud. Finally, his brow furrowed with concentration, he snapped open his eyelids and announced the phrase with bold, assured tones.

“Simul ire, ad Terram!”

The temperature of the tree house plummeted, and Jonathan felt prickles of static erupt from his toes and travel unbidden up his entire body before enveloping him from the head down. His vision flashed briefly before being plunged into a liquid black void of emptiness as the floor seemed to swallow him whole with a burst of thunderous rage.

Epilogue: A New Path Revealed…

Jonathan pulled himself awake from the turbulent throes of travel and found himself slumped in an unfortunately spiny bush nestled in the corner of a, thankfully familiar, city park. He picked himself painfully from the shrub's grasp and brushed aside the spines that stubbornly remained, a little embarrassed at his amateurish entry, then did a quick look round just in case anyone had seen him materialise and was going to ask awkward questions. Once he was satisfied that there was little in the way of onlookers Jonathan breathed a sigh of relief and started to walk towards a nearby path that he vaguely remembered, and hoped that it would help him to orientate himself now he was back in his own world. As he wondered however there was something at the back of his mind that was suspicious that something was not quite right, and the more Jonathan observed the more apparent that became. The air was a too cold for the time of year and was laced with a thin, bitter rain, there was nothing in the way of bird-song nor even the sounds of busy activity that would be common within a city of this size, most disturbingly, as he cleared a row of trees, the sky above his head sulked, heavy with swirling chunks of violet cloud that cast dour shadows upon the nearby buildings. Jonathan became more and more worried with each step, his mind springing up red flags that he hoped beyond hope were incorrect. A frigid blast of wind threw an old newspaper across his path and he stooped to pick it up, silently wishing for the ragged paper to settle things once and for all. He brushed a patch of dirt from the front cover and squinted at the date. His blood froze and his heart dropped like a leaden stone.

"That can't be right…" He muttered, his voice spread thin with disbelief. "I wasn't gone that long." His eyes wandered down the muck stained print and settled onto the front-page story, and his thoughts were forever sunk as he read the title of the article.

'UK Conditions reported overseas. Single entity to blame?'

Jonathan's pupil's, raw and animal-like with wide-eyed panic, flitted across the story and came to rest upon a single, impossible name that reported to have been repeated by 'infected' individuals over and over again. Five, haunted, grievous letters spelling out something he'd hoped would never resurface.

S

H

E

O

L

42208020R00134

Printed in Poland
by Amazon Fulfillment
Poland Sp. z o.o., Wrocław